THREE RIVERS

RIO RUIDOSO

PRESTON LEWIS

FIVE STAR
A part of Gale, a Cengage Company

LIBRARY OF CONGRESS CATALOGING-IN-PUBLICATION DATA

Names: Lewis, Preston, author.
Title: Rio Ruidoso / Preston Lewis.
Description: First edition. | Farmington Hills, Mich. : Five Star, a part of Gale, a Cengage Company, 2020. | Series: Three rivers
Identifiers: LCCN 2019038786 | ISBN 9781432868420 (hardcover)
Subjects: LCSH: Lincoln County (N.M.)—History—19th century—Fiction. | GSAFD: Historical fiction. | Western stories.
Classification: LCC PS3562.E964 R56 2020 | DDC 813/.54—dc23
LC record available at https://lccn.loc.gov/2019038786

First Edition. First Printing: February 2020
Find us on Facebook—https://www.facebook.com/FiveStarCengage
Visit our website—http://www.gale.cengage.com/fivestar
Contact Five Star Publishing at FiveStar@cengage.com

Printed in Mexico
Print Number: 01   Print Year: 2020

In memory of
David McCollum,
college buddy
and
great writer

CHAPTER 1

Luther had been right!

The water from the Rio Ruidoso was about the sweetest Wes Bracken had ever tasted.

Cupping his hand and sliding it into the cool stream, Wes dripped water to his lips. He savored the wetness, sweet and cool. Of all the rivers from Arkansas to El Paso and into New Mexico Territory, none had tasted sweeter than the Rio Ruidoso.

It was just as his older brother Luther had written. Luther knew good horses and, unfortunately, good whiskey. But good water? Wes doubted a pint of water had passed Luther's lips in the eight years since he had returned from the war. But in the Ruidoso valley, the water was sweet, and the bottom land was dark and fertile. As Luther had written, it was a promising place to start over, a promising place to raise horses and cattle.

Wes squatted at the stream's edge while the three horses that would become the Brackens' foundation stock drank their fill, seeming to sense their long journey was almost over. The sorrel stallion—Wes called him Charlie—pulled his mouth from the water and tossed his head, rattling the bridle and lifting a powder of trail dust from his mane. Impatient for the mares to quench their thirsts, Charlie stamped his feet and pulled at the reins Wes held in his other hand.

Both mares, a black with a white snip between her nostrils and a bay with a black mane and stockings, carried sawbuck pack saddles and a load of supplies. Being with foal, the bay bore a lighter load than the black mare. The black's load included a nine-inch steel plowshare to put in a crop and the extra Model 1873 Winchester carbine, just out this year, for his brother, Luther Bracken.

Just follow the Rio Ruidoso until it converged with the Rio Bonito, his brother had written. There, where the streams united, the brothers would raise horses in peace, something they hadn't enjoyed in the eight years since Appomattox. Loyalties in northwest Arkansas remained divided by the war. Feelings ran high, and emotions didn't die, just kinfolks. Wes had lost two brothers to the Southern cause, one at Shiloh, the other disappearing some place in Virginia. After the cause had died, Wes had lost his parents to an arsonist, a sister to a bad marriage, one brother to a sniper, and another to a rope and a willow tree.

Except for the bad memories, all he had taken from Arkansas was close to a thousand dollars from the sale of the Bracken place. After buying the horses and supplies at Fort Smith, he had ridden west with half that, including two hundred dollars in gold coins in his saddlebags.

Wes slipped his hand into the stream, the waters shivering with the cold of the spring melt and shimmering in the afternoon sun, then savored a final handful. As Wes pushed himself out of his squat, the mares lifted their heads from the water, their ears flicking forward. Charlie jerked at the reins in Wes's hand.

"Easy, fellow, easy," Wes said, rubbing the sorrel's neck. "Way I figure it, that village we passed a ways back was San Patricio. We're less than four miles from our new home."

Shoving his boot in the stirrup, Wes grabbed his saddle and hauled himself atop the sorrel, which nickered and backed away from the stream, twisting around and tossing his head like he wanted to run.

"Not with the mares loaded down, Charlie. We'll run tomorrow."

Charlie danced forward until Wes yanked on the reins. The sorrel rattled his head in displeasure, then eased into a walk. As Wes whistled, the two mares fell into line behind the stallion and headed east along the Ruidoso. Charlie was a good-looking animal, sixteen hands high with a barrel chest, muscled shoulders, and slender neck. His sinewy legs gave him an effortless gait that would quickly outpace the mares if he were granted free rein. If he had a fault, it was the head which appeared slightly swollen at the cheeks, unlike the appealing narrow head of the black mare, the best-looking horse of the three.

As the stallion followed the trail, Wes studied the roughhewn mountains that cradled the Rio Ruidoso with limestone arms. Outcroppings of rock pockmarked the peaks, and dark green splotches of piñon and gnarled juniper, all more bushes than trees, pimpled the slopes. The good timber—great stands of pine—Wes had already passed, back deeper in the mountains along the Rio Ruidoso. Though it might be handy to be closer to timber for good lumber, the forests reminded him of Arkansas, where a man could never see where he was going for the trees, and where the woods always held the secrets and animosities of enemies. Here, at least, the country was open and honest, not holding secrets from anyone.

And if a man needed shade, the cottonwoods and willows along the Ruidoso provided all he could ever want and offered it within reach of those cool, sweet waters.

The trail veered away from the Ruidoso, and Wes stood in his stirrups, staring ahead for another line of trees converging with the stream. There he would find his brother. Wes stretched his lean six-foot frame to its fullest and shaded his gray eyes with his hand even though the sun was at his back. But the stream bent around a mountain blocking his view.

Wes settled back into the saddle, his free hand patting the thigh of his corduroy britches, which—like his faded, blue, woolen pullover shirt—showed the wear of all the miles from Arkansas to New Mexico Territory. His knee boots were scuffed, but his wide-brimmed wool hat, though powdered with dust, was unblemished and as new as the riding time from El Paso where he had bought it.

The gray of the hat matched the gray of his alert eyes, though not the steeliness. His bronze face was partially obscured by the brown whiskers that had thrived since El Paso and his last shave. And a thick mustache hid his lips beneath. He avoided wide smiles, as much to hide his emotions as to conceal the wickedly chipped front tooth, compliments of a Yankee rifle butt to the face at Murfreesboro.

As the trail veered back toward the Rio Ruidoso, Wes noticed Charlie's ears flick forward, then stiffen. The stallion had heard something. Wes leaned forward in the saddle, his free hand bracing himself against the saddle horn. Nothing. Wes relaxed, and so did the stallion's ears, but just for an instant. Then they stood up again and tensed toward the east.

Wes thought he heard a faint cry. He shook his head, turning one ear toward the soft noise. It came again, a soft, high-pitched cry from down the trail. Twisting in his saddle, Wes glanced at the two mares, both trotting up to the stallion, as if they sought protection from the unsettling noise. Wes guided the stallion toward the stream, the mares following. At a pair of willow saplings, he jumped from his saddle and tied each mare to a young tree. Pulling the extra Winchester from the black mare's pack saddle, he climbed back atop the stallion and touched his boot heel to Charlie's flank. The sorrel danced forward at a gallop until Wes eased back on the reins.

As he neared the bend in the stream, a woman's screams and

sobs grew discernible and louder. Then Wes heard the mocking laugh of amused men. Rounding the bend, he saw a modest adobe dwelling with a small cultivated field between it and the Ruidoso. And in front of the house, he spied a circle of four men around a Hispanic woman. A fifth man sat horseback, holding the others' mounts. All five were hurrahing the woman and someone else within their circle.

Wes held the stallion back while he studied the five men, all so intent on their mischief that not one had noticed their visitor less than a hundred yards away. Wes knew neither the dispute nor its cause, but he could see the odds were less than fair. He levered a cartridge into the Winchester, then shook the reins. The sorrel stepped forward, the gap between Wes and the men narrowing to eighty yards, sixty yards, then forty yards. Still the men remained oblivious to all but the prey within their small circle.

Wes watched a frail man stand up among them, only to be shoved back to the ground by a bigger assailant. The woman screamed and tried to help the victim, but another attacker grabbed her arm and jerked her away. She fell to the ground, then clambered toward the frail man. Everyone laughed, except Wes. He had seen enough.

"Get up, greaser, so I can plant you in the ground again," taunted one attacker.

At twenty yards, Wes eased back on the sorrel's reins. Swinging the barrel of his carbine toward the assailants, he shouted, "Afternoon!"

Five men flinched at the greeting, then stiffened. They slowly turned around, facing Wes, their hands frozen near the revolvers at their sides.

"What seems to be the trouble?" Wes called out.

The woman burst through the circle of men and rushed toward Wes. *"Gracias, señor, muchas gracias!"*

11

Her cry and the flash of her skirt spooked Charlie. The sorrel nervously backtracked a half-dozen steps. One man reached toward his pistol, his hand wrapping around the gun butt.

The Hispanic woman stopped dead still.

Wes jerked the carbine to his shoulder and fired over the foolhardy man. The fellow's fingers widened, and his arm went limp, releasing the pistol that slid back into its holster. His companions raised their hands away from their own sidearms.

The young woman's hand flew to her throat. "Please, *señor,* stop them from hurting us."

Wes nodded. "What's the trouble?"

One troublemaker stepped ahead of the others. He had a stiff neck, his whole body turning with his head. "No trouble. Until you showed up, fellow!"

"The young lady wouldn't agree, now would she?"

"She's Mexican. What's she know?"

"Enough to expect decent treatment from folks."

Stiff neck turned his whole body toward the others. "He damn sure ain't from Texas, now is he?" As they laughed, stiff neck twisted back to face Wes. "Hell, fella, you remember the Alamo? This greaser's kin likely killed good white folks there. We're just paying them back."

Wes shrugged. "That was near forty years ago, and this isn't Texas. You best forget the Alamo, ride on, and leave these folks alone."

Raising his fist, stiff neck advanced a step. "Fella, I don't know who you are, but you got no business interfering in what my bunch does. The name's Horrell, I'm Mart, and these are my brothers Tom, Merritt, Ben, and Sam. We'll ride out, but you remember the Horrell name if you're planning on staying in Lincoln County because we'll meet again when we ain't in such a good mood."

Mart Horrell stepped stiffly toward his horse, and the other

12

three brothers afoot did likewise. They mounted in unison, Mart sitting awkwardly in his saddle as he jockeyed his horse around to face Wes.

"Show me you Texans know how to ride," Wes commanded, his carbine nodding in their direction.

Mart shook his knotted fist, his head bobbing atop his starched neck. "You best hope you never meet up with us anywhere again, fella." Then he swung his arm forward and issued a command to his brothers, "Let's ride."

The five men trotted single file past Wes, and he could see the family resemblance in their narrow eyes, hard and cold. Wes stared back, studying their faces because he planned to stay in Lincoln County and would surely encounter them again. It would be like watching out for rattlesnakes: you seldom got bit if you were careful and knew what to look for. The men rode east, and Wes studied them until they disappeared down the trail.

When he turned to the adobe dwelling, he saw the young woman helping the old Hispanic man to his feet. His face bloodied, he stumbled a moment, then threw back his narrow shoulders, shook himself from her grasp, and stepped proudly to a stool by the adobe's door.

The woman watched him ease down onto the seat, then turned to Wes. He found himself admiring her lithe body in a simple dark skirt and her full breasts pushing at a white blouse. Her dark eyes overflowed with tears and defiance. Her lips were full and red, and there was an invitation in her smile.

She sighed. "So far from heaven and so close to Texas."

"The Texans all that bad?"

She nodded. "*Gracias, señor,* for helping this poor family."

Wes stared at this young woman with the raven hair and alluring eyes. Since he had left Mesilla, he had seen but two white women, both married. White women were as scarce as good

13

horses in New Mexico Territory, but this olive-skinned woman in the simple clothes could make him forget any woman in the fanciest clothes anywhere.

"Please let me prepare you a meal before you leave."

"I would like that," Wes answered. "I've got a couple more horses upstream. I'll get them and return."

The young woman nodded and stepped toward the house, then spoke shyly over her shoulder. "My name is Sarafina."

"I'm Wesley Bracken," he replied, aiming the sorrel toward the mares. Reaching them, he slipped the extra carbine back into the pack saddle, untied the two mares, and retraced the trail to the dwelling, where Sarafina was offering the old man water from a clay cup.

"Is your father okay?" Wes asked as he dismounted and tied the horses to a primitive fence at the side of the house.

Sarafina turned meekly to Wes, her head bowed.

"He is not my father, *señor*. He is my husband."

CHAPTER 2

"Me llama Bonifacio Zamora," the old man said as he opened the door for Wes. *"Muchas gracias, muchas gracias!"*

Sarafina knelt before a bell-shaped fireplace in the corner of the modest adobe dwelling. Without looking over her shoulder, she spoke softly. "My husband says his name is Bonifacio Zamora. He offers his thanks for saving us."

Zamora closed the plank door, then offered his hand to Wes as well as a broad smile, a white slash across his bronzed face.

Wes took the old man's hand, studying his gray-flecked beard and the deep-lined face. Callused from hard work, Zamora's hand rested limply in Wes's grasp. Beneath bushy eyebrows his dark eyes glowed with integrity and pride. He was a decent man, but an old one. Releasing Zamora's fragile hand, Wes figured him at least forty years older than Sarafina and maybe more.

Zamora motioned toward a roughhewn bench against the back wall. Taking off his hat and placing it on the bench beside him as he sat down, Wes studied the single-room dwelling. Though simple, the room was immaculate, from the rough woolen rug covering much of the hard-packed dirt floor to the corner that served as the kitchen. The plastered walls shone a brilliant white as afternoon sunlight poured through open windows. Bedding was rolled up in the corner opposite the fireplace. The bench, a pair of stools, and a wooden trunk were all the furniture. From the ceiling beams hung strands of dried corn and peppers as well as goatskin containers of water.

The room felt cool despite the glowing embers in the small fireplace. On the circular hearth in front of the fire, Sarafina worked a yellow paste in her hands and periodically checked the long-necked earthen vessel that cooked on a circular metal griddle standing six inches above the coals. She had boiled coffee in a pot and set it aside for the grounds to settle. Pinching balls from the yellow paste, she flattened each with her palm and then dropped them to cook on the sizzling griddle. As she took each tortilla from the griddle, she covered it with the bean and meat concoction simmering in the long-necked vessel.

Sarafina spoke in Spanish to her husband. He picked up a stool and placed it in front of Wes. Zamora moved with an aged grace and perhaps pride that a man as old as he could have a wife as young and pretty as Sarafina. Wes envied Zamora his wife and felt foolish for that jealousy.

Sarafina stepped to Wes, her dark, proud eyes staring straight into his. She placed an earthen plate on the stool before him. "Please, eat." A slender smile pulled at the corner of her full lips, then she retreated meekly to the hearth and poured him coffee in a clay cup.

Wes bit into the rolled tortilla and nodded his approval as she placed the cup on his plate. "It's good. Won't you eat?"

"We had eaten when the Texas *diablos* rode up," Sarafina replied, lowering herself gracefully to the floor to sit while her husband fetched the other stool and seated himself beside her. Both watched him eat.

Wes felt their gaze with every bite. The food tasted good and countered his gnawing hunger. He accepted a second helping and two more cups of coffee. Finishing, he wiped his mouth with his sleeve and turned to Zamora. "Your wife is a good cook."

Sarafina translated for her husband, who shifted on his stool and smiled again. Taking her hand in his, he nodded his agreement. Sarafina rested her head against her husband's side, and their genuine affection and respect touched Wes, yet he feared for their happiness. "The Horrells may return."

Sarafina translated for her husband.

"Diablos." Zamora spat out the word like he would rancid food, then continued in Spanish.

Though not comprehending the words, Wes understood their intent.

Sarafina frowned. "Mean men, new to the Ruidoso valley. Upstream, they have a place. Some say they ranch. Some say they steal cattle. No one is safe from them! They destroyed our *acequia,* our irrigation ditch, then trampled our meager field with their horses. Bonifacio is not a young man, but he is a worker. They destroyed his work and my brother's, too. Thank God Carlos was gone to gather wood."

Wes had seen the Horrell type in Arkansas, bad to the core and intent on ruining everything they touched.

"And you, Wesley Bracken, where will you go?" Concern touched Sarafina's words.

"I'm staying in Lincoln County."

"Then you must be cautious." Sarafina seemed both worried and pleased. "But where will you live?"

"Perhaps we are neighbors. My brother has taken a place where the Rio Ruidoso joins the Rio Bonito."

Sarafina's hand flew to her mouth, and her eyes widened. "Oh, no," she said, her words muffled by her hand.

Wes slid to the edge of the bench. "Has something happened to Luther, my brother?"

Her head moved from side to side. "No, not that."

Wes felt his muscles relax as a breath of relief slid out of his mouth.

"The adobe where your brother lives was home to a man

17

killed there by the Apaches," Sarafina continued. "His spirit still lives in that adobe and brings bad luck to those who disturb it. Living there will bring you much trouble, you must believe me."

Wes picked up his hat, unsure how to counter a superstition.

"You do not trust me, I can tell, but it is dangerous for you to live there. No good will come of it." Sarafina then translated the conversation for her husband. He, too, shook his head.

"If the land is good like my brother says," Wes replied, "I can build a new house."

Suddenly, the door flew open and banged against the wall.

Sarafina screamed, and Zamora turned fearfully toward the entrance.

Wes tossed his hat aside, grabbed for the Colt at his waist, and bolted up from the bench, knocking over the stool before him. As the dishes shattered at his feet, Wes saw a serape-draped figure with an uplifted arm, swinging a pistol in his direction.

The figure at the door screamed. "*Diablo*, you ruined our field! You will die!"

Sarafina scrambled to her feet, blocking his aim. "No! Carlos, he is our friend."

Wes cocked the hammer on his revolver, his trigger finger but a hair's breadth away from sending a bullet into the enraged youth. Sarafina clambered between them.

The man in the door seemed confused, even more so when Sarafina lunged at him. Grabbing him, she wrapped her arms around him. "Carlos, he saved us, Bonifacio and me. Do not harm him. He is our friend. The Texas *diablos* did this to our land."

Zamora issued rapid commands in Spanish, and the young man lowered his pistol.

His finger sliding from the trigger, Wes released the hammer on his revolver and slid the gun back into its holster.

18

"Wesley Bracken, this is my brother, Carlos," Sarafina said as she released him and backed away.

Though Carlos looked no more than sixteen years old, his eyes flared with the fury, if not the experience, of an older man.

Wes picked up his hat from the floor, then offered his hand to Carlos, but the young man spun around on his heels and marched outside.

"I've work to do," he called over his shoulder as he stomped outside.

Zamora spoke rapidly, and Sarafina translated his apologies for Carlos's behavior. Then, she added her own regret for Carlos's rude intrusion.

"Carlos is hot tempered. He hates what the Texans are doing to the valley. I fear for him. And, I fear for the valley."

With good reason, Wes thought as he put on his hat and squatted by the overturned stool to gather the pieces of the shattered plate and cup.

Sarafina bent down and took the shards from his hand. "That is for me to do. You've done enough for us. Please do not hold my brother against our kind."

Wes studied her dark eyes. "And, do not hold the Horrells against my kind."

Sarafina answered with a smile.

"I must find my own brother now." Wes nodded to Sarafina, then Zamora. "How far am I from his place?"

"Two miles, no more," Sarafina replied, carrying the dish fragments to the hearth.

Wes shook Zamora's hand and stepped to the door, pausing long enough to spot Carlos repairing the irrigation ditch.

"*Adios,*" Zamora called out.

Wes walked outside toward his horses, checking the mares' pack saddles. Taking Charlie's reins, he mounted the sorrel and doffed his hat at Zamora and his wife. "*Adios,* neighbors," he said, pointing the sorrel east toward his new home and the direction the Horrells had ridden. The mares fell in line behind the stallion.

It felt good to be nearing a place he could call home, even if he had never been there before. By now Luther had probably plowed up a couple acres of land to plant corn and hay so they could set aside winter feed for the horses. And, Luther had likely begun a corral for the horses. It might be too much to ask for him to have started a barn, but it was good to know the place came with a dwelling, even if haunted by a dead man's spirit, as Sarafina feared.

Within the first mile, the valley narrowed. To the south, Wes could see a solid mountain ridge. The Rio Bonito must come in from the north, Wes figured as he topped a rise. From there he could see where two ribbons of water, glimmering in the late afternoon sun, converged.

Wes slowed the sorrel and studied the land, but it didn't square with what he had imagined. He saw an adobe dwelling, but it looked abandoned, and no fields had been plowed, ever. Nor did Wes see any improvements in the angle where the streams met beyond a dilapidated adobe. Had Luther given him poor directions? But Sarafina had said less than two miles to his place, and Wes approached that distance.

Jiggling the reins, Wes sent the sorrel angling toward the abandoned adobe. He glanced over his shoulder once to make sure the mares were keeping up, but mostly he stared at this place. Cottonwoods and willows lined the dark and fertile land along the stream, and a carpet of spring greenery extended to the base of the mountains only to stop in awe of the limestone heights. The abandoned dwelling was about a hundred feet from the Rio Ruidoso.

Drawing near the adobe, Wes shook his head. Surely this was not his place. Refuse littered the dwelling's perimeter, and the naked windows lacked shutters or other covering. Riding around to the front, Wes noticed the dwelling needed a door as well. He dismounted and tied the horses to a hitching post that had fallen over against the side of the house.

One corner of the house was melting away where water had collected on the roof, then overflowed. Rainfall had pitted parts of the walls, too. Stepping to the door opening, Wes bent and stuck his head inside, seeing blue sky between two roof timbers in the bad corner of the house. Wes shook his head. Surely this could not be the place Luther had written about?

A dozen empty cans lay scattered on the floor, and a couple blackened ones hid in the corner fireplace. In the adjacent corner, Wes spotted a bedroll, then his gaze went back to the fireplace. Dying embers. Someone lived here. Could it be Luther?

Striding to the unfurled bedding, Wes toed at the blankets and uncovered an empty whiskey bottle. Luther had not changed. And this was not the home Wes had been expecting.

Wes spat in the fireplace, which sizzled for a moment, then spat back. He stomped back outside, considering whether to take the horses and the five hundred dollars and just leave Luther on his own to squander his lazy days on whiskey. That would not be the right thing to do, but neither was this.

He walked from the adobe to the Rio Ruidoso, stopping occasionally to dig out a handful of soil and crumble it between his fingers. The soil was dark and rich. Like the adobe, it held promises unrealized.

Wes strolled along the Rio Ruidoso all the way to its union with the Rio Bonito. He was standing under a cottonwood tree, figuring his options, when he saw a rider approaching along the trail from the east. Even at a distance, Wes recognized the set of Luther in the saddle, slumped shoulders and a drooping head that always looked at the ground beneath him instead of the country before him.

Wes angled back toward the adobe and almost reached it before Luther spotted him. When he did, his older brother whooped, took off his hat, and slapped it against the flank of his chestnut.

"Wesley," he shouted, "you finally made it!" He rode up at a canter, then reined hard against his gelding. He jumped from his horse, stumbled as he hit the ground, and ran to Wes.

Wes wished he shared Luther's enthusiasm. He offered his hand to his older brother, and Luther pumped away at it.

"Glad to see you, Wes! You look fine, a sight for sore eyes."

Saying nothing, Wes just stared at Luther. His eyes may have been sore, but his muscles certainly weren't because Luther had hardly worked on their place. Even so, Luther had lost weight. His gaunt face showed red, watery eyes. And Wes thought he detected a hint of whiskey on his breath.

"And you brought supplies, Wes?" Luther glanced at the mares. "Bring any whiskey with you?" Luther released his brother's hand, scurried over to the black mare, and unstrapped the load.

"Hold on," Wes said, retreating to the sorrel and opening the saddlebag with the gold. "I've a bottle here."

Luther strode over before Wes could free the bottle. When the bottle emerged from hiding, Luther grabbed it from Wes, unplugged the cork, and lifted it to his lips. He gulped down the amber liquid, then came up for air and sighed. "Sorry I wasn't here when you arrived, Wes."

Wes shrugged. "What difference would it have made?"

"I rode down river with some friends," Luther offered, then laughed. "They had trouble at a greaser's place with some yahoo riding through." Luther took another slug of whiskey.

"Could your friends be the Horrells?"

Luther broke off his kiss with the bottle. "Yeah. How'd you

know, Wes?"

"I'm the yahoo they had trouble with."

Luther jerked the bottle to his lips again, then took a deep draw of the liquid and lowered the vessel. His flushed cheeks paled. "They said they would kill you, Wes!"

CHAPTER 3

So much to do and so little daylight. Wes rolled out of his bedding and reached for his boots. He shook the cobwebs from his head as he pulled on his footwear. Hunger nibbled at his stomach, and he recalled with pleasure Sarafina's hearty meal because he had missed supper, but he was still too mad at Luther to waste time fixing any breakfast.

And Luther had only smiled, as addled as a steer on locoweed, never comprehending Wes's anger. Now Luther snored in his corner, sleeping off the one bottle Wes had brought from El Paso.

Wes toed at Luther's bedroll. "Get up, Luther. We've work to do."

Luther groaned and slid deeper into his blankets, his refuge from the crisp dawn air and Wes's boot.

Wes stared out the naked entry where a door should have hung. The dark sky was just paling with light around the fringes. The sun was as slow arising as Luther, but Wes had faith the sun would begin its workday. He had his doubts about Luther. He shoved his boot in Luther's side, harder than he should have but not as hard as Luther needed. "Work to do, Luther!"

His brother grunted, got his arms tangled in the blanket, then gave up the fight and snored again.

Drawing his foot back, Wes kicked Luther in the butt, hard like he deserved.

Luther grumbled in his covers, twisting toward the wall.

"Time to get up, Luther, or I'll kick you in the head like I should've done yesterday." Wes cocked his foot until he noticed movement.

Luther sprouted from his cover, not as a man, but as a dog, pushing himself up on his hands and knees, his head hanging between his shoulders. He swayed like a tree in a breeze. "Damn, it's early, Wes. Give the sun time to warm up."

"Early don't last long," Wes replied, strapping on his revolver.

"It didn't come this soon yesterday," Luther answered.

Wes grabbed Luther by the collar and yanked him to his feet. "We're going for a walk."

"My boots," Luther protested. "Dammit, Wes, what's got into you?"

"A hell of a lot less liquor than's gotten into you, Luther."

His brother resisted weakly, his arm swinging against Wes's chest, then falling limp when Wes tightened his fingers around the back of his brother's neck.

Steering him through the door, Wes aimed Luther for the Ruidoso.

"Ouch! Damn!" cried Luther. "My boots. I need my boots."

"Not where we're going."

Luther gave up and stumbled beside Wes toward the stream. At its bank, Wes shoved Luther to his knees. Before Luther could protest, Wes grabbed him by the scruff of his neck and dunked his head in the frigid water. Luther struggled against the wet shock, then fought Wes's iron grip. He flailed for air. Wes jerked him from the Ruidoso.

Gasping for breath, Luther threw a punch, his fist grazing Wes's shoulder. The cold wetness and the invigorating morning air put vinegar in Luther's resistance until Wes grabbed a handful of his hair and dunked him again. The water bubbled with Luther's last breath, and his windmilling arms splashed water everywhere. Still, Wes overpowered him with the sober strength

25

of his hands and muscled arms. When his brother's resolve and resistance weakened, Wes yanked his head from the water.

Luther gagged and heaved, spitting water into the stream. He coughed and sputtered and wheezed for a dry breath.

His hands still controlling Luther, Wes waited until his brother mumbled, then shoved his head back into the water. Wes finally released him and backed away from the stream bank.

Luther burst from the liquid, sucking in the morning air and screaming at Wes. "You trying to drown me?"

"As little work as you've done, it's a cinch you won't drown in your own sweat." His hands resting on his hips, Wes glared at Luther.

"I didn't mean no harm."

"You didn't do any good, either." Wes spun around on his heels and stomped back to the adobe.

In his wake, he heard Luther filling the air with curses. Wes didn't care. Things must change, or he would split with his brother.

Charlie bolted down the trail and splattered through the stream without losing stride. It was the run the sorrel stallion had been waiting for, and Wes gave him free rein. The stallion's gait was long and powerful. Chores awaited back at the place, but Wes knew Luther was a brooding soul when he got his nose bloodied. Wes wanted to give him a little time to think about his abrupt awakening this morning.

And, if this were to be his home, Wes figured on meeting his neighbors to the east. He looked over his shoulder past the trail that paralleled the Rio Bonito to the northwest, and he stared eastward as Charlie galloped along the path. Once the Rio Ruidoso merged with the Rio Bonito, the stream became the Rio Hondo.

Five miles from the Bracken place, he yanked on the reins,

even though Charlie wanted to run more. But up ahead stood a huge mill and several small buildings. A few folks moved about, starting fires and beginning the day's chores. No sense in alarming his new neighbors with a hell-bent gallop past them. The stallion despised the decision to walk, tossing his head and pawing at the trail with his front hooves.

Built on the brow of a hill near the stream, the mill was a long, imposing two-story adobe building. The sloped plank roof was made of good solid timbers. Portholes had been cut in the walls, and Wes spotted but a single wooden door. A ditch from the stream sent water shooting over a twenty-foot wheel that revolved lazily to its own music of creaks and moans. Another ditch carried the spent water back to the Rio Hondo.

Beyond the mill two smaller adobe buildings sprouted from the same New Mexico Territory soil from which they had been constructed. Behind them three fields had been plowed. In a corral by a barn someone was yoking a team of oxen to do more plowing. Cattle grazed along the stream. Wes envied the proprietor for his industriousness and wished it were as contagious as the smallpox so he could leave Luther to catch a dose.

Wes skirted the mill and approached the larger of the two adobe dwellings as a bearded man came out. He was a big, imposing man whose beard parted in a smile, and his black eyebrows arched with pleasure. The eyes were dark, but guileless. The extended hand, like the invitation, was sincere. "Morning, sir! Welcome to Casey's Mill. Robert Casey's the name."

Easing the sorrel up to a hitching post, Wes slid from the saddle and tied the reins. "I'm Wesley Bracken, new in these parts; perhaps you know my brother, Luther?" Wes said, grabbing Casey's big paw of a hand.

Casey nodded, gnawing his lip as if disappointed in the connection. "Know him well. He buys whiskey here. On credit."

Wes shook his head. Casey knew Luther all right.

Casey stroked his beard a moment, staring at Wes, then the stallion. "Fine looking animal you rode in on. A few men passed by yesterday, talking about meeting a man on a sorrel."

"That's me. You a friend of theirs?"

A smile cracked open Casey's beard again. "I'm friends with everyone. You run a store, you don't want to be running no business off. Fact is, your brother rode in with them, and he let them buy him a drink."

"Luther'd let anybody supply him whiskey. What do you know about the Horrells?"

"They ain't been here long. Gossip has it they started feuding in Texas and got chased out," Casey said, scratching his chin. "The Horrells being so rough a crowd, I'd hate to meet the curly wolves that scared them away."

Behind Casey, the door opened. "Breakfast," came a female voice, followed by the woman herself, emerging into the crisp early morning air. Seeing Wes, she stopped and patted her cheek. "I'm sorry for yelling," she apologized. "I didn't know we had an early visitor." A handsome female with dark eyes and black hair primly parted in the middle and tied in back, she advanced with a slight limp to Casey's side and took his hand.

Casey introduced his wife, Ellen.

Wes tipped his hat.

She smiled at the courtesy. "You just passing through Lincoln County?"

Before Wes could answer, Casey interrupted her. "He's Luther Bracken's brother."

Her smile stiffened, and she failed to find words.

"The war drove Luther to drink. I'm not proud of it, ma'am, but he's still my brother."

Ellen Casey nodded, the starch draining from her grin until it was natural again. "We sell flour, and we sell whiskey. Some men buy more flour, some buy more liquor."

"I'll settle his account before I leave," Wes offered.

"Would you join us for breakfast?" she asked.

Wes accepted the invitation, then followed the Caseys into a room crammed with merchandise. The smells of coffee and tobacco mingled with the aroma of harness leather and jerked beef. From the ceiling rafters hung pails, bridles, a variety of tools, and a saddle. Sacks of flour and sugar lined the wall, leaning against each other like bloated dominoes. And the tables were stacked with canned sardines and oysters selling for fifty cents a tin and other less expensive canned goods. Along the back wall stood a bar loaded with bolts of cloth and boxes of soap. Wes was pleased to have such a well-stocked merchant so close to his place.

"I can tell we'll do business, Robert Casey," Wes said, closing the door behind him and leaving his hat on a wall peg. "You the only store in these parts?"

Casey nodded. "A lot of the Mexicans keep a few goods and whiskey at their places and call it a store, but this is the only real store, save for the post trader at Fort Stanton. Lawrence Murphy's his name. An Irishman, he is, like me, but so dishonest he's being kicked off army property for cheating the government. Murphy's moving everything to Lincoln, up Bonito canyon from here. Fact is, he cheats everybody. I think he even sold your brother a deed to land he doesn't own."

Wes gritted his teeth but said nothing. What else had Luther not told him? What other surprises awaited him? Wes followed Robert and Ellen Casey through a door into the kitchen. Two young girls were putting a platter of bacon and a pot of coffee on the table beside the plate of biscuits and the bowl of gravy. Wes settled into the chair Casey had motioned toward just as a young boy plodded into the room, wiping the sleep from his eyes. In unison, the Casey family joined Wes at the table.

Wes ate more than his share of breakfast, Ellen Casey enjoying his ravishing appetite, which surprised even himself. He finished the meal off with a final cup of coffee and a request. "Explain how Murphy swindled my brother."

Casey shrugged. "The land along the Ruidoso, Bonito, and Hondo has yet to be surveyed. Nobody owns the land until it's surveyed. Nobody owns anything other than the improvements on the land until the surveys are done. Folks can file patents for the land, but that means nothing unless the surveys are complete and official. I hear your brother got a quitclaim deed from Murphy, but all that does is say the buildings aren't Murphy's and he won't claim them. For instance, I could sell you a quitclaim deed to New Mexico Territory, and it's worth nothing if somebody else owns it. Rumor has it your brother may have even sold the quitclaim deed back to Murphy, who may now have a claim to the land he didn't have before."

"Sold it back for drinking money, I suspect," Wes said.

"Likely so . . . much of it spent in my place."

"How much does he owe you now?"

"I figure around sixty dollars, but I'll have to check the ledger."

"What's your whiskey cost?"

"Two bits a pint."

Wes whistled. "Almost two hundred and fifty pints worth! I'll settle with you, Robert, on one condition . . ."

"Anything within reason."

"Don't sell any more liquor to my brother."

Wes reined up at the little adobe and tied Charlie to the broken hitching post. Luther was nowhere to be seen, yet his gelding and the two mares were grazing by the stream. A ribbon of smoke wafted from the chimney, wrapping around itself in vaporous knots. Something was different about the place, though Wes couldn't figure it out initially, not until he stepped into the doorless entryway.

The trash and empty cans had been removed from inside. Glancing behind him, Wes realized the debris that had been piled around the outside had been cleared as well. Luther was hunkered down by the corner fireplace, bouncing a sizzling skillet over the hot coals. The sweet aroma of frying meat greeted Wes, but not Luther, who never looked back. Luther would brood awhile, if the liquor hadn't pickled his brain, but he'd get over it in time. After all, Luther had a commonsense head on his shoulders as long as he stayed sober.

In the corner by the fireplace, Luther had stacked the supplies Wes had brought with him. Luther's bedroll was laid out straight on the earthen floor, and the blankets were smoothed atop it. Wes had not touched his bedding after he had gotten up, yet it was smoothed out as well. Maybe the baptismal at the river had converted Luther, but Wes wondered how long before the backsliding began.

"When you've finished with your meal, I want you to look over the breeding stock, Luther, see if you approve," Wes offered.

"This was a skinny rabbit, Wes, but there's enough meat for two," Luther grunted.

His stomach was heavy with the Casey breakfast, but Wes understood he shouldn't refuse Luther. "I'll do with a bite."

Luther pulled the skillet from the fireplace, dropping it on the ground at his feet, forking a hunk of rabbit onto a tin plate, and offering it to Wes. "I borrowed your plate. It's the only one between us."

Damn, Wes thought, Luther had given away most of his belongings from tools and harnesses to his eating utensils. It must have been a strong urge, that liquor, to bite him. Wes waved the plate away. "You use it, let me grab a piece out of the skillet."

Luther slid to the ground and attacked the strips of rabbit meat with his fingers.

Squatting by the frying pan, Wes snatched a chunk of the sizzling meat. As he did, he studied Luther's gaunt face and his sunken eyes flitting from side to side. The eyes were blank, all emotion drained away. Maybe it was the liquor, but possibly it was the war that had siphoned off so much of the South's spirit. Wes chewed on the tough meat, remembering how he had always looked up to Luther and had admired his oldest brother's riding skills and especially his instinct with horses.

Luther gobbled away at the meat on his plate, then finished the remaining strips in the skillet. Leaving his tin dish on the floor, Luther stood up and stretched, never looking at Wes. "Any work you want me to start on now, Wes?"

"Let's step to the Ruidoso for some cool water to wash down our lunch."

Shrugging, Luther walked out the doorway. "I've had enough river to drink for one day."

"Then look over the horses I bought us," Wes responded, following him outside.

"Meet you at the animals," Luther said, walking away from the adobe toward the two hobbled mares grazing in the midday sun.

Wes untied Charlie and led him to the stream, where both quenched their thirst. Next, he mounted and rode over to the mares, reaching them just after Luther.

The older brother walked around each mare, opened their mouths, and forced apart their jaws to inspect their teeth. He nodded periodically and occasionally mumbled something to himself. Luther spent the most time with the black mare with the white snip between her nostrils, confirming Wes's opinion that the pretty mare was the best of the lot. When Luther completed inspecting the mares, he motioned for Wes to get off Charlie and then complained that it was hard to evaluate a horse with a saddle on his back. Luther spent considerable time, holding the stallion's head, studying the broad nose and bulging jaws. Wes awaited a verdict on the stallion.

Without looking at Wes, Luther offered his assessment. "Two out of three ain't bad."

"The stallion?" Wes asked.

"Nope," Luther replied, folding his arms across his chest like a man with a secret. "The stallion's got good lines, good lungs. He's a bit wide in the head to be a pretty horse, but he'll do for everything but looks. The mistake was the black."

"What?" Wes cried.

"It's the head again. A pretty head, with good lines. Only problem is its size. It's too small."

Wes shook his head. "I don't see it."

Luther ambled over to the black mare and grabbed her head, twisting it toward Wes. "Look at her nostrils. See how narrow they are next to the stallion's?"

Wes shot a glance at the stallion. The sorrel's nostrils were bigger and rounder, not slender crescents like the mare's.

"Small nostrils limit the air she breathes. She'll get winded quick in a run," Luther said, his hands sliding away from the mare's face. "A tiny head creates another problem." Luther bent over and un-hobbled the mare. As the binding came loose, the animal trotted fifteen yards away. "Now mount your stallion so you can catch the mare when I finish your lesson."

Luther was curing his wounded pride by humbling Wes and his knowledge of horses. Wes figured he had it coming for giving Luther a bath in the river. As long as Luther stayed sober, Wes would tolerate his arrogance. Silently, he mounted.

"Small head means less bone and less weight," Luther

Preston Lewis

lectured. "A horse needs a weighted head for balance." Standing, he whistled, and the black mare darted for the river. "Look at her stride. There's a hitch in it, gives her poor balance, makes her tentative, and all because her head is too small."

Wes nodded. He had noticed the mare's perky gait before but thought it a sign of a positive spirit rather than a running liability. Luther could teach him much about raising and trading horses, if he remained sober.

Wes clicked his tongue, and the stallion bolted after the mare, quickly passing her and turning her back toward Luther. The mare stumbled on the turn, confirming Luther's assessment of her balance. Wes rode up beside the mare, grabbing her mane and slowing her to a walk. He herded her back to Luther, who was waiting to re-hobble her.

When that was done, Luther glanced up at Wes, a superior sneer on his face.

Angering at Luther's condescension, Wes grimaced, then spoke. "We've got more business than horses to discuss, Luther. Let's meet back at the adobe to talk about who has title to our place."

34

CHAPTER 4

Wes sat on his bedroll, his gaze drifting from one side of the furniture-less room to the other, taking in the doorway without a door, the window openings without glass, shutters, or canvas coverings. Outside were fields unplowed, fences unbuilt, irrigation ditches undug. And the tools for that work, even the tin utensils for eating his meals, were gone, Luther trading them for liquor. The wagon and team that had brought those belongings from northwest Arkansas were missing. A trail of whiskey bottles and bartered Bracken possessions likely littered Luther's trail from Arkansas. But besides their wagon, implements, and belongings, Luther had squandered something more valuable than money. He had wasted time. By hard work a man could earn his dollars back, but he could never regain lost hours.

As Wes waited, his fingers impatiently tapped the saddlebag beside him. Inside were the greenbacks and gold he had taken out of Arkansas. Half was his, half Luther's. But Luther would squander it, just as he had their belongings and, as a result, two years if not more of their future.

Maybe Sarafina had been right. Bad luck came to those who claimed the house of a dead man. Shaking his head, Wes heard a scratching at the door and looked up to see Luther shuffling his boots on the hard-packed ground, entering with his shoulders slumped, face strained, eyes downcast.

Luther angled to the corner farthest from Wes and leaned against the wall, raising his face until his eyes met Wes's.

35

Emotionless, his face blended into the shadows coating the plain adobe wall.

Lifting the saddlebag, Wes tossed it halfway between them, his brother flinching as it thudded to the dirt floor. "There's five hundred dollars, less your liquor bill at Casey's Mill, in my saddlebags."

Luther's eyes expanded with anticipation. He licked his lips.

"Where's the wagon and the team, Luther, the tools and everything you left Arkansas with?"

The glimmer of hope died in his eyes. Luther pushed away from the wall, taking a half step with his fists clenched, then thinking better of it and retreating. He lifted his chin defiantly. "I sold some, lost some in card games."

"Half of it was mine, Luther."

"I'd planned on repaying you," he rasped.

"What about your whiskey bill at the Casey place?"

"I was gonna repay it."

Wes pushed himself up from his bedroll. "And what about this fellow Murphy? Word has it you bought a worthless deed to this land. That so?"

"I don't recall for sure, Wes. I know I traded the wagon and team for papers on this land."

"And then you sold it back to him, for what, Luther—drinking money?"

Luther's shoulders slumped, and he heaved a sigh of guilt.

"You're worthless when you've been drinking."

Luther's lip trembled in anger as he stepped out of the corner toward the door. "I should ride out of Lincoln County."

"I need you, Luther, 'cause you know horses, but I need you sober. All the time!"

His older brother shrugged. "I don't take but a little whiskey now and again. I haven't had nothing to drink all day, Wes."

"You gotta give it up altogether, Luther, if you're gonna work our land with me."

"I got no reason to stay now, Wes, me owing you all my gold. I can be just as broke someplace else," Luther answered, standing in the doorway and staring toward the stream.

"Sweat out that whiskey urge with hard work here, and you can keep your half of the gold less the sixty dollars I paid the Caseys for your drinking tab."

Luther stood motionless, a man turned to stone from his hard thinking.

Just steps from the door was land that held promise if irrigated with sweat. Wes wondered if Luther could help fulfill that potential. But first, he must step away from the bottle.

Luther twisted around to face Wes. When he spoke, his answer lacked enthusiasm. "I'll stay, Wes."

Wes grabbed Luther's hand. "In a few years, Luther, we can have colts and fillies running all over our place. We can breed good horses, sell them to the ranchers or the army. We can raise cattle. Whatever mistakes you made, Luther, you didn't fail us on claiming a fine place. Good soil, good water, great potential."

Luther pulled his fingers from Wes's.

"Rebuild us a fire, Luther," Wes said, pointing to the corner fireplace where coals still glowed from lunch.

Without questioning Wes, Luther did as ordered. Wes opened the saddlebags, taking out his pouch of gold coins and his stack of greenbacks. As he divided the coins into two equal stacks, Wes noticed Luther glancing over his shoulder at the gold pieces.

"Four hundred and forty dollars Luther," Wes said, when he finished with the gold coins and divided out the bills. "That's two hundred and fifty dollars for me, leaving you a hundred and ninety dollars after the sixty dollars I reimbursed the Caseys for your liquor charges."

Luther extended his open palm to Wes for his share.

Wes shook his head. "Before you get it, you've got to prove to me you'll not drink."

"It's mine, Wes."

"I've got a claim on it, Luther, for the wagon and tools you lost. Now fetch me three tin cans from those you dumped behind the house."

Luther scowled, grumbling as he stepped outside to the back. After he disappeared, Wes reached in his saddlebag and pulled out two small squares of lead for molding bullets. He slipped the squares into his pants pocket, just as Luther walked in without saying a word. Wes strode across the room where the supplies he had brought from Texas were stacked. Digging through them, he uncovered two boxes of candles, long and milky white. He could feel Luther's puzzled gaze upon his back.

When Luther offered him the tin cans, Wes studied them a moment, nodding his good luck that all three were blackened from being heated over coals. Wes stepped to the fireplace, his brother following him. The embers glowed red as the two men squatted by the shallow hearth. Wes snapped the candles in thirds, Luther staring incredulously, as Wes dropped the gold pieces in two of the cans. The brothers exchanged no words as Wes slid both cans toward the embers, the silence broken only by the sputtering and cracking of the disturbed coals.

As the candle wax melted, Wes stood up and untied the bandanna from his neck. When the wax was molten, Wes squatted by the fire, reaching with his kerchief to retrieve a tin. Quickly he poured part of the milky wax into the third can, then returned the other to the heat.

As the wax solidified, Wes turned to Luther. "To show you my faith in you, you can have your entire share in gold. I'll take mine in the bills and remaining gold. Hand me your portion of gold."

Luther picked up from the floor a hundred and ninety dollars in coins, squeezing them in his hand.

Wes held up the tin with the congealed wax. "Drop them in."

A look of confusion wandered across Luther's face until Wes shook the tin. As if they had rusted shut, Luther's fingers slowly, reluctantly parted over the can's mouth. Then the coins clinked one by one inside. Next Luther held his palms toward Wes as if he expected to be accused of hiding part of the money. With his bandanna-wrapped hand, Wes reached into the fireplace, taking the fuller of the two cans. Through the thin bandanna, the heated metal stung his fingers as he hurriedly poured the molten wax over the gold coins, which gradually disappeared in the waxen murkiness as it cooled.

Placing the hot tin by his boot, Wes pulled the wick strings out and let the wax solidify. "The money's yours, Luther," Wes said, pointing at the tin, "but I'm not letting you have it until I'm sure you won't buy whiskey. Find me a place to bury it. As long as the gold stays buried, we're partners."

"Damn you, Wes," Luther said, reaching for his tin of gold.

Wes grabbed his wrist. "Take your knife and go dig a hole. I'll bring it to you."

Luther jerked his arm from his brother's grip and stomped outside with anger in each step. When Luther disappeared, Wes yanked the lead squares from his pocket and dropped them into the other tin can at his boots. Then he retrieved the tin still heating on the fire, pouring the rest of the wax over the bullet lead. That can he would use as a decoy for Luther. The other, the one with Luther's gold, Wes would hide. Sorry thing, when a man couldn't trust his brother, but Wes saw no other way to keep Luther from squandering the gold on whiskey.

Wes returned the greenbacks to his leather pouch and tucked it into his britches pocket. Then he grabbed Luther's gold and stepped outside. Observing Luther on his hands and knees under a willow near the Ruidoso, Wes walked around the cabin and tossed the gold-bearing tin up on the roof.

Returning inside, Wes grabbed the water bucket by the door and then the decoy can. He ambled toward the river, wondering if he might not have been better off just claiming Luther's money as his own instead of creating this deception.

Luther was on his hands and knees, jabbing with his knife and clawing with his free hand at a hole eighteen inches deep.

"That'll do," Wes said.

Luther sat back on his knees as Wes dropped the tin can into the void. Luther's eyes were those of a whipped and hungry dog watching a fresh bone being buried out of reach. With his boot, Wes scraped the dark earth into the hole, mounding it up, then stepping on it. Luther stared wordlessly, motionlessly. Wes carried the water bucket to the stream, filling it then returning to where Luther gazed blankly at the ground.

As Wes dumped the water, Luther remained motionless, even when water splattered him. By pouring water over the freshly turned dirt, Wes knew Luther could not dig it up without leaving signs of what he had done. Luther spat at the puddle, pushed himself up from his perch, spun around, and marched back to the adobe.

Wes knew Luther would brood the rest of the day. For himself, there was work to do.

Over the next week, Wes checked that spot under the willow tree daily. Each day Luther went without a drink, he dropped a fist-sized stone over the burial site. Other than the growing pile of stones, Wes found no sign of tampering because he had kept Luther busy. Together they had traveled to the Casey place so Wes could buy supplies. He purchased a team of mules and harnesses from one of Casey's neighbors. Needing tools, Wes acquired an iron hoe, shovel, rake, ax, saw, and hammer, as well as hinges for a door and a couple pounds of nails. After adding to his bill a blanket each for himself and Luther, a pot, eating utensils, plates, and foodstuffs, including dried beans, tinned oysters, jerked beef, canned peaches, and a sack of flour, Wes knew there would be little money left for buying more horses. He still must purchase seed for a crop to last their small herd through the winter, and he needed more lumber to repair the adobe.

Because good timber was rare except farther up the Ruidoso valley, Casey's Mill did not cut lumber. Wes negotiated with Robert Casey to borrow his wagon for the twenty-mile trip to Dowlin's Mill up in the mountains where the pine trees were plentiful. Since Casey also needed lumber, he agreed to the loan if Wes would deliver Casey's lumber on the return trip.

Wes wanted to make the trip sooner, but he still didn't trust Luther to keep up with his plowing and other chores without supervision. After a week, Luther remained sullen, but his eyes had cleared of their redness, and his face had fleshed out from regular meals. Each day Luther had gone about his plowing at sunup and stayed at it until dusk. Not once did Wes see him wander over to the willow tree by the Ruidoso.

The morning of the trip to Dowlin's Mill, Wes arose with Luther to share a pot of black coffee and pieces of jerked beef for breakfast. Luther never said much unless asked and just sat on the floor and stared at his tin plate. He had finished his meal and was rising to go plow when Wes broke the early silence.

"You'll be on your own for the next few days, Luther."

A sneer crawled across Luther's face. "You figure I forgot where the gold's buried?"

"You've pulled your weight, Luther, this last week. I've no complaint."

"And no trust, watching me like a buzzard looking for a meal," Luther replied. "It'll be good to do my work without you standing over me like you're my pappy."

Even in the early morning light, Wes could detect the anger

41

on Luther's face. "I'm taking the stallion over to Casey's place and borrowing his wagon, for a trip up to Dowlin's Mill for lumber."

Luther's eyes widened, and his mouth dropped as his face paled. "You can't," he stammered.

This was the first emotion Luther had shown since they buried the tin. "Why not?"

"You've got to pass the Horrell place. They'll kill you, Wes; they'll kill you!"

The wagon rumbled down the trail and splashed through the water at the Ruidoso crossing. To his left, Wes observed Luther following the two mules along newly turned furrows in the field. Luther ignored Wes's passing, though he had seemed concerned when Wes had mentioned the trip to Dowlin's Mill.

In his lap, Wes carried his Winchester '73, loaded for the Horrells or other trouble. He wasn't looking for a fight, but he wouldn't run from one either. A man that's looked across a battle line and seen hundreds of advancing Yankee soldiers, all seemingly headed straight for him, wouldn't frighten from a handful of Texas siblings. When he had swapped his sorrel for the Casey wagon, the storekeeper repeated Luther's warning about the Horrells and gave him without charge a box of cartridges, insurance that Casey would get his wagon back. Wagons were valuable in this part of the country as in most of New Mexico Territory, which still thirsted for its first railroad to trickle out of Colorado.

Back at the cabin, Luther kept plowing while Wes loaded the wagon with his bedding and grub, including a tin of peaches and oysters for Sarafina Zamora and her husband, a small gift for their hospitality and an excuse to stop for a moment to enjoy Sarafina's unadorned beauty.

As he started the wagon for Dowlin's Mill, Wes waved at

Luther, who continued to ignore him. In the springless wagon, every bump or hole in the trail jarred Wes's spine. Where the valley narrowed, the road veered away from the gentle Ruidoso and brushed against the side of the jagged limestone slopes. Erosion's refuse littered the trail, the rocks too many to miss and the team of mules hitting most with hoof or wheel, increasing Wes's discomfort. Rounding the river bend, he spied the Zamora place.

Two men worked in the fields, which glistened with irrigation water channeled through *acequias* from the Ruidoso. That was how the Bracken land should look, Wes thought. The trail edged away from the mountainside and angled for the Zamora adobe. Wes straightened in his seat and slid the Winchester from his lap onto the floorboard. One man in the field looked up and pointed toward Wes, then dropped his hoe and ran to the adobe.

By the man's agility, hopping among the irrigated furrows, Wes knew it must be Carlos. Wes heard a whistle and saw Carlos wave his arm toward the river. In an instant, he observed the flash of a doeskin dress emerging from bushes by the stream. Sarafina scampered into the adobe, leaving behind deformed brush, bloated and splotched with blacks and browns and a sprinkling of whites. It was her laundry, left on the shrubs along the stream to dry.

From the field, Bonifacio Zamora came as well, his gait little more than an awkward walk. Reaching the adobe, he paused at the corner, as if he were catching his breath, then made it the rest of the way to the door. Carlos followed him inside, returning moments later with a rifle cradled in his arms.

As Wes turned the wagon off the main trail toward the Zamora place, he watched Carlos stiffen. When the wagon drew within twenty-five yards of the cabin, Sarafina darted out of the house to Carlos. Wes could hear her excited voice, issuing her

43

thoughts in Spanish. Reluctantly Carlos lowered the rifle to the ground.

Sarafina motioned for her husband to come out, and the three stood together as Wes drove up, pulled back on the reins, and grabbed the brake lever. A smile as warm as the morning decorated Sarafina's face. Her husband's gray beard revealed a grin. Only Carlos stood sullen before him, lean and muscular, the dark eyes of a predator silently watching Wes. Behind those eyes, though, was the fear of inexperienced youth. With maturity, Carlos would be a strong man. Or, an evil one.

"*Buenas dias, Señor* Bracken," called out Bonifacio Zamora, hobbling out to help Wes from his wagon.

Wes tipped his hat to Zamora and nodded to Sarafina, who seemed to read his mind.

"The Texas *diablos* are a plague upon us. We must take care these days, when white men approach," she said, her voice filled with concern more than fear.

"If they trouble you, come for me," Wes answered as he climbed from the wagon.

"On foot, on donkeys?" Carlos spat out the words with contempt. "They would shoot us like dogs, and you would laugh like they laughed at Bonifacio."

"*Silencio, Carlos, silencio!*" Sarafina stamped her feet. "*Señor* Bracken saved my husband."

Grabbing Carlos's arm, Bonifacio jerked him around with surprising strength and spoke heatedly in Spanish.

Carlos shouted back words Wes could not understand and pulled himself free, stumbling inside the adobe and slamming the door behind him.

Anger boiled in Sarafina's eyes. "Think not of his rudeness. You are always welcome at our home."

Wes reached into the back of the wagon for the canned peaches and oysters. He offered them to Bonifacio, but Sarafina took them from his hand, her soft fingers touching his for a moment.

"We are grateful," she replied. "We must return your favor."

Wes nodded. "Can your husband or brother repair our adobe roof? You can see the sun and stars through one corner."

Sarafina shrugged. "Both can, but it's bad luck to make your home in that of a dead man, I told you."

"But it's worse luck for it to rain in your house," Wes replied.

"Perhaps my husband will, but Carlos would never do it." Sarafina spoke with great concern in Spanish to Bonifacio, who glanced from his young wife to Wes, then pursed his lips as he stared at a cloudless sky overhead. He answered in Spanish that Sarafina interpreted.

"He says the spirit of the dead man might not escape the house if we cover the hole. But he will do it to repay your kindness. We ask only that you escort us from here to your place and back so the Texas *diablos* will not trouble us."

"Agreed," Wes said.

"Stay and I'll fix you food," Sarafina offered.

"I'm sorry, but I must go to Dowlin's Mill for lumber."

Her hand flew to her mouth, and the two cans tumbled to the ground. "You will pass the place of the *diablos*."

Wes nodded. "I need lumber." He pulled himself back into the wagon. "I'll come back in a few days for you," he said, untying the reins from the brake handle. When he shook the lines, the mules jerked against the harnesses, and the wagon lurched toward Dowlin's Mill.

The valley before him widened, and the trail swung away from the stream. South of the road, a big adobe house with gun-ports in the walls brooded in the shade of three cottonwood trees. Recognizing some horses in the corral as those of the Horrells, Wes patted the Winchester in his lap and studied the terrain well. All he noticed was a white woman, her hands on her hips, scowling as he passed. The Horrell women, evidently, were as sour as their husbands. Several times, Wes glanced over his shoulder but saw nothing alarming, and the trip unfolded uneventfully into the high country where timber was plentiful.

He reached Dowlin's Mill about dusk and explained his mission to Paul Dowlin, a middle-aged man with a warm handshake and an honest smile. Dowlin enjoyed a visitor as much as he liked doing business. He fed Wes, put him up for the night in his mill, and then helped him load the lumber so Wes could leave the next day before noon.

Spurning the offer of lunch because of the time he would lose, Wes made the return trip much more slowly because of the heavy load. He passed the Horrell place as safely as before, though he noticed the horses were missing from the corral.

Darkness descended on him before he reached San Patricio. The Zamora adobe was dark when he passed it. A full moon made the night travel easier. When he neared his place, he called for Luther, half expecting to find his brother sleeping off a two-day drunk, but a match flickered in the open window of the adobe. Moments later, Luther appeared in his boots and union suit to help unload the Bracken share of the lumber. Luther spoke only when spoken to, and Wes was too tired to attempt conversation.

When the pair finished unloading the wood beside the adobe, Wes told Luther he was taking the wagon to Casey's Mill, where he would stay the night. Luther grunted and returned to his bedroll.

Wes made it to Casey's Mill by midnight, unhooked the mules and put them in the corral, then rolled out his bedroll under the wagon and let the sheer exhaustion put him to sleep.

Come morning, fatigue still lingered in his bones, but Mrs. Casey helped him further with a big breakfast and begged him to stay a bit longer. Wes declined. He was eager to race home astride Charlie and evaluate Luther's plowing progress by daylight.

On the ride home, he gave Charlie free rein, the sorrel maintaining full speed until he splashed across the Rio Ruidoso and stepped onto Bracken land. The fields were empty, Luther nowhere to be seen, and the plow mules missing.

Cursing, Wes reined Charlie up at the house and jumped to the ground. "Luther!" he yelled. "Why the hell aren't you out in the field?"

Before Wes could say anything else, Luther appeared at the door, his own Winchester '73 in his right hand, a bloody bandage around his left arm. "You figured I'd been drinking, didn't you, Wes? Check the gold, dammit, it's still there."

Wes stopped in his tracks. "What happened?"

"Horsemen last night came in after you left, took the mares, the mules, and my gelding. I tried to stop them, but you can see what happened," Luther said, staring sadly at his arm.

"Was it the Horrells?"

"I don't think so," Luther said, shaking his head, then his bloodied arm. "The arm's not as bad as it looks, but I guess there goes our chances of raising horses."

"Not yet, Luther, not yet," Wes answered.

CHAPTER 5

Wes was tying his bedroll behind his saddle's cantle when he spotted the three riders, their horses standing in the Ruidoso with heads bowed over the water.

"Get your carbine, Luther," Wes commanded, as he studied the trio. They sat stiffly in their saddles, no frivolity in their posture. They meant trouble for someone.

Luther emerged from the adobe, his right hand clamped around his Winchester and ready for business. His left arm was gimpy from the bullet wound, but Wes had re-bandaged it for him and confirmed that it was only a flesh injury.

Wes pointed to the three men watering their horses. "They don't look like Horrells. You seen 'em before?"

"Nope."

"You positive you didn't see them last night?"

Luther exploded. "I'm sure, dammit. I ain't had no whiskey, Wes, so I ought to know what I seen."

When their horses finished drinking, the trio advanced, not along the trail, but straight for Wes and Luther.

Wes pulled his carbine from its saddle boot, cradling it in his elbow, and stepped around the sorrel to meet them.

They reined up an easy distance from Wes, the man in the middle removing his hat with his right hand, his gun hand by the set of the Colt on his hip. He pointed at the stallion.

"Looks like you're taking a little trip, mister. Might I be right?" the stranger asked.

Before answering, Wes took in the man's reddish-brown hair, his wide eyes, his broad face, and the stubble on his cheeks. His motions avoided anything sudden or threatening, not out of fear, Wes figured, as much as care not to create any unnecessary problems.

"Perhaps," Wes answered.

A sliver of a grin worked its way across the rider's face. "Might you be going after horse thieves?"

Wes nodded.

"They hit you, too, did they? How many'd you lose?" The man replaced his hat on his head.

"Two mares, a gelding, and a team of mules," Wes answered, slowly letting the barrel of the carbine slide down his left arm until it pointed toward the ground.

The man's grin widened into a full smile. "Jesse Evans is the name." He introduced himself and the pair beside him as Ansel and Clem. "We work for John Chisum."

"Don't know him," Wes replied.

"Then you ain't been long in Lincoln County, mister."

"I'm Wesley Bracken, fellow behind me is my brother, Luther," Wes explained. "I'm new here."

"John Chisum runs cattle all up and down the Pecos River. He says he's the biggest rancher in the entire territory, and I'm not one to question him that. Chisum's got more cowhands taking his pay than most of the so-called ranchers around here have steers. And for a ranch so big, funny thing is, he don't own any property, just claims the Pecos. In these parts, the man that controls the water controls the land." Evans looked about for a moment. " 'Course you must've figured that out, settling here."

"You're his hands, then?" Wes asked.

Ansel and Clem snickered.

"Yeah," Evans replied as Clem and Ansel laughed. "You might say that. Fact is, a man with so much land and so many cattle

49

needs a few hands to help him keep what's his. We're out to bring back the twenty or so of his horses stolen a few nights ago."

"They hit us last night," Wes said.

Evans nodded. "Way we figure it, it's the Mes brothers from La Boquilla. They say they're farmers, but they never produce a crop of anything except mischief. Couple times a year, they round up as many of Chisum's horses as they can and run down to Mexico to sell them. Chisum's got more horses than he and his hands can use, but if he don't go after his losses, every two-bit outfit in the territory'll be stealing what's his. You're welcome to join us, Wes, even up the odds, as if they mattered."

Wes turned and shoved his carbine back in its scabbard. "I'll throw in with you." He pulled himself aboard his saddle.

Evans laughed. "The boys, here, are as talkative as a couple pine trees, but they know horses, and they know horse thieves and don't care to talk about either. Now me, I'm the best talker in Lincoln County. I know my job and most other things. What I don't know, I make up so you'll never lack for conversation."

Wes shook his head. "We riding or talking?"

"The boys just ride," Evans chuckled. "I do both."

Turning to Luther, Wes winked. "Don't hitch that plow up to your shoulders and try any plowing until I get our mules back."

His brother stood erect, wearing the red-stained bandage on his arm like a badge of honor. "I'll find something to keep me busy, Wes."

Wes tipped his hat to Luther, feeling comfortable for once about leaving him.

Luther replied, "Good luck, Wes."

"Let's ride," Evans whooped, using his hat to slap the flank of his gray gelding.

Spurring Charlie, Wes whistled as the stallion bolted ahead

with long and powerful strides. Even so, the sorrel gained little on the trio. They knew horses all right, and they knew speed, all of them mounted on good horseflesh. Wes wondered how the four horses would fare against each other with an equal start. Beneath him, Charlie seemed invigorated by the full run. Though this was a race, it was not one among themselves, but against the horse thieves that had at least an eight-hour lead.

The quartet passed the Zamora place at a gallop. Wes glimpsed Sarafina, working in the garden plot beside the adobe, then racing inside at the sound of the galloping horses. Wes wondered if she recognized him. She was the last pleasant thought he would have for hours as the men rode deeper into the valley.

Just as Wes was wondering whether or not he had overestimated Evans's horse sense, the gun hand backed off on his gray gelding, and the others slowed their mounts, Charlie passing them before Wes tugged on the reins, easing the stallion into a trot. Throughout the morning the riders alternated between a gallop for speed and distance and a lope for rest, each time Jesse Evans seeming to know how far to push the horses without crossing over that line into the exhaustion that could ruin an animal.

All the while the four men plowed farther into the timbered slopes of the high country where the trail narrowed between walls of pines. They passed Dowlin's Mill about noon, stopping long enough to water their mounts and grab a few bites of jerky and a few sips of water for themselves before remounting and leaving. Paul Dowlin had reported hearing a herd of horses pass in the night, but that was evident from the chewed-up path they were tracking.

Farther up the valley, a lesser trail angled off to the south. Though the horse tracks continued along the main route, Evans cut to the left, taking the narrower trace. The horses fell in line single file, Evans in the lead, then Wes and the other two. Wes wondered why Chisum's men were leaving the main trail.

Evans seemed to read his mind and glanced back over his shoulder. "We know where they're going, and this trail'll get us there faster."

"Why didn't they take it?" Wes called back.

"This route cuts through the Mescalero reservation. Those Apaches can steal horses better than you can speak English. The Mes brothers'd be lucky to ride out with their mounts, much less the herd."

That was solid information, Wes thought, in case he ever had more horses stolen or brought a herd into Lincoln County. Wordlessly, the four rode for more than an hour, the trail widening into a spacious valley, lush with the greenery that follows the spring melt.

Up ahead was a mill and past the stream the buildings of the Indian agency, neatly aligned with military precision and plainly designed with the low-bid architecture that gave government structures their unadorned sameness. At one building, Wes guessed two hundred Apache women and children had lined up with empty bowls in their hands and vacant looks on their faces. Beyond them, the men congregated, their pride stronger than their hunger, their envious stares following the four horsemen as they trotted past.

"Those bucks sure like the cut of our horses, Wes!" Evans hollered, whooping his gray gelding into a gallop, the other animals pounding after him.

By late afternoon, the upward slope leveled out, and the horses had an easier time. By dusk, the quartet had reached a great precipice that looked over a vast expanse of white sands to the west and rough basin country to the southwest, where broken mountains jutted like granite teeth from the earth.

Wes eased his stallion to the edge of the cliff where Evans sat on his horse studying the basin that shimmered with the lingering heat of late afternoon. Wes couldn't figure the trail from here, not with three hundred feet between him and the ground at the bottom of the mountain.

"Good trail up to now, Evans. We fly from here?" Wes asked, easing his stallion back from the cliff's edge.

Jesse spit over the precipice and waited as if expecting to hear an echo when it hit ground. "Pretty view, ain't it?"

"I didn't come for pretty."

"Come morning, when the air is clear and crisp, we'll be able to see the Mes brothers if they're around anywhere. We'll know how hard we'll have to push our horses. You missed the trail cutoff about a mile back."

"You've got it all figured out?"

Nodding, Evans grinned. "I've done this before." He pointed southwest to the jagged peaks. "I figure we'll get our horses back this side of the Organ Mountains." Evans shook his head, then spat over the cliff again. "Some folks say those mountains look like the pipes of an organ. Me, I think the folks that named them had never seen an organ."

"You've no imagination, Jesse."

Evans shrugged. "Oh, I've got imagination. I've wondered what it would be like to be as wealthy as old John Chisum. I've thought about what I could do with a spread a hundredth the size of his place and a herd of cattle to graze it. It's not imagination I lack, Wes, it's money."

"And horses."

"That'll change, come tomorrow," Evans replied. With a sweep of his arm, he pointed to tall trees a hundred yards back of the cliff. "We'll toss our bedrolls there."

Wes glanced that direction, seeing Ansel and Clem already unsaddling their horses and pitching their bedding. They had the stern look of men who knew their business and took grim satisfaction from it.

"Go on and join them," Evans offered. "We'll pitch a cold camp and watch for their fires below, then get an early start come morning."

At the encampment Wes was greeted by the two men's silence. He tended and hobbled the stallion, then unfurled his bedroll over a layer of pine needles. He eased his aching muscles down onto the bed and stretched out on his side, propping his head up in the palm of his hand and studying Clem and Ansel across from him.

Clem, the bigger of the two, wore a plaid shirt over ox-like shoulders that tapered into thin, whippet-like arms. His ruddy face, stubbled with whiskers and distorted by a chew of tobacco, bore a smile that looked like a rip in cheap cloth and revealed tobacco-stained teeth.

Ansel carried a thin frame and head that seemed too small for the bug eyes that bulged out of their sockets like they took in everything ahead and behind him. He had a habit of shaking his gun hand and wriggling his fingers like some deadly ritual.

Both men toted well-greased revolvers in well-oiled leather holsters, and neither appeared as much cowboy as law officer. Or, outlaw.

Gradually, the cool breeze blew out the light to the west, and the night crawled in with a chill on its breath. For more than an hour, Evans sat on his horse at the edge of the precipice, as still and quiet as an equestrian statue.

As Wes took off his boots and slid under his blanket, Jesse Evans rejoined the others.

"Didn't see a thing," he said. "We'll do better in the morning, when the air is clearer." He dismounted and prepared himself and his horse for the night.

Shortly Evans was in his bedroll and breathing heavy from

the quick onset of sleep. Wes gradually faded away into rest, though it was a mite cold to be comfortable.

Come morning, he heard Evans stirring, and he arose with him, both men pulling on their boots and stretching as they jumped up from the frigid ground. Evans ambled toward the cliff, Wes following closely.

The eastern sky behind them was trimmed in pink at the fringes, but at the precipice everything to the west was black like a great abyss at the edge of the earth. They stood in silence as the darkness evaporated, a layer at a time, and the whole heavens lightened in shades of pink.

Jesse pointed to the northwest and whispered, "Camp fires."

Wes squinted at the basin and could just make out the two pinpoints of light, likely a couple miles apart.

"I figure the Mes brothers are the northernmost fire. We'll catch them on the mountains. I hope your aim is as good as your sorrel."

"Charlie's a fine one."

Evans nodded and whirled around. "It's time for us to be moving."

Wes trotted back to camp with him.

The other two men had saddled their mounts and now checked the loads in their pistols and carbines.

"Looks like you're a little anxious, Ansel," Evans said to the man with the bug eyes.

"I aim to be ready for any opportunity I get to shoot a few greasers. Clem feels the same way," Ansel replied while his partner in the plaid shirt grinned.

Wes studied them a moment as he tied his bedroll. "You boys from Texas, by chance?"

"Yep," Ansel answered, "and proud of it."

Wes thought so. He turned and saddled the stallion, finishing up with Jesse. Wordlessly, they mounted and rode toward the trail that led from their camp into the basin that separated them from the distant mountain ranges.

During the ride, Wes kept telling himself he was after horse thieves, not Mexicans. He wasn't sure Ansel and Clem made that distinction. How Evans felt, Wes could not be sure, but he had a better sense about Jesse than the other two. During the descent down the mountain trail and the gallop across the dusty flats, Wes reminded himself he was after his horses. If it took a killing to get them back, so be it. If not, that would be fine, too. Or at least as long as the thieves learned their lesson and left his stock alone in the future.

During the ride, he wondered what Sarafina would think if he had to kill one of her people. He worried, too, that he should even be thinking of a married woman on a hard journey across New Mexico.

CHAPTER 6

Jesse Evans reined up his gray gelding and licked his dry lips as Wes drew beside him atop the mountain pass. Both took swigs from their canteens and savored the wetness even if the water was hot and musty. Behind them the flats shimmered in the afternoon heat. Before them stretched the road to Mesilla, and they could see for miles.

A sly grin on his lips, Evans nodded at Wes as he pointed at the afternoon sun. "No riders with horses, Wes. We topped San Augustine Pass first." Evans laughed. "Now we'll just ride back down the trail. The Mes brothers will be so busy looking over their shoulders, they won't figure on us riding in from the west."

Evans slid his Colt from his holster and examined the load, then repeated the process with his carbine. Wes did likewise.

Approaching Wes, Ansel and Clem checked their guns for what must have been the sixth time since dawn.

"We can ride easy now, boys. It's downhill all the way to the Mes brothers and a little fun." Evans grinned. "And, I feel a good conversation coming on."

Ansel and Clem shook their heads, jiggled their reins, and trotted past Evans.

"If those two birds won't talk to me, that just leaves you, partner."

Wes shrugged and shook the reins. "Your jabber's a small price for getting my animals back." Evans pulled beside him, his talk vigorous, his manner easy. Evans remained casual until he rounded a bend in the trail and saw riders ahead. His face stiffened, and his hand dropped to his Colt.

Three horsemen approached, one of them a young boy. The only horses with them were their mounts. Wes watched the tension drain from Evans's face.

Ansel and Clem slowed their mounts until Jesse and Wes caught up and passed them. Within hailing distance of the oncoming fellows, Evans reined in his gelding and took off his hat with a magnanimous sweep of his arm.

"Howdy," he called, and they nodded back their silent answer, the freckle-faced boy trotting his mount up beside a man that was likely his father. Then all three pulled up on the reins. "Heading Mesilla way?"

The father nodded, his lean face drawn with suspicion, his eyes moving nervously behind wire-rim glasses. Wes had the distinct feeling he was carrying considerable money somewhere on himself or his horse. Finally, he spoke. "Afternoon, gentlemen."

"Jesse Evans is my name," he replied. "We work for John Chisum."

The connection with Chisum eased the man's fears, but still he stared at Evans. "It's no business of mine," Evans continued, "but did you fellows cook breakfast in the basin this morning?"

A puzzled expression distorted the father's face. He nodded suspiciously. "Odd question to ask a man."

"We're to meet up with a herd of horses for Mr. Chisum, just curious if you might've seen them," Evans continued.

"A few fellows with horses spent the night two, three miles from us," he replied.

"Thank you, kindly," Evans said, replacing his hat atop his disheveled hair. "They must be our men."

Clem and Ansel chuckled sinisterly behind Wes, drawing a nervous stare from the boy Wes pegged for thirteen years old.

"We'll be riding, gents," Evans said to the trio. "We're grateful for your help. Have a safe journey." Evans nudged his gray gelding forward, the animal dancing ahead, followed by Wes, then Clem and Ansel.

Wes nodded as he passed the two men and the youth. He noted the relief in their eyes.

A hundred yards down the trail, Jesse Evans chuckled. "That fellow was hiding something. You could see it in his expression."

"And he knew by our eyes we were seeking trouble," Wes answered.

"But he told me where I would find the thieves and our horses," Evans said, his voice cocky and confident.

"Tell me what you heard that I didn't."

Evans grinned. "The Mes brothers camped behind them last night and gained no ground on them today. Those Mexicans have seen no sign of anyone trailing them, so they're going easy. They'll stay the night at an abandoned ranch a couple miles off the trail in the foothills. There's little left of the ranch building, but the corral is still standing. They'll pen the horses there and get a good night's rest. Come tomorrow, they're planning a leisurely ride over the mountain and into Mesilla. Only problem is, they aren't expecting visitors tonight."

Wes studied the land before him and glimpsed the ruins of an adobe hidden among the foothills and deep afternoon shadows ahead. Evans's prediction had been right because Wes next spotted the corner of a corral, before a hillock screened it and Wes from ruins. By the motion of Evans's hand, Wes understood they were about to confront the horse thieves.

"This isn't every man's slice of beef, Wes," Evans offered.

Wes figured it was a final check of his bravery more than a genuine offer for him to stay behind. "I play my cards like they are dealt."

Evans nodded, then pulled his carbine out of its scabbard. Wes tugged his Winchester free as well. No one checked their loads this time. They were ready, had been since morning. Nudging their mounts forward, the four men lined up abreast and advanced at a steady, deadly walk.

Rounding a nub of a hill that skirted the trail, Wes saw a corral filled with maybe three dozen horses. In an instant, he glimpsed the black mare, recognizing her peculiar gait. Then, Evans's horse nickered. Out of the corner of his eye, Wes caught a sudden movement. He twisted his head that direction.

Beside the broken and eroded walls of the abandoned ranch house, four men dove for their carbines or grabbed their pistols.

"This is it, boys!" Evans yelled, spurring his gray gelding. The horse lurched ahead, Evans shouting his lungs out. Crack! His carbine exploded, and one of the Mexican men tumbled over the wall, screaming in agony.

Before Wes could get off a shot, Clem's and Ansel's carbines roared to life, puncturing flesh or splattering dirt at the surprised horse thieves. Wes discharged the carbine from his side, ejected the hull, then fired again.

The three Mes brothers still on their feet staggered but returned gunfire, the lead buzzing overhead like deadly bees.

Wes ducked low in the saddle and headed straight for the thieves. Their guns spat fire at him. He leaned over Charlie's neck and swung the carbine at the closest of the three thieves. He pulled the trigger, and the carbine's recoil rammed the stock into his side simultaneously with a scream.

A red splotch appeared on the chest of his target. The man's hand drooped toward the ground, the pistol it held exploding with a shot that plugged the earth at his own feet. The gun slipped from his feeble fingers and hit the dirt as the thief dropped to his knees and tumbled forward on his face.

With his stallion quick upon the two surviving men, Wes

twisted to fire at them but stared into the dark forever of a pistol barrel sighted at his nose. With a grimace, he braced himself for the expected impact of lead against his flesh, then saw his would-be assassin quiver and collapse to the ground, the side of his head a bloody pulp.

The sorrel raced ahead, and Wes tugged the stallion around to charge again, but a dozen gunshots erupted one after the other into the evening air. By the time Wes had changed directions on the stallion, all was quiet except for the pounding hooves and his throbbing heart.

It had started quickly and ended the same. Wes caught his breath and tried to give his mind time to sort through what had happened and just how close he had been to death. The air was rank with gunpowder, and Wes felt a cold sweat pimpling his forehead and ice stiffening his spine. Relief drained his body. He remembered fights during the War Between the States, but nothing ever as sudden as this.

While Ansel and Clem dismounted to inspect the dead, Evans rode over to Wes and slapped him on the back. "Hell of a fighter, Wes, charging right into them."

"I owe somebody for shooting that one that was aiming at me," Wes said, his voice still breathy from the scare.

Evans laughed. "He was mine. I figure any fool that'll charge into a crowd like that needs a guardian angel watching out for him."

"I never figured you for much of an angel, Jesse, but I'm obliged anyway."

Evans laughed, then responded, "Let's check the horses."

Wes rode toward the corral, passing Clem and Ansel as they looted the dead men's pockets, a final indignity for the thieves and a small reward for Clem and Ansel, who were satisfied with the kills alone. Wes had never grown accustomed to killing Yankees during the war and found this incident no different, even if the victims were horse thieves.

The horses in the corral milled nervously, flicking their ears, tossing their heads at the smell of human blood. As the horses danced about the pen, Wes spotted the bay mare with foal and the two mules, then Luther's gelding. He had redeemed what was rightfully his and would take the animals home, knowing the Mes brothers would never again steal them.

"You lost five animals, wasn't it, Wes?" Evans asked.

Wes nodded. "They're all there." He pointed them out for Evans.

"Somewhere the Mes brothers picked up another dozen besides yours and Mr. Chisum's. Several lack brands, including yours. When you get back to the valley, have the blacksmith at Casey's place fix you one and register it with the county. It simplifies reclaiming your stock. In Lincoln County you have to recover them as much as feed them."

"The horses will be less skittish tonight if we moved them away from the smell of death," Wes said.

Evans scratched his chin and nodded. "True, but they'll be easier to keep inside a corral than out. I'll have Clem and Ansel move the bodies downwind; maybe that'll calm them some. If they're still anxious in the morning, we'll let them run a while and work out their edginess. Fact of the matter is, Wes, we've only done half our job. We've recovered them, but now we've got to get them home where they belong."

Come morning, the men started the horses back to the Ruidoso valley, taking the long route and avoiding the Mescalero reservation. Except for the early morning gallop to let the stock work off their skittishness, Evans and Wes pushed them lightly. Their own mounts, driven hard to catch the Mes brothers, needed the rest. The slower pace kept them an extra two days on the trail, so Wes was relieved to reach the mountains and finally dip into the Ruidoso valley. It was near dusk when they approached Dowlin's place, so they spent the night there and had their first hot meal in days. They tossed their bedrolls on mats of hay in the barn beside the corral where they penned the recovered stock.

With morning's light the men rode out. The nearer Wes got to home, the more he wondered how Luther had been doing, if the flesh wound to the arm was okay, if he'd done any work, if he had gotten into whiskey, or, worst of all, if he had dug up his tin of gold to find he had been duped. That would be tough to explain.

As the morning wore on, Wes and Evans gradually rode point for the herd while Clem and Ansel trailed behind to keep the stragglers moving. As they neared the Horrell place, Wes's nerves grew taut, and he forgot about Luther. One thing he had not forgotten was the Horrells' threat to settle their score.

As the road rounded the mountain and he could see the Horrell property, Wes breathed easier. Their horses were gone from the corral, and no sign of women or children was discernible from the road. Wes found the tightness gradually evaporating from his gun hand the farther they moved from the Horrell house.

A half hour down the trail, though, he tensed as five riders approached from the east. By the rigid saddle profile of the lead rider, Wes knew it was Mart Horrell, the one with the stiff neck. Wes pulled the revolver from his holster and confirmed the load.

Jesse Evans observed Wes, then nodded toward the riders. "Friends of yours?"

"The Horrell brothers. They've threatened to kill me."

"The Mes brothers and now the Horrell brothers? Is there any family you get along with around here?"

Wes left the question unanswered.

Evans filled the silence. "Hell, if they'd seen you against the Mes brothers, they'd know not to fool around with you."

Ahead the five Horrells recognized Wes, as there was much pointing and standing in stirrups. They halted fifty yards ahead in the road and lined up five abreast, blocking the trail. Evans reined his gray gelding in front of Wes's mount and trotted to the Texans, stopping a dozen yards in front of them.

"Gentlemen, you're blocking our trail," Evans called. "We'd be obliged if you moved out of our way. We've got a skittish bunch of horses here that's had a rough go of it."

Mart Horrell nudged his horse ahead of the rest. "We're not interested in you or your horses, fellow, just one of your hands." Mart twisted his shoulder and stiff neck until he stared at Wes. Mart aimed his finger at Wes. "Turn him over to us."

"Why, gentlemen, I couldn't do that. This man's too good a fighter."

"Fighter?" Mart spat. "He's a meddler."

"You'd think otherwise if you saw the way he tore into the Mes brothers over in the Organs. He charged the sons-a-bitches and shot one or two of 'em."

Mart spat again, his voice dripping contempt when he replied. "Killed greasers, did he? We were funning some ourselves along the Ruidoso when he butted his nose into our business. Odd, ain't it, a man protecting *some* greasers and then killing *others*?"

"Horse thieves," Wes called, edging his horse toward Mart Horrell and drawing up beside Evans. "Whale of a difference from what you were doing."

"The difference is you were messing with us Horrells, and we intend to teach you a lesson you'll never forget. It'll give you a chance to go to hell and visit with the Mes brothers."

"Cool down, mister," Evans said, his warning issued softly.

"Us Horrells have no quarrel with you, mister."

"Jesse Evans is the name, fellow. And I've no quarrel with

you unless you interfere with my horses or my hands. And if you do, you've got a spat not just with me and the boys here, but also with Mr. John Chisum."

Mart Horrell swallowed hard.

CHAPTER 7

Mart Horrell stared wide-eyed at Jesse Evans. "We ain't got a fight with you or with John Chisum. Just Wes Bracken. Shame he ain't a good man like his brother."

Wes worried about his back. For an instant, he took his eye off Mart Horrell and glanced over his shoulder. Clem and Ansel were behind him, their carbines drawn and pointed at the Horrells. Suddenly, he had a better appreciation, if not estimation, of Clem and Ansel.

"My boys don't take kindly to you delaying our progress to Mr. Chisum's place," Evans said, a swagger in his voice. "They haven't slept on a soft bed for a week, and they're edgy, their trigger fingers shakier than usual."

Mart Horrell spat toward Wes. "We'll catch you alone some day and settle up then, Bracken."

Evans laughed. "Five against one? That should be about even, considering what he did to the Mes brothers. Now you boys see if your get-along can take you on down the road before we lose our patience and our tempers."

"Evans, you didn't make no pals for yourself or John Chisum today," Mart Horrell said.

"John Chisum don't need friends, and I despise your kind."

Mart Horrell's face reddened. Behind him his four brothers wore matching family scowls. When Mart motioned for them to ride forward, they did, each staring at Wes with wordless hate.

Wes and the Chisum men watched until the Horrells had

66

moved a safe distance away, then started the horses toward Wes's place. By early afternoon, they reached the Zamora land. Carlos and Bonifacio worked in the field, but Wes failed to spot Sarafina. He fought disappointment, then foolishness for this fixation on a married woman. But few women lived in Lincoln County, and a man couldn't help the stirrings that a pretty one could raise.

As the horses rounded the last bend before home, Wes was surprised at what he saw—Luther working beside the house, building something from the lumber Wes had brought from Dowlin's Mill. The closer he got to the adobe, the more pleased he grew. His brother had installed shutters at each window and hung a door over the entrance.

Luther stopped sawing and wiped the sweat from his brow with the sleeve of his shirt. He shook his right arm and bent to retrieve his tool but paused as if something were amiss. Looking around, he spotted the riders and stared at them for a moment, then jerked off his hat and waved it at Wes.

Maybe being partners with his brother would turn out okay after all, Wes thought. "Howdy, Luther," he called. "Looks like you've been doing a passel of work."

Plopping his hat back on his head, his brother nodded. "A bit."

"I returned your plow mules."

"What about the mares and my chestnut?" Luther called. "Them too?"

Wes nodded as Evans ordered Clem and Ansel to water the horses at the stream.

"I've been thinking it over, Wes," Evans said. "John Chisum lost twenty-four horses. We came back with forty-two animals. Less your two mules, two mares, and chestnut gelding, that leaves thirteen more than John Chisum lost. I figure I should let you keep those head. If anybody claims them, give them to him. If not, keep them for a spell, then you and I can split them or any monies you make on them. Any objections?"

"Generous, Jesse. I'll be glad to look after them for you," Wes replied.

"For us, Wes. It's a partnership; we divide up the horses or the profits. If we lose them, so what, but maybe they'll give me a stake at starting my own place someday."

"It'll provide me more breeding stock. We had money for starting a herd, but we had a run of bad luck," Wes said, instantly regretting his words as Luther's head drooped. Damn, Wes thought, why did he keep bringing up things that stung his older brother?

"Then it's a deal!" Evans announced.

Wes nodded, and the two men shook hands.

"When they're done watering, we'll cut out your horses and mules and the unclaimed stock," Evans said. "Keep an eye on them. It's a shame the Mes brothers weren't the only horse thieves in Lincoln County 'cause our problems would be over."

"I've learned Lincoln County has enough problems to go around," Wes answered.

"You're a good man to ride with. *Adios!*" Evans flicked the reins against the neck of his gray and trotted toward the Ruidoso.

Wes watched him separate the horses, driving Chisum's to the east and sending the others to graze in the lush grass along the stream. Finishing the division, Evans waved his hat and started for Chisum's spread.

Then Wes eased out of the saddle, wincing at the stiffness from so much time on the trail. "It's good to be home."

Luther took the reins and tied Charlie to a new hitching post. Luther neither spoke nor looked at his brother.

Wes stretched the kinks out of his legs and arms, noting the hitching rail. "The doors, the shutters, the hitching post. You stayed busy, Luther."

"And sober," Luther answered, a challenge in his words.

"All I'm asking, Luther, is for you to stay sober and pull your weight. From what I've seen you've done that."

Wes gathered his bedroll and carbine, carrying them to the adobe, pushing the new door open. It swung around easily. Luther had performed a good job, but Wes was in for more surprises inside. The room smelled of new wood and was dotted with furniture: a table and two benches near the corner fireplace and two wooden bedsteads with rope lacing to support a mattress or a bedroll.

The place was shaping up as a legitimate dwelling, except for the hole in the roof where sunlight still seeped through the eroded opening. "I'm pleased with all your work, Luther," Wes called out. "I've arranged for old man Zamora to patch the roof once I get around to bringing him over. One day we'll have decent quarters. Damn, if we won't make a go of this yet."

Luther stepped inside the door, carrying Wes's saddle. He draped it over a bench by the table. "Mart and Ben Horrell rode by day before last, you ought to know."

Wes studied Luther's face, gauging the worry in his watery eyes. "I encountered them on the road coming in."

"I told them you were my brother and didn't mean no harm by breaking up their fun."

Luther cringed. Wes detected fear in his face.

"I couldn't talk them out of killing you, Wes. You'd be safer elsewhere."

"I'm not dead yet, and I'm not leaving Lincoln County. I left Arkansas, not running from trouble, just tired of finding it. Now I'll go where trouble takes me, and we'll see who dies or leaves Lincoln County first."

In the following week, Wes and Luther sweated out chores from dawn until dusk, Luther plowing more of the fields and helping

Wes dig irrigation ditches. Wes traveled to Casey's Mill to buy field corn for planting and more tools—a posthole digger and a sharpening stone. With Luther, he had decided on the "Mirror B" brand—a capital B and its mirrored reflection joined at the spine—for their horses and cattle. While at the mill, Wes gave instructions on the branding iron to the blacksmith and arranged with Casey to borrow his wagon again to haul the seed back home and to go into the high country to cut fence posts. With all the stock now, he would need a corral to protect them from thieves. When Wes returned the wagon, he would pick up the branding iron.

Back at the place, he put Luther to planting corn, and he loaded the wagon to head into the high country for timber. Luther didn't understand why he was leaving mid-afternoon rather than the next morning, but Wes preferred to pass the Horrell place in the dark to avoid trouble.

Wes loaded tools and supplies enough for four days, then saddled Charlie and tied him behind the Casey wagon and team. For the first time since he had arrived in the Ruidoso valley, he felt confident about leaving Luther, who had earned his respect. The wagon rattled westward without pausing at the Zamoras' adobe, though in the field Wes made out Sarafina and Carlos scowling at him. He waved, but they ignored the gesture.

Darkness had drawn a curtain across the sky by the time he reached the Horrell place, the wagon rattling and creaking with every bump in the road. He cradled his Winchester in the crook of his arm as his hands gently held the reins and his eyes studied the Horrell house by the stream. Lamplight spilled out of two windows, then suddenly went dark. The Horrells were a suspicious bunch, Wes thought, if they feared a wagon passing their property at night. Maybe they had made more enemies than just him.

An hour beyond the Horrells', he stopped for the night in a

clearing off the road, sleeping under the wagon. Before sunrise, he was on the trail again, heading to the tall timber but stopping first at Dowlin's Mill to visit with the proprietor and tell him of his plans, then moving deeper into the valley. By mid-afternoon, he had found a stand of young trees the right size for fence posts and near the stream to provide easy and plentiful water for himself and the animals. There were enough pines to keep him busy the next two days. After unhitching and cross-hobbling the team, he tended to Charlie, staking him in the middle of an adjacent grassy meadow.

Taking a deep breath, Wes picked up the ax, saw, and sharpening stone and threw himself into the chore, attacking the timber with every fiber of his muscles, the wood chips whizzing in the air like buzzing hornets, the thud of the sharp ax echoing down the mountainside, the periodic crash of timber reverberating through the valley. He felled trees two to four inches in diameter, so it required little skill beyond stepping out of the way when they dropped. Then, he trimmed off the slight limbs and decapitated the tops. Starting at the base, he cut the trees in six-foot lengths for posts and the narrower portions up the tree he chopped into ten-foot lengths for railings. To give his aching muscles a rest, he would load the new lumber in the wagon. He repeated the process time and time again, until he lost count of everything but his soreness.

Come nightfall, he watered the mules and checked their hobbles, then fetched Charlie from the meadow and tied him to a wagon wheel for the night. He pitched his bedroll under the wagon and cradled his Winchester beside him, falling into an exhausted sleep that ended much too soon the next morning with the noisy call of a mountain jay complaining about his poor breakfast findings.

Wes ate a handful of jerked beef again and ambled down to the stream, tossing cold water in his face and sitting for a while on the big boulders that lined the noisy waters and disrupted their course to the Pecos River. The rush of the water over the rocks and the gentle breeze rustling through the trees made soothing music. Wes looked around, noting the contentment of Charlie and the mules that had found good grazing and water near enough even for their hobbled feet. Wes pushed himself up from his perch. Time was a wasting. Hadn't he himself told Luther that early didn't last long? The grass was moist with the morning dew, and the piney fragrance of the trees drifted on the gentle wind like a mountain perfume.

In the cool dawn air with his hands still stiff from yesterday's exertion, Wes picked up the ax. The first swing took a mighty exertion, but gradually Wes's muscles and his mind warmed to the task ahead. With each downed tree, the stack of lumber in the wagon grew, and Wes noted the fruits of his work nearing the top of the sideboards.

After high sun he had chopped another victim into the proper lengths and was carrying more fence posts to the wagon. He loaded them, then picked up his canteen, which hung over the wagon seat railings. Uncorking the canteen, he tipped his head and let the water roll down his throat. Plugging the container, he turned to hang it back over the wagon when he realized how silent the valley had become. Just as he hooked the vessel's strap over the seat railing, he heard a twig snap behind him.

He dove for his Winchester under the wagon.

The thud of a bullet plowed into the wagon where he had stood. Then he heard the explosion of the would-be assassin's rifle.

Wes grabbed his carbine from atop his bedding and rolled out from under the wagon. He scrambled to his knees and jumped to his feet, every moment watching the puff of gun smoke drifting from the trees. Wes expected to hear the retort of other guns, knowing the Horrells usually traveled in bunches.

He fired a shot into the trees to answer theirs, then spotted a flash of movement through the pines.

An instant of recognition struck him. He caught his breath. It wasn't the Horrells.

It was Carlos!

CHAPTER 8

His anger boiling, Wes Bracken squeezed off a carbine shot at Carlos to scare him away. But why had the boy tried to kill him? Wes heard hoofbeats and knew Carlos was escaping and would not return. Against the five Horrell brothers, Wes would have been lucky to escape an ambush, but Carlos was not the threat they were. But why was he a threat at all? The question kept coming back to him as he propped his Winchester against the wagon wheel and returned to his ax and the next tree destined for his fence.

By late afternoon, Wes had filled his wagon with as heavy a load as he dared. He hitched up the team and tied Charlie behind for the return trip. The wagon groaned under the load, and the mules strained against their harnesses. Travel was slow, and it was night when he reached a darkened Dowlin's Mill.

Behind the building, the water wheel creaked in the darkness, and the door opened slowly. Wes saw a gun barrel peek out, then Dowlin.

"It's Wes Bracken," he called and watched the gun barrel lower to the porch.

Dowlin cleared his throat, trying to laugh, but a nervous giggle came out instead. "You must be the most popular man in Lincoln County, Wes Bracken."

"How's that," Wes answered, setting the brake on his wagon.

"The Horrell brothers came by looking for you, saying they wanted to repay a debt. Hell, I told them they owed me money,

74

and by paying me they could save themselves a trip. They didn't see no humor in that, and I didn't see anything funny in them."

"I never saw them."

Dowlin laughed nervously. "Nope, I guess not. I told them I understood you'd gone over to Tularosa. I ain't looking forward to when they come back through. On top of that, a Mexican boy rode through, saying he needed to find you. Then this afternoon, he comes galloping by like the devil was on his tail, never stopping, nothing. Did he find you?"

Wes nodded. "He found me."

"Hope it was nothing bad."

"Nobody hurt."

"Glad to learn that, Wes. You're welcome to spend the night."

His muscles aching, his fingers and hands stiff from the work, Wes wanted to stay and rest, but if the Horrells were returning from Tularosa, they might overtake him. Wes knew he'd best keep moving. "Let me talk you out of a cup or two of coffee and a bite of whatever you got to eat. Moon'll be up in a bit, and I need to get back as soon as I can."

"Sure, come on in."

Wes hopped down from the wagon, landing awkwardly on his feet, his tired muscles giving him little help to maintain his balance. He stumbled up onto the porch and inside the door, just as Dowlin was hanging his shotgun on a pair of pegs beside it. He lit a candle as Wes collapsed in a chair at the table.

"Certain you wouldn't rather stay the night?" Dowlin said, putting a coffee pot on the stove, then adding small strips of wood to the glowing embers in the stove's belly. "It's coffee left from supper. It won't be too bad. Only thing I can offer you to eat is cold biscuits and taters."

"It's better than I've had in three days," Wes answered, taking a couple hard biscuits and a boiled potato from the tin plate Dowlin placed before him. He gobbled down a biscuit, then broke the potato in half and grabbed the box of salt on the table. Sprinkling salt on each bite, he consumed the potato quickly.

When the coffee boiled, Dowlin poured him a cup and placed the tin vessel before him. Dowlin returned the pot to the stove and then slid into the chair opposite Wes.

"The county's going to hell, Wes. These Horrell boys threatening the Mexicans and good folks like yourselves. Everybody's up to mischief in Lincoln, trying to drive the smaller stores out of business and to control what little money there is floating around."

Wes sipped the strong coffee. "Lawrence Murphy as much as swindled my brother, selling him land that wasn't his to begin with, and Luther sold the claim back to him."

Dowlin laughed, then caught himself. "Don't take that the wrong way, Wes, but I understand he did the same thing to the Horrell brothers, and they were out several hundred dollars they picked up from the sale of their place in Texas."

Wes chuckled himself. "I must meet Lawrence Murphy." He finished the rest of his potato with his second biscuit and downed a refill of coffee. Pushing himself away from the table, he stood up slowly, his muscles complaining all the way. "Grateful for the food."

"Wasn't much, Wes. You be careful 'cause one of these days you'll run into the Horrells."

"Big as Lincoln County is, it's not big enough for me to hide," Wes answered.

"Hiding wouldn't be in your constitution."

They shook hands, and Wes stepped outside, his eyes adjusting to the dark and taking in the full moon to the east.

"Good night for a ride," Wes said.

"Or an ambush!" Dowlin answered.

★ ★ ★ ★ ★

The Horrell place was dark, the corral empty and Wes exhausted when he passed. But, he wanted distance between himself and their home. Safely beyond their house, he drove another hour, then pulled off the road to a copse of trees by the river. He tied the brake, grabbed his carbine and bedroll from the floorboard, and stepped onto the soft grass. After unfurling the bedding, he collapsed atop it, the Winchester at his side.

He awoke before dawn, figuring he'd had two, maybe three hours sleep at most. Sliding his carbine and bedroll into the wagon, he climbed onto the seat and headed for home. The sun was well above the eastern mountains when he rounded the bend in the stream and saw the Zamora house, smoke floating from the chimney. Wes directed the wagon toward the modest adobe. Drawing up in front of the cabin, he tied the brake and stepped down onto a wagon wheel and then on the ground. "Hello."

The door cracked open, and Bonifacio Zamora poked his head out, his face lined with worry. Behind him, the door swung open, and Sarafina emerged. Her eyes were cold, and she stood silently for a moment.

"Where's Carlos?" Wes demanded.

At the mention of Carlos's name, Zamora flinched.

Sarafina crossed her arms over her breast. "You've no need for Carlos!"

Wes studied the husband and wife, then glanced at the adobe, glimpsing a sliver of a shadow by the window. Carlos was watching.

"I want to know why he took a potshot at me."

She shook her fist at Wes. "You're like the rest!"

Puzzled by Sarafina's anger, Wes climbed back in the wagon. "Tell your brother at the window that I'm leaving. If he wants another shot at my back, here's his chance."

Sarafina's mouth flew open, and her hand leapt to cover it. "No! No!"

"His aim was as poor as his courage."

Bonifacio turned to Sarafina, imploring her to translate Wes's words for him.

Wes stared hard at Sarafina. "Your husband promised to fix my roof. If he does that, your debt's cleared with me."

"He doesn't want to," Sarafina replied defiantly.

"He agreed, provided I accompany him there and back. I'll be here day after tomorrow," Wes said, pulling the reins free of the brake lever and shaking them against the flank of the team. "Hiya!" he yelled and turned the wagon in a circle as tight as his nerves.

Together Wes and Luther unloaded the wagon in an hour, stacking the fence materials against the back of the house where they would build the corral. Wes preferred to erect it farther away, but proximity made it easier to detect potential thieves, should they strike. Wes wasn't proud of his part in slaying the Mes brothers, but he didn't mind word getting around either that men who stole his animals would suffer the consequences.

Luther, sensing his brother's exhaustion from the trip, worked hard beside Wes, unloading twice as many lengths of fencing. "The fields are planted, Wes. I've been working steady while you were gone."

"I can tell, Luther."

"You want me to take the wagon back to Casey for you, give you a chance to sleep?"

Wes shook his head. "I'd best do it."

Luther dumped a load of lumber onto the pile. "Still don't trust me, do you? You figure I'll buy whiskey and get drunk on you."

"Damn, Luther, I've got other reasons, none related to your drinking."

"Are we partners, Wes, or am I just your damn field hand?"

"You know the answer to that, Luther. It's just that I'm in charge."

"And I'm doing all the work."

Wes studied his older brother standing there with a defiant chin and head cocked forward in antagonism. "If you'd done more work before I got here, you'd've been the boss. You squandered that chance, and I'll decide when you get another opportunity, Luther."

His brother tossed the last of the fence posts onto the pile and stormed away.

Wes untied Charlie from the hitching post and retied him behind the wagon, then crawled aboard, regretting that it had turned out so badly with Luther. He whistled and shook the reins, the wagon lurching forward, the team fairly dancing under the empty load.

At Casey's Mill, Robert Casey came out to greet him. He stopped for a moment, studying the wagon, then scratching his chin. He pointed at the bullet hole. "That wasn't there when you left. Horrell brothers?"

"Somebody else," Wes answered sliding out of the wagon and untying Charlie.

Casey shook his head. "I figure it'd take a fool to try that after hearing how you charged right through the Mes brothers, firing like you were a Gatling gun."

"Don't believe everything you hear, Casey. You got my branding iron done?"

Casey headed toward the blacksmith shop, Wes beside him, leading Charlie. The clanging of hammer against anvil grew louder as they approached the smithy. The strong smell of red-hot metal singed their noses. Casey grabbed a new branding rod leaning against the door and lifted it for Wes to inspect.

Wes liked what he saw. "The Mirror B," he said to himself.

Casey nodded. "One day it will be a big brand in Lincoln County."

As he reined up Charlie in front of the Zamora adobe, Wes felt his fist clench, anger still knotting in his stomach over Carlos and his unprovoked ambush. He doubted Bonifacio would live up to his promise to repair the roof, but he would force the issue, maybe angering Bonifacio and his wife, making it impossible for him to think of her again. That might be the best thing that could happen, though Wes had a hard time convincing himself of it.

The couple had been working in the field with Carlos as he rode up, and now all three were marching toward him. Wes studied Carlos, looking for a weapon. The kid wore no gun belt, unless it was hidden beneath the baggy shirt that reached below his waist.

Wes tipped his hat to Bonifacio. "You planning on keeping your promise?"

"No," Carlos shouted.

"*Silencio, Carlos,*" Sarafina scolded. "Have you no manners?" Turning to Wes, she nodded. "Bonifacio has tools and wood strips to take for the repair. Carlos," she commanded, "bring the donkeys and your horse."

"When did Carlos get a horse?" Wes asked, unprepared for the answer.

"Last week," Sarafina replied, her eyes flaring with rage. "A gift from our cousins, the Mes brothers."

CHAPTER 9

Wes toed at the ground with his boot. His palms felt clammy, his throat tight. Denying the killings would only compound the harm. He could not refute it because it was true. He could not apologize for what he had done because that, too, would be a lie. He could only stand in silence, guilty as accused.

"We thought you an honorable man," Sarafina said, pointing a finger at his nose as if she were aiming a revolver. "But we were wrong. A man that rides with Jesse Evans—the biggest horse thief in Lincoln County—cannot be respectable."

Lifting his head and looking full bore into Sarafina's dark eyes, Wes answered softly. "Jesse Evans didn't steal my animals. Your cousins did. I got back what was mine."

Sensing the simmering rage in Wes's low voice, Bonifacio stepped to his wife. He spoke harshly to her in Spanish.

"No!" She stamped her foot on the ground and crossed her arms over her breast. "No!"

The lines furrowed in Bonifacio's leathery face, and his black eyes narrowed with anger. His voice deepening, he scolded her. His arm waved from her to Wes and back. When he finished speaking, he cocked his head at Sarafina.

Her lip trembled, not so much in fear as in embarrassment. When she spoke, Sarafina glanced timidly from Bonifacio to Wes.

"My husband says to tell you that my cousins may not have been good men, but they were no worse than others in Lincoln

81

County. If they were bad, they at least deserved a trial instead of being killed like animals. You Anglos kill our kind, and the law does nothing. But if we even defend ourselves against an Anglo, we must suffer from the law or any Texan that wishes revenge."

Wes felt Bonifacio's gaze as if the old man were gauging his reaction. "Tell your husband what he says is true."

Sarafina translated his comment.

Bonifacio's tilted head straightened, and the deep lines in his face softened.

"Let your husband know," Wes continued, "that I respect him as an honest man, one who speaks his feelings and knows the truth."

As Sarafina interpreted the words, Bonifacio's gray beard parted in a narrow smile. *"Gracias, señor, muchas gracias."*

Wes detected in Bonifacio's troubled eyes that he had less regard for the Mes brothers than did his wife. Even so, he was uncomfortable, like he was standing with a pebble in his boot. The silence between them was loud, and Wes was relieved when Carlos rode up on his new horse, leading two donkeys.

Anger brimmed in Carlos's eyes. In the crook of his arm rested a single-shot, breech-loading rifle made years before the War Between the States. Wes studied the weapon. No wonder Carlos had fired but one shot at him. That was all he had!

One donkey carried twin gunnysacks, tied at the neck by opposite ends of a rope draped across the animal's back. The other donkey wore but a halter. Upon this donkey, Bonifacio gingerly helped his wife. Then, slowly and awkwardly from age, he climbed on the donkey with the burlap bags.

Wes mounted Charlie and pointed east to his place. Bonifacio nudged his donkey with his knees, and the animal plodded ahead. Wes nodded to Sarafina, the fire in her eyes burning low now. She slapped her donkey, which jumped forward at an awkward gait.

Carlos and Wes sat on their horses staring at each other, waiting for the other to fall in behind the donkeys. Wes finally shook his head. "I don't care to have you at my back with a gun in your hands."

Carlos spat at the ground. "You were lucky!"

"You, too. If I had come after you, you'd've been a dead boy."

"A man!" Carlos answered defiantly.

"Dead, just the same."

Carlos slapped the reins against his dappled gray and passed Bonifacio and his sister.

Charlie pranced forward, wanting to race, but Wes held him in check. Shortly, the stallion caught up with the two donkeys, and Wes rode beside the Zamoras.

The valley was quiet with nature, the water of the Rio Ruidoso gushing toward the Pecos, the willows and cottonwoods waving in the breeze as it ambled by. Overhead wisps of clouds wandered silently eastward, shadowing the stream.

No one spoke during the two-mile ride, and Wes was glad when the adobe came into view around the bend. Carlos had passed the house and was watering his dappled gelding in the stream. Out in the field, Luther was working on a lateral from the new irrigation ditch.

Reaching the cabin, Wes dismounted, tying Charlie to the hitching post, then offering Sarafina a hand in getting off the donkey. She accepted his offer. She looked pale, exhausted even from such a short ride.

"You're welcome to go inside, out of the sun," he offered.

She shook her head. "It is unwise to stay in this place where a man died from the Apaches."

Wes knew he could never convince her otherwise. Instead he shoved the door open and fetched a blanket from his bed. "You can rest on this. You look tired."

"I am," she answered simply.

Wes considered tossing the blanket beside the house in the strip of dwindling shade, but reconsidered. "Not enough cover. It's better under a cottonwood by the stream."

For the first time this day, Sarafina smiled at him. She said something to her husband, who nodded his answer, and then she started toward the river.

Wes noted a fullness in her hips and a clumsy hitch in her step, different from the doe-like grace he had previously admired in her movements. Wes caught up and accompanied her to the stream. With each stride, he could feel Carlos's hard stare boring into him. The youth mistrusted Wes's intentions toward Sarafina. Perhaps he was right, Wes thought.

Beneath the cottonwood tree, Wes spread out the blanket for Sarafina. She settled gently upon it, nodding her thanks as he turned back to the house.

Further up the river, Luther worked diligently, knee-deep in the irrigation ditch. Beyond him the horses grazed peacefully in the lush grass the spring moisture had spawned. It was a beautiful sight, fine horses on good land. It would be even more striking when the bay mare foaled and a gawky-legged progeny was dancing on Mirror B property.

Back at the house, Bonifacio had found the single pole ladder Luther had made and was propping it against the corner of the adobe. When Wes reached him, the old man was emptying one gunnysack of thin, roughhewn wooden shingles. He pointed at the sack, then the ground, repeating the gesture several times.

"Dirt, fill it with dirt?" Wes asked, confused for a moment. He next toed at the ground, then picked up a pinch of soil and dropped it as he pointed at the sack.

"*Sí!*" Bonifacio said, handing the burlap bag to Wes.

He tossed it over his shoulder and strode out to the irrigation ditch where Luther stood resting his hands and chin on the shovel handle.

"Who's the kid on the dappled gray?" Luther asked.

"Carlos, Sarafina's brother."

"He's carrying a mad around for somebody."

Wes nodded. "Me. The Mes brothers were his cousins."

Luther whistled, then laughed. "Guess that ruins any chance you'll have with his sister!"

As Wes jerked the shovel away from his brother, Luther stumbled forward with a taunting laugh. Wes's face burned with anger.

Luther's chuckle carried a hard edge. "I'm not blind, Wes. Even when I'm drunk, I can still see. You've taken a shine to her since you've been here. Don't matter if she's married or not."

Wes impaled the shovel into a pile of freshly turned earth, much like he would use a spear on an enemy, then dumped a spade full of dirt into the bag. "Shut up, Luther!"

"No, dammit! You've ridden me hard, Wes, harder than you should have. I'll do my share of the work . . . no, I'll do more than my share, but I'll not have you telling me what I can and can't say about you or that greaser girl."

Dropping the shovel, Wes stepped toward Luther, his fists knotting. "If you call her a greaser again, I'll beat some manners into you."

Luther pointed his finger at his chin. "Go ahead, slug me, Wes! Do it now, while she's watching."

Wes's anger raged, and he admitted to himself that he would have punched Luther, were she not nearby. Instead, he grabbed the shovel and bent over the sack. His words came as a low growl, as he had intended. "Mind your tongue, Luther, or I'll rip it from your throat."

Luther spat beside the gunnysack. "You've been gone a lot, Wes, while I've been working here. Have you been staying over at the señorita's place and getting liver for your pup?" Luther sneered.

Wes gritted his teeth and dumped a shovel of dirt in the sack, then another. When he finished, he pitched the spade at Luther's boots. Luther was right, dammit, and that made his words even more galling. Wes jerked up the bag by its ears and carried it toward the adobe.

Reaching the cabin, Wes was winded from both the load and the anger. Bonifacio stood on the ladder at the bad section of the cabin, the wooden slats stacked beside him atop the slight adobe parapet encircling the roof. He pointed at one of the beams that protruded through the wall at the corner.

As Wes dropped the sack, he realized it wasn't a beam, but rather a wooden drain pipe. Bonifacio pushed his hand into the drain and pulled out a bird's nest. Bonifacio studied the nest a moment, then tossed it to the ground. The nest had blocked the roof spout, slowing the drainage and allowing water to collect in that corner. Gradually, the water soaked through, weakening the roof until the corner collapsed from the erosion.

Bonifacio grabbed one of the slats and leaned over the parapet to begin the repairs. Wes slipped inside the house to the damaged corner and watched the opening disappear as Bonifacio worked wooden shingles between the jagged edges of the hole and the *vigas* that supported the roof.

Bonifacio eased onto the parapet and then onto the roof when he was confident it could hold him. Wes returned outside and wrestled the dirt-filled bag up the ladder and plopped it on the parapet near the old man, who gestured for him to dump it on the roof. As Wes poured the dirt onto the wooden slats, he stared at the flat roof that was nothing more than dried mud well baked by the New Mexico sun. In the opposite corner, Wes saw a blackened tin can and nodded to himself. Luther's gold was safe there.

When the sack was empty, Wes tossed it to the ground.

Bonifacio pointed at the water bucket outside the door.

"Water?" Wes asked, pointing to the stream.

Bonifacio nodded.

Wes made two trips to the Rio Ruidoso for water, letting Bonifacio soak the new dirt at the corner of the house, then shape it with a crude trowel. Shortly, the old man completed the work, tossed his implements to the ground, and climbed down the ladder. Bonifacio put his few tools back in the sack.

"Gracias," Wes told Bonifacio. At the stream, he saw Sarafina arise from the blanket, then gather and fold it. She walked toward the adobe. Farther down the Ruidoso, Carlos was riding among the animals on his horse.

Though Bonifacio was old and bent, he straightened when Sarafina stepped to him and patted his arm. Bonifacio whistled shrilly, signaling Carlos. Moments later, the youth came trotting up on his dappled gray. Anger still resided in his eyes.

As Bonifacio tied the two sacks over his donkey, Sarafina handed Wes his blanket and spoke to her husband, who nodded at her.

"I believe we have everything and can return home," she told Wes.

"No, we don't," Carlos challenged. "We don't have our horses."

"What horses?" Sarafina asked, looking from Carlos to Wes and back again.

"Four of the horses in his herd belonged to our cousins. Now they should belong to us. We're their kin," Carlos replied.

"Have you proof?" Sarafina asked Carlos.

"He doesn't need any," Wes interjected. "If he says they belong to your people, take them."

"Gracias, muchas gracias," Sarafina replied. "All four of us thank you."

"Four of you?" Wes asked.

"*Sí*," she nodded. "I am with child."

Wes stood stunned for a moment, the silence as gripping as the knot in his gut. "Congratulations," he managed, but he wasn't sure if he meant it.

CHAPTER 10

Unseasonably cool, the spring air stung his bare hands and nipped at his nose and ears as he rode toward Lincoln in the fading light of dusk. Foolish though it was, Wes Bracken had left his coat at the adobe. He refused to turn around and fetch it, even after he realized the night would have an extra bite to it.

Occasionally, he shivered in the saddle, then stiffened his resolve to let neither the weather nor Sarafina's pregnancy bother him. He had to admit he was failing on both counts, the cold gripping his body, her pregnancy seizing his thoughts. To stay at the adobe in this mood would only have heightened the tension between him and his brother, who still smirked over Wes's infatuation with Sarafina. Luther had correctly judged Wes's feelings for her, but his insinuations that Wes had been less than a gentleman in dealing with her had burned like the new Mirror B branding iron. And from now on, Luther would pester him about it with snide remarks, his way of fighting Wes's strong hand in running the place and in stopping his drinking.

Rather than endure the ragged tensions between him and his brother, Wes opted to visit Lincoln and meet Lawrence G. Murphy, the county's economic kingpin who had sold Luther a worthless deed and had as much as stolen the Bracken wagon, team, and tools from him.

The trail to Lincoln meandered beside the Rio Bonito, which joined the Rio Ruidoso at the Mirror B to form the Rio Hondo that fed into the Pecos River. Upstream a dozen miles was Lincoln, county seat for the southeastern quarter of New Mexico Territory. Wes had hoped to reach the town before bedding down for the night, but the cloud cover from the late spring cold front had shortened the daylight. Wes preferred not to travel in the dark on an unfamiliar trail. When the final light seeped out of the clouds, he directed Charlie some thirty yards off the road to a grassy patch, where he pitched a cold camp and crawled into his bedroll and blanket.

The chilly night was long. In his fitful sleep, Wes thought morning would never arrive. And when it did, it was veiled in a heavy fog that made the night seem even longer. Wes arose and gathered his belongings, cinching them to Charlie's back, then riding on toward Lincoln, figuring it would be mid-morning at the earliest and possibly even noon before the heavy mist burned away. He could make out the trail okay and let Charlie advance at a canter. With the fog for cover, however, he didn't have to worry about the Horrell brothers ambushing him.

Arriving in Lincoln, Wes had expected more of a town. It wasn't much unless more buildings hid somewhere behind the fog. What he could see, though, was a smattering of nondescript adobes and pole *jacales* strung out along a dusty street for at least three quarters of a mile. The town's inhabitants, likely enjoying the warmth of the piñon fires that perfumed the heavy air, seemed to have abandoned the outdoors to a few chickens, pigs, dogs, and goats. From somewhere up ahead carried the pounding of a hammer at work and the Spanish words of its unseen master, commiserating with each other that in all of Lincoln only they should be at work.

As Wes passed an abandoned freight wagon loaded with lumber at the side of the road, he spotted through the haze a faded sign identifying the Wortley Hotel, an unadorned adobe building as plain as the weathered lumber that trimmed its door and windows. The squat structure, thirty feet from the road, would have melded into the fog except for one window wearing a golden halo of light diffused by the mist. In the glow Wes could see a burly man, likely the teamster belonging to the wagon, at a table taking his breakfast.

Jostling the reins, Wes aimed Charlie for a hitching post beside the road, dismounted, and tied his stallion. He rubbed his hands of the chill and followed the hardened path to the door, which answered his push with the moan of thirsty hinges. The room's warmth enveloped him as he closed the door and took in the petite registration desk, three round tables, each covered with a red-and-white checkered cloth, and the small corner fireplace typical of the adobe buildings. From the window table, the burly man, his eyes hiding behind the greasy brim of his weathered hat, nodded less at Wes than at his plate of bacon and biscuits. From a door at the room's back emerged a narrow man with thin shoulders and slight eyes, a steaming pot of coffee in his hand.

"Breakfast?" he asked as he passed Wes on his way to the customer by the window.

"Just coffee," Wes replied, ambling to the fireplace. He stretched his hands toward the dancing flames and wriggled his fingers in the heat. The warmth gradually thawed his fingers and worked its way up his arms, the stiffness melting away. Wes turned his back to the fire to flush out the lingering cold that had hidden in his muscles there and studied the narrow man approaching him with a cup of steaming coffee. His eyes watered from work over the kitchen stove, and his high brow receded into a spotty crop of brown hair. His flesh was tight against his bones, as if he ate none of his own cooking, and his long arms moved with a spidery precision.

He handed Wes the cup of coffee. "This'll take the chill out of your innards."

Nodding, Wes cupped the tin in both hands, enjoying the feel of the hot metal against his fingers, and downed the searing liquid. The coffee was strong, like a man needed on a cold morning, and it warmed Wes up in places that the heat from the fireplace could never reach. "Another cup," Wes commanded, extending the tin toward the coffee pot.

"I can float you in Arbuckle's, if that's what you need," the man answered as he dumped a second load of the strong liquid into the cup.

"What I need is to find Lawrence G. Murphy," Wes said.

The man's eyes narrowed, glancing from Wes's face to the gun at his side and back to his face. His lips were taut when he spoke. "You one of his men?"

"What difference does it make?"

The man swallowed hard, his bony Adam's apple bobbing in the drawn flesh of his throat. "All the difference in Lincoln County."

"Nope," Wes replied, "I only know Murphy by reputation. His men must be worse, huh?"

The tension seemed to drain from the fellow's countenance, but he gave a noncommittal shrug to Wes's question. "It just makes a difference," he said, reluctant to reveal his meaning to a stranger.

Wes tipped the coffee cup to his lips and let the steaming liquid slide down his throat. He stared a moment at the proprietor, then drained his cup the second time. "Tell me what I owe you and where I can find Murphy."

"Up the street about fifty yards. Mr. Murphy's making sure his hands are putting in a full day, even in unseasonable weather." The fellow shrugged. "Coffee's always free on your first visit to the Wortley."

Wes touched the brim of his hat. "Obliged," he said, lingering a last moment in the fire's heat, then aiming for the door. Quickly, he headed up the street toward the hammering noises.

Visibility was murky, and in one instance he could see nothing, and in the next he spotted a fortress looming before him. Thick and twice as tall as a man, the adobe walls jutted skyward, awaiting the completion of the second floor and a roof. A lot of work remained, but even so this would become the biggest structure Wes had seen in New Mexico Territory. Nearing the store, Wes saw a wagon at the far corner and marched to inspect it, grimacing when he recognized the wagon he remembered from Arkansas. The vehicle was filled with lumber and construction supplies. Wes clinched his fists, angry at Luther for losing it.

The pounding of the hammer punctuated conversations in Spanish, all the noise coming from behind the building. As Wes rounded the corner, he heard a forceful voice, tainted with Irish vigor. "Ye boys 'urry about the work I'm paying' ye for."

Just ahead, Wes made out a ghostly figure that with each step came better into focus. Standing akimbo, the imposing man turned toward the sound of Wes's footsteps. Wes took in a daunting man, fastidiously dressed in a black suit, clean linen shirt, and black cravat. His auburn hair was a receding flame on his pale forehead, and the closely trimmed red beard and mustache circling his dictatorial mouth set his pallid cheeks afire. Stopping short of the man, Wes detected the aroma of whiskey.

"Should I know ye?" the man asked, lifting his hands from his hips and folding his arms across his chest. The hammering stopped behind him, only until he scowled over his shoulder at two forms barely discernible in the fog.

"Wes Bracken's the name, Mr. Murphy."

"I've 'eard of ye; the 'orrell boys seen to that, as much as they talk about ye. And the Bracken trade's been going to Bob Casey since ye came to Lincoln County."

Wes nodded. "Seems you know most that goes on in these parts."

"I know Luther traded with me before 'is brother showed up and took the Bracken business to Casey." Murphy uncaged a low laugh. In its wake Wes could smell liquor on his breath.

"I find no profit in doing business with a man who sold my brother a worthless quitclaim deed on our place."

"Ye'd be please to know I sold the 'orrell brothers a quitclaim deed on their place as well."

"Worthless, all the same."

Sweeping his arm toward the unfinished structure, Murphy answered, his voice low and ominous. "Take a look at the biggest building in Lincoln County. Money and influence built it. A quitclaim deed is not a worthless piece of paper when signed by the most powerful man in Lincoln County."

"From what I hear," Wes countered, "John Chisum holds that honor."

Murphy's squinty eyes widened a moment, and a frown fractured his face. "Maybe in 'is mind, but 'e don't 'ave friends 'ere or in Santa Fe." He paused as he mulled over his next words.

Wes issued a challenge first. "You robbed Luther of our wagon, team, and tools with bartered liquor. I saw the wagon out front. I want it back."

Murphy rocked on the heels of his polished shoes. "I'm Irish and a drinking man meself. I'd never dealt with your brother without first me 'aving some liquor meself. Besides, I got a bill of sale for the wagon. Ye best remember who ye're talking to; I'm not some 'orsethief like the Mes brothers. I run Lincoln County, and by me grace you can live on your place. I got the contracts for beef, corn, and flour with the Indian agency. I got the contracts with the army for beef and hay at Fort Stanton. Ye want to do business in Lincoln County, ye've got to deal with me, not Bob Casey, not the army, not the meskins."

"Threats don't scare me, Murphy."

"No threat, just fact, Wes Bracken. Only fools like the 'orrells threaten folks. I ruin folks like yerselves."

Wes touched the brim of his hat. "I'm a survivor, Murphy."

"A survivor, are ye?" Murphy's hands clenched into pale fists. "Ye never survived the potato fog back in Ireland in eighteen and forty-six. A thick and ominous fog like this, it was, but it smelled like the outhouse pit, and it brought the potato famine with it.

"Me mother, me father, me brothers and sisters took sick after the potato fog and me with them when we 'ave nothing to eat but rotten potatoes and nothing to drink but blood we drained from the cows of our English landlords while they're bedding their wenches and making more bastard English vermin." He paused and spat at Wes's feet.

"Ye ever see family become walking skeletons with purple gums that bleed to yer touch, with legs that fester and turn black, with eyes as 'ollow as a gourd? And when they 'ave no food and must relieve themselves, they splotch blood on the ground. Me mother watches 'er children die, breaking 'er 'eart until she dies, too. At fifteen I some'ow survived the potato fog and came to this country, made something of meself." Murphy crossed his arms over his chest again, his squinting eyes staring beyond Wes into the past. " 'Less ye want to remember this fog for bringing ye bad luck in Lincoln County, ye best act more civil."

Wes shook his head. "I'll tend to my business, you tend to yours."

Murphy sneered. "In Lincoln County, yer business is my business or no business at all, Wes Bracken, and ye best walk on my sunny side, maybe rustle a few of John Chisum's cattle to show me ye know who runs things here."

"I abide by the law, Murphy."

"There's no law but me in Lincoln County," Murphy replied,

laughing. "Right now, Wes Bracken, yer brother, Luther, and yer friend Bob Casey are no threat to me, but if ye ever become a bother, I swear by the broken 'eart of my dead Irish mother ye'll wish ye never set a foot in Lincoln County."

"I don't scare."

"Ay," Murphy nodded, "that I know about ye for not letting the 'orrell boys run ye out, but a brave man bleeds as much as a coward, no matter that 'e gets it in the gut 'stead of the back."

Wes felt his jaw tighten. "Nobody, not you, not the Horrells, not anybody'll run me out of Lincoln County. I'll not pick a fight with you, but I'll not run from one either. Mark my words." Wes spun around and retreated into the anonymity of the fog. Behind him, he could hear Murphy cursing at his workers and the resulting flurry of hammers pounding nails into the biggest store in Lincoln County.

The air was still damp and cool, but the angry blood pulsing through his veins insulated him against the chill. A pang of hunger twitched in his stomach, reminding him it had been yesterday noon since he had last eaten. He strode back toward the Wortley and encountered the teamster cajoling his mules westward to the music of his rattling wagon. Wes planned to eat at the hotel, then return to the Mirror B in time to handle afternoon chores.

He picked out the yellowish glow from the front window and noted that Charlie had been joined by five other horses at the hitching rack. So much for a solitary meal, Wes thought as he walked by the stallion and slapped his flank. He marched across the plank stoop and stomped his boots against the worn lumber. His nose perked to the aroma of fresh biscuits, savory bacon, and strong coffee. It might not be any better than his or Luther's cooking, but at least someone else was preparing the meal for a change.

Wes heard hearty voices inside as he opened the door. When

he stepped in, he froze, and the room went silent. Sitting at the far table near the fire were five men—the Horrell brothers.

Motionless they sat but an instant. Then boots scraped and chair legs grated against the hardwood floor as the Horrells jumped from their chairs and slapped at their coats for the pistols on their gun belts. Wes scampered outside.

Cursing, Mart Horrell jerked his revolver free.

Wes bolted for the hitching post. Behind him the doorway exploded, once, twice, four times with the sound of gunfire.

Spooked, Charlie reared the length of his secured reins, jerking them tighter against the hitching post. Wes fumbled to loosen them, but they resisted. He tugged his revolver from the holster and in one smooth motion fired at the door frame. Beside Charlie, the other horses were fighting against their reins, making it impossible for Wes to untie Charlie. Wes saw a shadow at the window and swung his pistol that direction, squeezing off a single shot. The sound of breaking glass bracketed a scream and curses.

"Get him!" Mart Horrell yelled.

Wes jumped around the hitching post and grabbed Charlie's bridle strap, jerking on the stallion's head until he had enough slack to pull the reins free with his gun hand.

Inside the Wortley, the room suddenly went dark except for the flickering light of the fireplace. Wes stuck his foot in a stirrup and pulled himself aboard Charlie. Balanced in the saddle, he thumbed the hammer back on his revolver and fired into the doorway, then a second shot into the window.

He jerked Charlie's reins and galloped into the mist. Behind him the Horrells spilled outside the Wortley.

"He's getting away!" yelled Mart Horrell.

Wes wondered if they'd be fool enough to follow him in the fog.

CHAPTER 11

A trio of chickens squawked as the sorrel galloped down the street of Lincoln. The fog was thinning but remained thick enough for Wes to disappear from the Horrells' sight and to find good cover to make a stand. Charlie sprinted past the last hovel in Lincoln and by the cemetery, his pounding hooves throwing up dirt and pebbles as his legs churned toward the Mirror B.

Wes glanced over his shoulder, seeing nothing but the fog. The trail angled to the Rio Bonito and twisted with it around an outcropping of limestone boulders. Wes reined up Charlie. The stallion tossed his head, displeased that he could not gallop onward. Bringing the horse to a trot, then a walk, Wes guided him among the rocks, hurriedly tying the reins to a dwarf juniper.

From down the road, Wes heard galloping hoofbeats. He jerked his Winchester from its saddle scabbard and pulled a box of cartridges from his saddlebag. He scampered atop a couple of rocks and took a perch between two higher boulders, throwing his shoulder against one rock to steady the carbine as he sighted in on the trail as far back as the mist allowed. The sound of racing horses grew louder, and the muffled noises of excited men reached him.

Like apparitions, the riders appeared out of nothingness in the fog. Wes aimed at the first horseman, his finger tightening against the trigger until the weapon exploded with noise and smoke and slammed against his shoulder. Wes cursed at the ineffective shot, at himself for misjudging the distance. He levered the smoking hull from the Winchester and pulled the wooden stock tighter against his shoulder. At his finger's contraction, the carbine spit fire, and the nearest horse staggered, then tumbled forward, its rider cartwheeling over his neck.

The Horrell brothers cut loose a volley of lead, but their misdirected shots landed nowhere near Wes. A pair of riders stopped to help their downed brother, who was staggering to his feet, and two more rode straight at Wes. Aiming at the nearest rider's head, Wes fired. Instantly, the hat flew off the target. Damn close, but not close enough. Wes cursed.

The hatless rider savagely jerked on his reins. "Let's get out of here!" he shouted. He and his accompanying brother circled their horses around and galloped back to their mounted siblings, who were helping their horseless brother onto the back of one of their animals.

Wes sighted in on the nearest rider's spine and squeezed off a final shot. The gun exploded, and simultaneously the target grabbed his arm. Wes cursed again. Either his aim was off, or the fog was distorting his vision. He should have hit at least three, but at best he only nicked two. The five men on their four horses evaporated into the haze. The fifth horse thrashed on the ground, then managed to stand on three legs. With a hind leg broken, he tottered in a circle. Wes needed to put the animal out of his misery, but he stayed in his perch in case the Horrells doubled back.

Behind Wes, Charlie nickered, and the injured animal, a yellow dun with a black stripe down his face, stumbled ahead. The dun whinnied and whimpered until he stopped on the trail beneath Wes and looked around for the horse he had heard.

Wes tilted his carbine and took aim between the wounded

horse's wide eyes. The dun was a good-looking mount. Holding his breath, Wes pulled the trigger with regret. The dun dropped in his tracks without a whimper. Wes exhaled, pondering the irony that he had intended to kill the Horrells without a second thought, yet could not destroy an injured horse without a pang of conscience. Survival in Lincoln County had a way of warping a man's values.

After another dozen minutes without sign of the Horrells, Wes marched around the boulders to the dead dun, sprawled on its side, its broken leg angled beneath it, its good hind leg sticking up in the air. Wes rested his carbine in the cradle of his arm and studied the horse, then untied the worn flap on the saddlebag and fished around. He pulled out a box of cartridges and a knife and scabbard. Shoving the ammunition in his pocket, he jerked the hunting knife from the scabbard and studied the seven-inch blade. It was fine steel, well honed, a knife that might come in handy. Wes wondered if it were as sharp as it looked. Figuring the Horrells planned to return for the saddle, Wes hooked the knife under the leather fender and shoved his foot in the stirrup. The knife sliced through the worn leather from one side to the other, and the now useless stirrup came loose. Wes kicked the stirrup free from his boot, and it sailed across the trail. Next, he cut through the cinch straps. At least one of the Texans must now buy a new saddle. And a new rifle. Wes focused on the stock of a Henry rifle. He shoved the knife back in the scabbard and untied the rifle boot from the saddle.

With his spoils, he turned around for his sorrel. The horse was nickering behind the boulders, likely whiffing the blood of the dun. Charlie's eyes were terrified, and he was stamping his feet. Wes shoved his carbine in its scabbard and stroked the stallion's mane. He slipped the knife under his belt and tied the Henry to his saddle. Charlie's spirit improved when Wes untied him from the bush and mounted. Guiding him from among the rocks, Wes steered him onto the trail and touched his heel to Charlie's flank; the horse darted ahead. He let him run.

Gradually, the visibility improved as the fog burned away. The trail ran parallel to the Rio Bonito, which meandered through the valley before joining with the Ruidoso at the Mirror B. As layer after layer of the fog dissipated, Wes could see the mountains shoulder to shoulder on either side of the river. When the sun finally broke through the clouds, the Rio Bonito glittered like a giant necklace upon the earth. As the sun's warmth seeped into his skin, Wes felt his muscles surrender their stiffness.

By high noon the fog had burned away, and only scattered clouds remained from the unseasonable weather. As he rounded the final bend in the trail where the Rio Bonito joined the Ruidoso at the Mirror B, Wes eased Charlie into a trot. No sense alarming Luther with a hell-bent gallop toward the place.

The fields were green with their crops. Alfalfa and knee-high corn stood at attention like emerald sentries keeping watch over the Rio Ruidoso. The bay mare was bloated with foal, and soon her young offspring would join their horse herd, the first of what Wes hoped to be many fine Mirror B horses. Next to one field, Luther was digging another irrigation ditch. The Mirror B cropland was gradually being laced together by a lattice of water channels to irrigate the best bottomland in southeastern New Mexico. Whatever his other faults, his brother knew horses, and he recognized good, fertile land.

Luther tossed his shovel aside and angled for the adobe. When Luther started work, he seldom left the field except for lunch or quitting time. Wes's stomach—with nothing in it except the Wortley Hotel coffee since the day before—told him his timing was perfect. Luther reached the cabin, pausing for a moment to stare in Wes's direction, then disappearing into the adobe. Wes figured Luther had spotted him but preferred to ignore him.

By the time Wes approached the adobe, he saw smoke coming out the chimney and sniffed bacon frying. The aroma smelled good enough to eat, and his stomach churned with anticipation. Dismounting, he felt the knife rubbing against his side, and he pulled the scabbard from his pants, fingering the belt loop in its back. He unbuckled his gun belt and slipped the scabbard over its leathery tongue before re-buckling it. He slid the blade around the belt until it was comfortable riding on his left hip, a counterbalance to the revolver on his right.

As he stepped to the door Wes coughed to keep from startling Luther when he walked in. Pushing the door open, he saw Luther hunched over the fireplace, forking slices of bacon, then stirring a pot of beans.

Without offering Wes an acknowledging look, Luther spoke softly, as much to himself as to his brother. "Always here in time for lunch, but seldom around to put in a full day's work."

Wes pretended not to hear. "Howdy, Luther, glad to see you."

Luther grumbled incoherently and snapped his spoon against the metal pot with the bubbling beans.

Tossing his hat on the table, Wes stretched his arms and yawned as Luther stood up from the fire.

Luther took two tin plates from the shelf by the fireplace and turned to the table. He tossed the plates opposite their usual seats, and stared full into his brother's face. His gaunt eyes showed disgust, and his words were embittered. "Glad you made it back today, Wes. It's not like there's not enough work for us both here."

Wes shoved his hands on his hips and glared at his brother. "I met Lawrence G. Murphy, the man you let sell us a worthless deed, the man that gave you a few quarts of whiskey and drained away our wagon and team."

"You never forget a mistake, Wes."

"And you never let up on me, Luther." Wes lifted his left hand from his belt and let it rest instead on the grip of the Horrell knife.

"You ain't carried a knife before. You planning on gutting me?" Luther challenged.

"Damn you, Luther, quit riding me. If you don't trust me, you can have the damn knife."

Luther flinched when Wes jerked it free of the scabbard and tossed the blade onto the table. The knife slid to the opposite side of the slab and clattered against Luther's plate. Luther reached for the blade, his fingers stopping just inches away from the bone handle with the embossed stag's head. Luther glanced from the knife to Wes, uncertainty in his eyes.

"Where'd you come by this knife, Wes?"

"Found it—"

Luther interrupted, his voice trembling. "This resembles Mart Horrell's knife, one he's damn proud of."

"—in the saddlebags of one of the Horrells," Wes finished.

"Damn, Wes, you're crazy, stealing a knife from him."

"I got his Henry rifle outside, Luther."

"Damnation, Wes, they're mean, and there's five of them and only one of you."

Wes shook his head. "I figured there was two of us against them, Luther?"

Luther shrugged. "I ain't got nothing against them. I always considered them my friends until you came along and spoiled it, Wes."

"Luther, anybody that'll buy you a drink is a friend of yours."

"And you've been riding me hard because I like a drink now and again." His lips curling with anger, Luther shoved the knife back across the table at Wes. "You come here with all the answers. Taking my share of our money, burying it. I could've

103

dug it up, Wes, a thousand times, but I didn't. I haven't taken a drink since that day."

"And the place looks a world better for it. The cabin has doors and shutters now, a crop's planted and growing, and the irrigation ditch is taking shape." Wes grabbed the knife from the table and shoved it back in the scabbard. His nose sniffed at an odor permeating the room. "Your bacon is burning."

Luther spun around and bent over the corner fireplace. He took the skillet handle and jerked the pan from the flames. "Ouch!" he shouted, licking his fingers from the burn. Grease splattered over the skillet's rim and flared in the fire. "Damn you, Wes!" Luther shook his singed hand. He snatched a fork and fished a dozen pieces of blackened bacon from the grease, dropping them in pairs on a tin plate.

Wes stepped around the table and fetched two coffee tins from the shelf with their meager eating utensils. He wrapped his hand in a rag and reached over Luther for the coffee pot.

Luther grumbled under his breath as he forked the last slice of bacon from the pan. "As long as you're helping, take this to the table." Luther thrust the bacon platter toward him.

Wes put the two coffee tins under his arm and grabbed the plate with his free hand.

"A little help is all I've been getting from you."

Wes slammed the coffee pot onto the table, dropped the bacon tin with a clatter, then plopped down each coffee cup at its place. When he turned around, Luther was at his side, elbowing him out of the way and dropping the hot pot of beans on the table.

"Help yourself," Luther taunted.

"Burnt bacon don't appeal to me."

"Then cook it yourself." Luther drew back his fist and launched it for Wes's head.

Surprised, Wes dodged awkwardly, his chin taking a solid

blow for his slow reaction. He stumbled backward toward the open door and outside. Luther followed him into the sunlight. For a moment, the sun's glare muddied Wes's mind. Slowly, his eyes focused on his brother's raised fists and his defiant jaw.

"Come on," Luther sneered, "let's see who's boss of the Mirror B, and who does all the work."

Wes rubbed his jaw, then clenched his teeth. He unbuckled his gun belt and let the revolver and Horrell knife slide to the ground. Then he nodded as his fingers knotted into fists, and he circled Luther, both men measuring each other, both looking for a weakness that would vent their frustrations with the other.

Wes feinted toward Luther, then jerked back. His brother ignored the ploy, waiting for a true opening. Wes moved in, and Luther stepped to meet him, both men swinging their fists, both absorbing blows to the jaw. Wes shook his head and retreated a step. Luther's reactions weren't muddled by liquor, and his muscles were hardened from the field work. Luther might not be as easy to take as Wes thought. He was no longer a clumsy drunk.

Luther advanced, his eyes afire. He swung wide with his right.

As Luther's right split the air, Wes jumped toward him, realizing too late the miss had only been a ploy. Luther's left fist caught him under the chin, jarring his teeth and rattling his brain. Wes staggered backward, and Luther rushed him, his fists flailing with wild anger. Planting his feet, Wes lowered his head and bent forward to meet the charge. Luther came in hard but gasped when Wes's shoulder caught him beneath the breastbone and staggered him backward as Wes stumbled forward.

Reeling into the side of the house, Luther hit the wall hard with his head. In the instant he took to catch his senses, he absorbed Wes's right fist in the nose. His face exploded with blood, and his whole body blew up with anger. He leaped for Wes, grabbing him around the neck and falling atop him.

Together the two brothers rolled across the ground, pummeling one another, slamming each other into the dirt, both inflicting pain, but neither dispatching the other. They tumbled near Charlie, and the terrified animal fought the hitching post and kicked at the two men. Realizing the danger to them and to Charlie, Wes and Luther broke from each other's grip and rolled away.

The sweat of exertion stung Wes's eyes and the abrasions on his face. He tasted blood trickling from his mouth. Through the blood and sweat, he examined Luther, his brother's face a bloody pulp, though his gaze remained as determined as ever.

Both men, their breaths heaving, scrambled to their feet and lunged for one another. Again they tumbled to earth, neither gaining an advantage that was not offset by the strength or determination of the other.

Luther pinned Wes to the ground and struck at his face, but Wes dodged the blow and Luther hit the hard-pack instead. As his brother howled, Wes marshaled his remaining strength and shoved him away. Sapped by the exertion, Wes sat up, prepared to take Luther's next charge. But Luther, too, seemed spent as he rolled over on his back, panting.

Wes felt his muscles melting, and he reclined as well on the blood-spattered earth.

"You had enough, Wes?"

"Plenty, Luther. How about you?"

"Enough to last a few months."

"Call it a draw?"

Luther wiped his tender nose. "Okay, as long as you don't bring up my drinking again."

"A deal, provided you don't mention Sarafina again."

"Agreed."

Both men sprawled on their backs for several minutes before getting to their knees and helping one another up. Shoulder to shoulder, they staggered back to the cabin, stopping long enough for Wes to retrieve his gun belt. Depleted of energy, they limped through the door and crawled into their chairs at the table.

"How about some burnt bacon, Wes?"

"Sounds good, Luther."

Both men laughed.

CHAPTER 12

With plenty of work to do, Wes never ventured from the Mirror B for the three weeks after his fight with Luther. Though nothing had been settled by the fisticuffs, both men had vented their frustrations. Afterwards they tolerated the other's faults without exchanging harsh words.

Handling chores side by side, day after day, strengthened their brotherly bond and spruced up the Mirror B. The work was a strong salve for Wes, the sweat washing away his thoughts of Sarafina and proving to Luther he would handle his share of the work. They extended the irrigation ditches beyond the cornfield to the alfalfa, and they finished the corral next to the house, providing a more secure area to keep the horses at night.

At the end of each day's work, Wes and Luther walked the property from the tree where Luther believed his money was buried to the junction of the Ruidoso with the Bonito, driving the horses toward the corral. No one had claimed the nine remaining horses Wes and Jesse Evans had recovered from the thieves, and Wes came to view them as his own to split with Evans. When he studied those horses, he wondered if Carlos's claim was true that the other four he had returned with had truly belonged to the Mes brothers. One evening late, Wes saw Carlos gallop by on a black gelding, but that was the last he had seen of the four horses or of anyone from the Zamora household.

The nine remaining horses were good stock, though not the quality of Charlie or the two mares he had brought from

Arkansas. All the animals were eating well on the alfalfa and the natural grass that grew along the valley. Their coats were sleek and shiny, and their spirits frisky, though the bay mare was sluggish with foal. She had filled out fully, and it was only a matter of days until a long-legged foal would be dashing across their land.

In the dwindling light of dusk each day, Wes had found himself becoming more optimistic about the prospects of the Mirror B, now that he didn't have to contend with his brother's drinking and resentment. Luther, too, seemed to relish the new atmosphere between brothers and, as always, to adore the equines.

"We haven't done bad for horses, Wes," Luther said. "You know my favorite?"

Wes shook his head, then twisted Luther's way. The answer surprised him.

"The black mare. Like I told you, her head is too small, so she doesn't have good balance or great lungs, but she's a pretty one to watch prance around, even if she's not a speedster."

Taking his hat off in disbelief, Wes laughed. "You want to keep her?"

"Hell no, Wes. She's nice looking, but I ain't in love with her. Sell her to the first fool that'll offer us more than she's worth."

"You're a sentimental one, aren't you?"

"Yep," Luther nodded, "Just 'cause I know horses."

They drove the herd toward the pen.

"Couple days at the most on the bay mare," Luther said. "We'll need to keep a close watch on her, in case she has trouble. She may be a little lean in the flanks for an easy birth."

The horses trotted into the corral, and Wes replaced the pole gate while Luther fetched from the adobe a pail of feed corn, which he held up to the bay mare's mouth after waving two other horses, including Charlie, away. "You'll be a poppa before long, Charlie," Luther chided. "Don't take food away from your son."

"You sure it'll be a stallion, Luther?"

"Half sure," he answered.

Wes laughed. "Once she foals, Luther, what you say we head into Lincoln, the two of us, have a time of it. As much muscle as we've put in this place the last three weeks, we deserve a little celebration."

Luther nodded. "I'm for it, as long as all our bruises are healed." He rubbed his nose, still tender from the impression Wes's fist had made on it.

"Agreed," Wes replied.

On the morning three days later, Luther and Wes pulled a gate from its wooden frame in the irrigation ditch and admired the flow of water trickling into the rows of chest-high corn. Luther dropped the gate beside the trench and paused a moment as he looked toward the field. "Uh-oh," he said, "may be trouble."

Wes spun around, his hand sliding the revolver from his holster.

Luther shook his head. "Not that kind of trouble. It's the mare."

Easing his pistol back into its scabbard, Wes spied the bay, dancing restlessly in the field, tossing her head, kicking her hind legs. She ran in circles, alternately lying down for a few moments, then struggling back up on her feet.

"Can't put my finger on it, Wes, but things don't look just right."

"How can you tell?"

Luther shrugged. "Can't for certain. Just a feeling I've got. You best mount Charlie and drive the mare into the corral."

Wes trotted toward his sorrel, grazing by the Rio Ruidoso, and gave a shrill whistle. Charlie lifted his head, and Wes whistled again. The stallion trotted toward him. "Good boy," Wes called as Charlie approached. Wes stroked the animal's neck, then grabbed a handful of his silky mane. "Easy, boy, this won't take long. You're about to become a poppa." Wes pulled himself atop Charlie's muscular back and straddled him. Leaning forward to stroke the stallion's neck, Wes tugged gently on the sorrel's mane. Charlie responded by moving in that direction. "Good boy, Charlie; let's get the bay into the corral."

Charlie trotted toward the fitful mare, tossing her head, dancing a jittery jig on a patch of grass worn by churning hooves. As Charlie cut behind the mare, Wes whistled. The bay continued to circle, ignoring the interruption. With his knees, Wes urged Charlie closer to the mare, but the stallion seemed confused by her strange behavior. The mare halted for a moment, bewildered and staring at the sorrel, as if plotting retribution for his part in her current discomfort. Jerking his hat off, Wes waved it without result, then threw it at the mare. Startled, the horse trotted toward the corral. Wes whistled, and she ran harder, Charlie giving chase.

The bay mare darted past Luther at the gate. He shoved three poles into their slots as the mare danced around the corral tossing her head, stopping and pawing at the ground. As Wes dismounted Charlie and retrieved his hat, Luther stood studying the mare and shaking his head.

Wes walked up beside him. "You don't like what you see, I can tell."

Luther pointed at the mare. "Look at her rump."

"Looks about normal to me."

"That's the problem. Both sides of the rump ought to flatten out, then actually sink, leaving a depression. This close to birthing the flanks should be looser. Something's wrong."

The mare charged at the Brackens but turned away from the fence at the last second.

"She don't like us watching. Most mares don't."

"We can't leave her like this until we know the problem."

Luther shook his head. "We can watch from inside the house through a shutter." He tapped Wes on the shoulder. "Let's get out of sight for a while."

Together the brothers trotted around the adobe. They shoved the door open and marched inside, Luther striding to a window facing the corral and cracking the shutter until he could watch the mare.

For thirty minutes, Luther stood transfixed, the slow hiss of his breath and the occasional batting of his eyelids the only indications that he was alive. This, Wes thought, was where his brother was of value to the Mirror B. Though Luther had said little, Wes realized the fate of the foal and even the mare might rest with Luther's knowledge of horses.

Leaving the sentry duty to Luther, Wes put a piece of firewood on the glowing embers in the corner fireplace and started heating a pot of coffee. He figured they both could use a cup after the mare foaled. If things didn't work out, then maybe something stiffer was in order.

As the coffee boiled, Wes fetched his cup from the table where he had left it at breakfast. Walking by Luther, Wes glanced over his shoulder at the pacing mare, now glistening with perspiration in the midday sun. She dropped to her knees and leaned over on her side.

"It won't be long now," Luther said, "but her rump still don't look right."

Wes grunted and marched to the fireplace to fill his cup. "Coffee, Luther?"

His older brother motioned for him to be quiet. "Her water just cut loose; it's getting closer."

Wes positioned himself behind his brother, watching over his shoulder at one of nature's miracles. The mare, her rump to the shutters, strained, and gradually the slick white membrane that surrounded the foal began to emerge. Luther pushed open the shutters and stared, leaning outside. "Dammit!" Luther shouted, pushing himself from the window, jostling Wes.

The collision spilled hot coffee down Wes's shirt. "Ouch!" he shouted as Luther darted around the table for the door, unbuttoning his shirt and pulling it off as if he were on fire or crazy. "What's wrong?" Wes called as he slapped at the hot coffee splotches on his own shirt.

"The foal's coming out backwards, maybe with just one leg. We gotta act fast or the foal will smother!" he yelled as he ran out the door and threw his shirt on the ground. "Stay in the house, Wes. We don't want to excite the mare any more than we have to."

Before Wes could move from the shutters, he saw Luther scrambling over the fence and into the corral. The startled mare fidgeted for a moment, then lay her head down and whimpered.

Luther fell to his knees by the animal's rump and grabbed the milky white sheath around the foal, squeezing it between his fingers. "Dammit, one leg, a hind leg." Taking a deep breath, Luther leaned into the mare's rump and started shoving the leg back up the birth canal. The mare flinched, her hind legs twitching. She melted into limpness as Luther pushed the milky membrane back inside. His right hand disappeared in the mare, and his arm followed. "Come on, come on," he yelled, his face flushing with exertion. "Where's your other leg, dammit?"

Luther jerked his arm out, shaking off the slick mucous and mumbling profanely. He clapped his two palms together, holding them and interlocking his fingers. Then gingerly he shoved both hands back into the horse and began to push and strain against the mare. "Come on!" he yelled. "Come on." Perspiration soaked Luther like the mare. "Yeah!" he shouted, as he extracted his arms, first one, next the other, each grasping a spindly leg shrouded in a milky pouch.

Exhaling loudly, Luther inched back from the horse, still holding the foal's legs and tugging gently, then more firmly. The newborn began to emerge, hind legs, rump, torso, head, and forelegs as the white membrane split. With its soggy coat gleaming in the sun, the foal lay motionless by the bay, giving no sign of life.

"No, dammit, no!" Luther yelled. He bent over the motionless form, imploring it to move. As still as a stone, the foal lay on the ground. Luther lifted his fist and pounded the newborn's chest in frustration. Luther leaned over the wet animal and sobbed.

Damn the luck, Wes thought, bringing the mare this far and losing the foal like this.

The mare stirred, lifting her head, twisting it around to see her offspring. The mare nickered.

Luther's sobbing turned to laughter, like he had gone mad. He pushed himself away from the newborn. Sitting on his knees, Luther laughed again.

Wes saw a hind leg twitch, then the other. The foal began to kick and whinny. The mare lifted her head higher, trying to get up, but she was still drained from giving birth.

"We got us a good-looking filly," Luther called, staring at the foal.

"You're the one that saved her, Luther. Good job."

Luther shrugged and squatted by the foal. Slipping his arms under her neck and stomach, he carried her around to the mare and placed the foal by her mother's neck. Luther stepped away and dodged the blur of the mare's leg as she attempted to kick him. Luther cut loose a hearty laugh as he avoided the bay's hoof.

Wes leaned out the window. "Don't see what's so funny about her trying to kick you."

114

Luther backed out of range. "Most mares turn mean after they give birth. Her disposition's normal, and she'll likely come through this without lasting harm. Our luck's holding up." He pointed to the mare, and Wes observed the bay nuzzling her offspring, licking her and cleaning her shiny coat. The filly lifted her head and stared at her new world.

"We've got plenty of reasons to go to Lincoln for a little celebration," Wes said.

Luther climbed over the fence and disappeared around the side of the adobe, reappearing in the door a moment later. "I'll take the cup of coffee now, Wes."

Wes obliged him with a tin of steaming coffee and refilled his own cup.

"I'd like a trip to Lincoln, Wes, to forget our worries, but you sure we can leave the place unattended, the filly and all? Hate to get her stolen."

Nodding, Wes returned the coffee pot to the fire. "I figured I'd ride over to Bob Casey's, see if he could spare a man to keep an eye on things Saturday night. Then we could have a good time and not worry."

Luther drained his coffee cup and slammed it down on the table. "Sounds like a fine idea, but before I think about anything else, I'm going down to the stream to take a bath."

"I'll saddle Charlie while you're doing that and be ready to ride over to Casey's when all's done," Wes replied.

Grabbing a cake of lye soap, Luther glanced through the shutter into the corral. "Look, will you?"

Wes checked outside. What he saw thrilled him. The foal stood on her wobbly legs, taking a few tentative steps, then a couple hops before combining the two gaits into an awkward dance around her resting mother. Her head bobbing like a fishing cork on rough water, the filly finally figured out it was easier to walk than hop. She stumbled around her mother, her gait

115

improving with each step.

Luther threw the remnants of a blanket they used as a towel over his shoulder and grabbed two wooden buckets as he headed out the door. "I'll bring back water for them," he called on the way to the stream.

"Maybe things are gonna work out all right between me and you," Wes said to himself as Luther strode proudly toward the Ruidoso, his head high.

Wes stepped outside into the sunlight and whistled. He looked for Charlie but saw no signs of him until he walked around the house. The stallion was grazing by the stream. Whistling again, Wes watched Charlie lift his head and stare toward the adobe. The animal came trotting toward the home. As he drew near, the mare sensed his presence and stood up, prepared to defend her foal. The little one saw Charlie and stepped to her mother's side. "That's your poppa, girl," Wes announced.

Charlie studied the bay mare and her offspring for a few moments, then trotted to Wes, who led him around to the adobe front where he kept his saddle and gear by the door.

Just as Wes finished saddling the stallion and strapping his carbine on, he heard a scream from the road. He glanced over the saddle, his muscles tensing, and recognized Sarafina, riding one of the Zamora donkeys and swatting it with a length of rope.

Grabbing the reins from the hitching post, Wes mounted Charlie and galloped to her.

Her eyes dilated with fear, she screamed, "Come quick! Save my husband and my brother. Four men say they will hang them."

"You stay here," he ordered Sarafina as he turned Charlie toward the Zamora place. "Tell my brother what is happening and where I'm going."

"Sí, sí," she said, her plump belly heaving for breath.

Wes slapped Charlie, and the stallion bolted west. Behind him he could hear Sarafina screaming something else. Wes wondered if this were a Horrell trick to settle their score. Leaning over in the saddle, he pulled his carbine from its scabbard and gritted his teeth for a fight.

CHAPTER 13

His hooves pounding the trail with each powerful stride, Charlie galloped with abandon. The sorrel would get Wes to the Zamora place as fast as any animal could, but Wes wondered if he might be too late to save the Zamoras or if he was riding into a trap. His gaze jumped from the clump of trees ahead to the boulders piled like giant marbles beyond that. His muscles were taut with anticipation, half expecting at any moment to hear the retort of rifles from ambush or, even worse, feel the hot lead of those guns piercing his flesh.

When he rounded the final bend before the Zamora place and could see the adobe, he loosed a long breath from his lungs. He glanced from the cabin to the fields. Nothing seemed amiss. His gaze moved to the stream and a stand of great cottonwoods, their sturdy branches reaching skyward. Cradled beneath those limbs was trouble!

Four horsemen sat stolidly on their horses, circling Bonifacio and Carlos, both standing with lengths of rope on their necks, their hands tied behind their backs. The ropes hung loosely over a hefty limb, and the quartet did not tighten them as Wes neared. Patiently, they looked his way as Wes studied them and breathed easier. They were strangers, not the Horrell brothers.

Pulling on the reins, Wes slowed Charlie to a canter, then a walk. He cradled his Winchester '73 in the crook of his left arm and advanced toward the men. They made no threatening or sudden moves, sitting as calmly as if they were waiting for a stagecoach. Wes looked around the tree for other horses and up in the branches for possible assassins, then glanced across the stream. All he saw were the four men and beyond them the horses Carlos had claimed from those Wes and Jesse Evans had taken from the Mes brothers.

Bonifacio trembled before the men, his eyes wild with worry and his lip quivering. Carlos stood defiant, glaring with hatred at his captors and with loathing at Wes. Carlos was as hardened as the Horrell brothers and Murphy, Wes thought.

A middle-aged man with a ruddy complexion and bent nose eased his horse away from the others and took a half dozen paces toward Wes, his yellow dun reminiscent of the horse Wes had shot from under Mart Horrell. "The little lady said you'd be here," he rasped, a slight smile cracking an otherwise hard shell. "She told us you could explain everything."

Wes studied the man, his clothes dusty from days on the trail, his revolver glistening with oil, and his holster sitting high on his hip. He was dangerous when riled, Wes suspected, and his unruffled demeanor contributed to the potential peril. "The Zamoras are good folk," Wes replied. "Not much more I can explain, unless I know what's bothering you."

The man nodded, his right hand patting his shirt's breast pocket, extracting a tobacco pouch. He offered the bag to Wes, then retracted it when Wes waved it away. His fingers moved nimbly, sprinkling a cigarette paper with tobacco. "I'm bothered by the four horses over yonder." He pointed at the quartet that Carlos had claimed as belonging to his cousins. "They are ours." Glaring at Carlos, Wes expected a denial, but the youth just sneered. He had lied! Carlos had known all along the animals never belonged to his cousins. If a youth ever needed common sense beat into him, it was Carlos. Perhaps Wes would take care of that later, but now, he had to save Carlos and Bonifacio. "No markings or brand on them. Any way to prove up your claim?"

"Four against one's all the proof I can offer."

"Those are good odds, but they don't always come up a winner," Wes replied. "Any solid evidence of ownership?"

The man pulled a match from a tin and lit his cigarette. Studying the four horses, he exhaled a cloud of smoke. "We work small ranches around Seven Rivers, southeast of here. The blacksmith there shoes our horses and marks all his horseshoes with a seven embedded in the right heel of each. Look for yourself if you don't believe me."

Wes shook his head. "Didn't say I didn't believe you, just could you prove it. Your word's good enough for me."

"I figured as much, the odds being four to one against you." The man laughed, but his fun ended abruptly at the sound of another voice.

"Two to one odds now," called Luther from across the stream, his carbine aimed at the cigarette in the man's mouth.

Damned if he wasn't glad to see Luther, Wes thought. Not so much because he expected trouble as much as the signal it offered that maybe the problems between them were over.

"Who the hell are you?" the old man asked Luther.

"His brother."

"Easy, Luther, we're only talking," Wes cautioned.

"Go ahead," Luther said. "My trigger finger's just listening should something go wrong."

"The odds and the truth still favor us boys from Seven Rivers," the man continued. "We'll take our horses, but the question about how these greasers got them hasn't been answered, and their future's looking mighty dim."

Wes leaned forward in his saddle, more at ease now with Luther across the stream for support. "Those horses are part of those I took from the Mes brothers on their last ride."

"Well, I'll be damned, boys, this here must be Wes Bracken. Word is you're a tough hombre."

"When I'm defending what's mine. These were unclaimed horses I brought back with Jesse Evans." Wes pointed to Carlos. "The boy there told me they belonged to his cousins. I believed him. The old man had nothing to do with it, so untie him."

The Seven Rivers man motioned to one of his companions. "Just the old man." A lanky fellow wearing a checked shirt and a straw hat slipped down from his saddle and pulled a hunting knife from its scabbard on his belt. With a flick of the blade, he freed Bonifacio's wrists.

"Gracias, señor, gracias," he said, rubbing his wrists at the rope burns.

The thin rancher next loosened the rope from Bonifacio's neck, lifting it over his head.

"Downstream at my place," Wes continued, "we've nine more horses that haven't been claimed. You're welcome to inspect them and take what's yours."

"Obliged," the leader said. "We'll do it." He turned to the two men still mounted and issued a command. "Go fetch our horses."

Carlos kicked at the dirt and jerked his head as if he could free himself from the noose. He spat toward Wes, his eyes still boiling with hate.

Bonifacio stepped tentatively away from Carlos as his lanky benefactor tugged the rope from over the tree limb and coiled it. "What about the young one?" the fellow asked Wes.

"I'll take care of him," Wes said, shoving his carbine back in its scabbard, then jumping from the saddle. Taking his time, Wes adjusted the gun belt at his side and fingered the handle of the knife that had once belonged to Mart Horrell. Across the stream, Wes saw his brother ready to help, if needed. Wes lifted his hand and waved at him. "Everything's fine, Luther. Head on back to our place and help those two look over the horses. I'll join you shortly to inspect those orphan horses, see if any of them are theirs."

Luther nodded and reined his chestnut toward the Mirror B. Wes watched him disappear along the stream bank before turning to Carlos, who was mumbling in Spanish. Though he didn't understand Carlos's words, Wes knew they weren't flattering. Wes walked to Carlos and grabbed the loose end of the lariat tied around the youth's neck and draped over the tree limb. Wes tugged the rope, and it tightened against Carlos's neck.

Carlos gasped and grunted, his Spanish curses caught in his throat. His Adam's apple bobbed in his neck, then went taut like the rope.

"That feel good, Carlos? And your feet are still on the ground. Think how it would be if you didn't have a foothold. Don't you ever lie to me again. It can get you killed, you fool." His fingers relaxed, and the rope slid through his hand.

Gasping at the rope's prickly release, Carlos tumbled forward, landing on his shoulder. He howled as much as his scarce breath would allow, then gritted his teeth, determined not to be humiliated any more.

Wes bent over him, loosened the noose from under his chafed jaw, and lifted it from his neck, roughing Carlos's ears with the hemp.

Carlos clenched his teeth.

Grabbing him under the arms, Wes jerked Carlos upright to his feet. He stood face to face with the youth, his finger pointing at his nose. "Don't you ever tell me another lie, Carlos!" He stepped behind him to cut the rope binding his hands behind his back.

His anger boiling over, Carlos twisted to face his neighbor, lifted his knee for Wes's groin, and spat at his face.

Wes jerked his left knee forward and deflected the blow aimed at his crotch but took the spittle on the cheek.

Carlos backed away, a wicked grin slithering across his face.

Wes drew the sleeve of his shirt over his cheek, advancing on Carlos and his triumphant smirk. With snake quickness Wes flung the back of his hand into Carlos's jaw.

The youth stumbled backward but maintained his balance. Carlos's smile skulked back to where it had come from, and he cut loose with a string of Spanish profanities.

Wes jerked the knife from its scabbard and advanced toward Carlos. Wes saw panic rising in Carlos's dark eyes as he retreated, slowly at first, then as fast as he could, but Wes matched him step for step. Finally, without his arms free for balance, he tripped and fell to the ground.

As Carlos scrambled to his knees, Wes stepped behind him and grabbed him, his powerful fingers digging into his neck and shoulders. Carlos started a scream but bit it off with a snap of his teeth.

With his knife hand, Wes held the dull edge of the knife against Carlos's throat. The youth trembled at the touch of the cold steel against the softness of his gullet.

"I should scar you up for that, Carlos. If you ever lie to me or spit on me again, I will."

Carlos stiffened, then threw up his chin, as if daring Wes to slit his throat.

Wes pulled the knife away from his flesh and lowered it along Carlos's back until he reached his bound hands. He worked the sharp blade between the tight loops of hemp around the youth's wrists, and, with a couple slices of steel, the rope fell free.

Carlos jerked his arms free and held them at his waist, wriggling his fingers to erase the numbness from his hands.

With his left hand still on Carlos's neck, Wes shoved him to the ground. "You'll never grow old like Bonifacio, if you don't change your ways, Carlos."

Muttering in Spanish, the youth stumbled away toward the adobe, passing Zamora and speaking harshly to him. Zamora shrugged, then glanced toward Wes, who detected shame in the old man's eyes. Carlos was at that age when his manly juices were rising in him and increasing his confidence that he was always right. Most men overcame those years if they lived that long. Wes wondered if Carlos ever would.

The leader of the Seven Rivers men took off his hat and wiped his brow. "That's one hot chili pepper."

Wes shoved his knife back in its scabbard and whistled at Charlie, not twenty paces away. The stallion came at a trot. "Carlos has a mad for white folks."

"That can be unhealthy for someone living in Lincoln County."

Grabbing Charlie's reins, Wes took hold of his saddle and pulled himself aboard. "Near everything can be bad for your health in Lincoln County," Wes replied.

The rancher drew his horse up opposite Charlie and extended his hand. "Hugh Beckwith's the name." He motioned to the lanky man, who was remounting. "That's Will Johnson, my son-in-law. The two fellows rounding up our four horses are my boys, John and Bob."

Wes touched the brim of his hat. "You fellows had plenty of time to hang them. Why didn't you?"

Hugh Beckwith laughed, then tossed aside his depleted cigarette. "Wanted to scare them, more than hang them. Other'n our four horses, only other animals they had on the place were jackasses. They weren't horse thieves, but they were keeping them for someone. We figured the *señorita* would flush the thief out. We were glad you came galloping in. A bluff can scare only so long."

Johnson herded the four horses Carlos had claimed over to Beckwith and reined up.

"You fellows care to ride to my place, help your boys identify any more horses that might be yours?" Wes asked.

124

"Sure thing," Beckwith answered, "but first, I got a question for you. How come an honest man like yourself would ride with a low-down skunk such as Jesse Evans? He's the biggest horse thief in Lincoln County, doing John Chisum's dirty work all the time."

"Same reason you fellows would threaten to hang a couple farmers you knew was innocent. You do what you have to do." Wes motioned toward the Mirror B. "Let's check out the other horses."

The riders trotted away, Bonifacio Zamora standing motionless behind them, not understanding that the danger had been less than it seemed. Beyond him in the adobe's door stood Carlos, his arms folded across his chest.

On the trip to the Mirror B, Hugh Beckwith did most of the talking, complaining about John Chisum and his stranglehold on the Pecos valley, about his cowboys who claimed all cattle in the basin as Chisum's, and about his special hired hands like Jesse Evans who, Beckwith kept repeating, filled the vast Chisum remuda with stolen horses.

"Chisum's trying to run us small fellows out of Lincoln County," Beckwith spat, "but we're like flies on a bull's butt, and we'll pester him to death. If we don't, he'll ruin Lincoln County for our type."

Wes cleared his throat. "I figure Lawrence G. Murphy's this county's main worry."

"No, sir," Beckwith replied. "Any man that takes on John Chisum is a friend of the small fellow in this county." Johnson grunted his approval.

"I've got enough troubles of my own with the Horrell brothers," Wes replied, "without sticking my nose in other people's fights."

Old Man Beckwith reached for his cigarette fixings again. "Horrell brothers won't bother you for a while, not during the summer when there's so many chores to handle. Come fall and winter, though, be on your guard."

As Beckwith lit his smoke, the Mirror B came into view around the bend. Wes could see the nine horses he and Jesse had recovered in the corral where Luther helped Beckwith's two sons examine all the animals.

Riding up to the adobe, Wes saw the jackass tied to the hitching post and Sarafina standing in the doorway shadows. "They're okay, your brother and husband," he called.

Sarafina emerged into the sunshine, her eyes reflecting fear of the Beckwiths. Her rounded belly gave her an awkward waddle as she stepped toward her mount. *"Gracias,"* she said, "but I must go check on them."

"Carlos has too much vinegar in his blood, Sarafina. You better caution him for his own good."

"I try," she answered meekly, giving no doubt to her lack of success.

Wes dismounted and offered her his hand.

She ignored it, untied the donkey's halter from the hitching post, and tossed the reins over its back. Her gaze swept over the Beckwiths and Johnson, then stopped at Wes. Her eyes were sad, her cheeks fuller than Wes remembered, and her belly bulged with her unborn child.

Wes still found her comely, even if she carried the baby of another man and even if that man was her husband. "Please let me help." Wes offered her his hand again, but she shook her head, her black hair bouncing.

Putting her arms around the donkey's neck, she leaned into it, lifted one foot until a brown patch of calf showed beneath her long skirt and hopped with the other foot. With the awkward grace of a pregnant woman, she pulled herself atop the animal. She sat a moment, trying to cover part of her leg that had been exposed by the skirt that was not made for riding. Failing, she settled for pulling her blouse down over her protruding stomach. Though embarrassed at having to mount before Wes and the others, by the lift of her head and the angle of her jaw she reflected a pride at accomplishing the task without help from any of them. With a tug on the reins, Sarafina uprooted the donkey and pointed it toward her home.

"She sure scooted up on that burro when we had ropes around her men's necks," Hugh Beckwith sneered.

Wes felt his face heat with anger, but he stood silent, watching Sarafina disappear down the road.

Luther stood in his stirrups, staring at Hugh Beckwith. "You boys care to join us or do you plan to talk all day."

"By damn with an invitation like that, I guess we'll have to look at those nags," Beckwith replied, riding over with Johnson. Wes followed.

Beckwith looked about and studied the Mirror B. "Good place you got, Wes. Good land's hard to hang onto in Lincoln County, unless you're willing to fight."

"Luther and I'll do what's needed."

Luther pulled three rails out of the fence so Beckwith and Johnson could join Beckwith's two sons in the corral. Once inside Johnson dismounted and walked among the horses, lifting a leg of each animal to check their horseshoes for that telltale seven imbedded in the metal.

"Three more of them are ours," Johnson called as he pointed the trio out to John and Bob Beckwith, who cut them out of the crowd and drove them out of the pen.

"What about the bay mare?" Beckwith inquired, pointing toward the animal and her new offspring.

"That one's ours," Luther stated matter-of-factly, "and only a fool would try to inspect her with a new foal. She'll bite your head off."

Beckwith rubbed his chin as he stared at Luther. "If you're

half as honest as your brother, then that mare and foal are yours for certain."

"Obliged," Luther replied, replacing the three fence rails after Johnson and the others rode outside with their horses.

"Just a warning for you Brackens," Beckwith said. "Lincoln County's not a safe place for honest men."

CHAPTER 14

The sky was fringed with dusk's golden glow when Wes reached the end of the last row of corn. His hands were stiff from handling a hoe all day, but the field was weeded. The stalks were shoulder high and the corn was tasseling. Good soil and good water made a good crop, and Wes knew he had both on the Mirror B.

Out in the pasture, Luther was driving the horses and mules toward the corral for the night. The frisky filly, now two weeks old, pranced ahead of the other horses, then darted back among them and finally reclaimed the lead. Not given to smiling because of the jagged front tooth, Wes grinned at the filly. He liked her playfulness. All newborns were frolicsome as they tried out their legs, but this one was plucky as well, charging headlong into her approaching elders and dodging their powerful hooves. The filly had inherited that spirit from her sire as sure as the sun was setting, for Wes had seen it in Charlie dozens of times.

The bay mare was still gimpy from the hard delivery, but her step in recent days had lost some of its caution, and she seemed to be returning to her old self. Luther, too, looked to be himself again, the way Wes had remembered him from Arkansas before the war. All the work had sweated the liquor out of his body, and the fight had eased his bitterness.

Wes propped his hands on his hoe handle and rested his chin atop them. He gloated at what he saw around him: a small herd of horses, a vibrant corn patch, a fine crop of alfalfa, and a brother that had come to his senses. Work still remained, like building a barn for keeping the animals out of the winter weather and for storing the crops once harvested. A smoke house would be good as well so they could raise hogs and have more variety to their meals. They had been so busy, neither Wes nor Luther had taken time for hunting, even though turkeys roosted along the river and deer came for water regularly. A tasty, hot meal cooked by someone other than himself or his brother seemed as appealing as anything Wes could wish for.

Luther drove the horses into the corral, then replaced the pole gate. He stood at the fence awhile, his arms draped over the top rail, and studied the animals. Luther observed them each night, not just because he liked horses, but because he viewed them as the commodities they were. Luther, the horse trader in the family, would be an asset when they started selling horses.

Wes pried the hoe from beneath his chin and headed toward their adobe, wishing they would have something other than bacon and beans for supper, hoping he still had enough light to go hunt up meat, a rabbit if nothing else. He figured Sarafina would have a good meal cooking tonight, and he envied Bonifacio.

Propping the hoe beside the door, Wes walked around the cabin to join Luther at the corral. Silently, both stared at the horses as the dregs of the daylight seeped away to the west.

"We owe ourselves a celebration, Luther, for all the work we've put in the last two months."

"I was wondering if you ever thought of anything but chores." Luther laughed.

"Occasionally I think about a little fun and a delicious meal."

His brother twisted his head toward his younger brother, and Wes just made out his smile. "You don't like my cooking?"

"I had worse in the war, but not since."

Luther tipped his hat. "You'll never get a wife talking about other people's cooking like that." There was no malice in his comment and no clear thought of Sarafina.

"About two weeks ago, I promised us a trip to Lincoln, once the mare foaled. It's time we treated ourselves."

"A little tonsil-painting sounds good to me, Wes, but I don't figure we both ought to be away from here at the same time, as much trouble as is always brewing in Lincoln County."

Wes nodded, pleased that Luther now took his obligations to the ranch seriously. "Let me check if Casey can spare a hand. We both deserve a night in Lincoln. Together."

"I'm game, Wes. It'd be good for us to have a little fun together."

Come morning, Wes saddled Charlie and headed toward Casey's Mill. The sun rose hot, and the early air was thin and still. For once, the stallion moved listlessly as if his spirit were as lifeless as the atmosphere. Even Casey's Mill seemed languid when it came into sight. Except for the smoke coming from the chimney of the main house and store, the compound would have looked abandoned and so unlike the vigorous and ambitious Casey.

As he rode in, Wes studied the stillness. The corrals held few horses, and the cattle that usually grazed on the far hills were gone. He wondered if anyone other than the Casey women were home as he drew up outside the store. Dismounting, he tied Charlie to the hitching post. His gun hand slid down to the butt of his revolver as he pushed open the door. The aroma of fresh coffee and new goods tickled his nose. He stepped inside.

"Come in, come in," called Bob Casey, easing up from a table by the bar. With him was a tall, angular man, who turned in his seat and studied Wes.

"Morning, Bob," Wes said, returning the stare of the stranger dressed in a new broadcloth suit with just a powder of trail dust on it. He had a thin face held together by a thick mustache and dark piercing eyes intense enough to see through mountains. His was a handsome, leathery countenance, flawed only by a pair of oversized ears. "Your place looks abandoned, Bob. Is everything okay?" Wes asked.

"Thieves hit us two nights ago, running off my cattle and quite a few horses. My hands took what horses remained to chase the bastards to see what they could get back." Casey hobbled past the table, using it for support. His pants leg was slit up the side, and a pink-stained bandage snaked around his left thigh just above his knee. "I took a flesh wound, or I'd be out chasing them, too, but I didn't feel much like riding after they plugged me. Mrs. Casey said I might bleed to death if I rode a horse very far."

"Wish I'd known, I'd've come to help. They missed my place."

Casey tossed off a laugh. "Nobody's gonna bother your animals after word got around how you attacked the Mes brothers. Now, I want you to meet my guest," Casey announced as the stranger rose from his chair.

"No introduction necessary, Bob," the tall man said, extending his hand to Wes. "I've been hearing what a fighter Wes Bracken was, and I'm glad to get a chance to introduce myself. I'm John Chisum."

Wes took off his hat and offered his hand to the cattle baron.

Chisum's big paw wrapped around Wes's fingers and shook them vigorously. "No matter what you've heard about me, I'm not as bad as they say. I just got here first and prospered most. Some men can't accept my good luck and their bad." As Chisum spoke, his gaze seemed to bare Wes's soul. When he released Wes's hand, the cattleman motioned toward the table. "Join us. We've been discussing all the two-legged snakes in Lincoln County." Chisum peeled off his broadcloth coat and folded it over the back of a vacant chair.

Wes watched Chisum's precise movements and envied his fine clothes as his gaze took in the cattleman's starched white shirt, his sharp-creased pants, and his polished boots. But something was amiss, though it didn't strike Wes until his eyes focused on his narrow belt. John Chisum, one of the most hated men in Lincoln County, wore no sidearm.

Chisum noticed. "You've seen I don't carry a pistol."

Wes nodded.

"It's been my observation that toting a revolver gets a man in more trouble than going without one," he explained, then folded his lean frame into a seat.

John Chisum had plenty of grit in his craw, Wes thought as he took a seat beside the cattleman, and Casey hobbled back to his chair.

"If it weren't for thieves, weeds, and cockleburs," Chisum laughed, "Lincoln County would be about as near heaven as you can get on earth. I suspect it's Apaches that took Bob's stock here and more than a hundred of my horses. A white man couldn't get away with that many, the way I see it."

Casey nodded across the table. "Uncle John here put Jesse Evans on the trail after them. My men joined up with him to reclaim our animals."

Chisum laughed. "I told Jesse to steal every horse on the Mescalero reservation. I'll show them they can't out-steal me!"

Wes tossed his hat on the table. "Thought you hated thieves, weeds, and cockleburs."

Throwing back his head, Chisum cut loose a deep laugh. "When I'm doing the stealing, I hate weeds and cockleburs. I hear you're a bear when some bandits take what's yours. Don't misunderstand me, Mr. Bracken. I respect an honest thief, like Hugh Beckwith and his boys. They're thieves and damn proud of every cow of mine they can alter the brand on. It's a thief like L. G. Murphy that I can't tolerate. He either steals by legal

133

manipulation—selling folks worthless deeds—or having others rob for him. I make no secret that Jesse Evans and his boys are on my payroll. I'll go to whatever lengths necessary to protect what's mine. Murphy takes what belongs to others."

Wes stroked his chin. "Murphy don't care for either of you."

"Me?" Casey asked, his eyes narrowing and his hands grabbing the edge of the table. "Where'd you hear that?"

"Murphy told me himself," Wes answered, "when I confronted him on selling Luther a worthless quitclaim deed to our place and stealing our wagon. Said as much as he'd drive both of you out of the county."

Chisum drummed his fingers on the table. "He's after you, Bob, because you run a store."

Casey's face reddened. "I do a lot of things, but my place can't compete with his, not with all the money behind him."

"No matter," Chisum replied. "He don't like *any* competition for what money there is in Lincoln County."

Wes leaned forward in his seat. "Murphy hates that I trade with you, even threatening me unless I gave him my business."

"Damn him," Casey cried, pounding his fist on the table, then grimacing at the pain from his wounded leg.

"Easy, Bob," Chisum cautioned. "Don't tangle with Murphy and his hired assassins."

Wes nodded. "He offered to buy from me any cattle I could steal, Mr. Chisum."

"That's how he fills the government beef contracts below cost," Chisum replied.

"It ain't right," Casey blurted out, the frustration tugging at the corner of his mouth.

"Right has nothing to do with it, not in Lincoln County," Chisum answered.

For an hour, the three men talked about the desperate situation that Lawrence G. Murphy was creating in the region. Few markets existed in the county except for the government contracts at Fort Stanton and the Mescalero reservation. A big rancher like John Chisum, with plenty of cattle and hands to look after them, could afford to drive them to El Paso or Denver, where the markets and the returns were better. But for most, the alternative was to sell their beef to Murphy at inferior prices if he didn't steal them first. Further, Murphy, being the only market for beef in southeast New Mexico Territory, could refuse to buy a rancher's herd. One condition before Murphy would purchase their cattle was that they had to do their trading at his mercantile. Thus, Murphy could buy their cattle cheap and force them to procure goods from his store at exorbitant prices.

Murphy also controlled the contracts to supply hay and corn at Fort Stanton and flour at the reservation. The farmers living along the Ruidoso, Bonito, and Hondo had no better options than the ranchers. They either sold their crops to Murphy, or they had to take them elsewhere, an inconvenience and a cost few of them could afford. Most honest folks in the region were in arrears to Murphy's store, and every visit to his mercantile sank them deeper into the quicksand of indebtedness.

"We'll not solve all Lincoln County's problems today," Chisum announced, unfolding his lanky frame from the chair. He offered his big paw to Wes and shook his hand. "I'm glad to have made your acquaintance, Mr. Bracken. You're always welcome on my ranch, and once you start selling horses, maybe we can strike us a deal. You'll find me better to do business with than the army or Murphy."

Chisum assured Casey that Jesse Evans would catch the livestock thieves and return his cattle and horses. "You'll get most of them back before it's over."

"Obliged, Uncle John," Casey said, hobbling with the cattle baron to the door. "Need help saddling your horse?"

"Hell, no," Chisum laughed. "I'm not that old yet!"

Casey shut the door behind him. "He's a tough old bird," he said, "but as good a man as you'll find in Lincoln County. His word's his bond."

"A man I can do business with." Wes picked up his hat from the table.

Casey squinted at Wes. "Can you still trade with me, or are you taking your trade to Murphy?"

Wes swatted at Casey with his hat. "You got my business as long as you'll have it. And this trip, I need five pounds of coffee."

"You didn't make this trip just for coffee."

"I came to borrow one of your men for a day, but I see you don't have any to spare if they're all out chasing thieves."

"You and Luther seem to get plenty of work done, so I'm surprised you need another man."

"We want a break, a night in Lincoln and someone to look after the place for a day or two."

Casey limped around behind the bar and pulled a bottle and two jiggers from beneath. Uncorking it, he tipped the bottle over the two glasses, letting the amber liquid fill each. He pushed one to Wes. "On the house."

Wes stepped up to the bar, fingered the jigger, then tossed the whiskey down his throat.

The storekeeper savored the liquor in his mouth, then swallowed it hard. "Need a hand for a night?"

Wes nodded.

"Unless he's left, there's a rider that came in yesterday afternoon, saying he was looking for work. Don't know a thing about him. Called himself Jace Cousins. I let him sleep the night at the mill. If he's still around and you'd trust a stranger standing guard at your place, try him. Otherwise, I'm too short-handed to oblige you."

The door swung open, and a tall, lean man with a rifle in his hand ducked his head and strode in. His work shirt bulged with muscles put to hard use, and his hat wore the sweat stains of a thousand past chores. Raising the rifle, he used the barrel to push his hat back on his head. A cleft in his chin matched the gap between his two front teeth when he opened his mouth to speak. "Came to settle up 'fore I ride on," he addressed Casey, then stared at Wes.

"We were just talking about you," Casey replied.

His lips tightening, the man lowered the rifle barrel and nodded at Wes. "Is your friend the law?"

"Neighbor," Case replied, "and a good one."

The stranger lowered his rifle further until the barrel pointed harmlessly at the ground. "Jace Cousins is my name."

Wes wiped his hand on his britches, then offered it to Cousins.

"That your stallion outside?" Cousins asked. "Best looking animal I've seen in New Mexico Territory."

"He's mine," Wes replied. "Hear you're looking for work?"

"You heard right, but I didn't hear your name."

"Wes Bracken. Me and my brother are starting the Mirror B Ranch upstream from here. Raising horses. Right now, we need a man to watch after the place a night or two while we relax over in Lincoln. There's a few dollars in it for you, a roof over your head for a night, but no permanent work."

Cousins walked to the bar as Wes sized him up. He had an easy manner about him, though his brown eyes were void of nonsense, and his lip had a peculiar curl about it at the corners.

"A drink?" Wes offered.

Cousins declined with a wave of his arm. "You must not be a popular man, if you can't leave your place without a guard."

"I've got some enemies."

Scratching his chin, Cousins looked from Wes to Casey. "We all make a few enemies along the way." He seemed to speak from experience. "How much is in this for me?"

"Two dollars," Wes answered.

"Not bad for a couple days' easy work. I'm your man."

"Get me that five pounds of coffee, Casey, and we'll be on our way."

CHAPTER 15

In the daylight, Lincoln was even less impressive than it had been in the fog. Had the buildings been bunched together around a common square with several streets feeding into it, Lincoln might have a legitimate claim to being a town. But instead, the structures were strewn out along a mile-and-a-quarter dusty trail, as if they had fallen from a slow-moving wagon with an open tailgate.

The buildings were draped in the common New Mexico drab of earthen adobe, weathered wood, and murky oilskin windows. The better adobes lined the street, and behind them were the privies and beyond them were the *jacales,* simple pole and mud buildings with flat roofs and blankets that quivered in the breeze for doors.

Lincoln's most distinguishing structure, save for the Murphy store visible at the western edge of town, was a round stone and mud tower twenty feet tall near the middle of the town. From the heavy wooden door hanging askew on rusted hinges and from the shoulder-high gun ports at the ground level and those ringing the upper perimeter, Wes knew the structure was a fortress from when the Apaches still roamed the region.

Opposite the *torreón* stood a modest adobe building with a broad door and wide windows. Thirsty weeds sprouted around it like beggars by a bank. The door was padlocked. Wes studied it, figuring it was the public meeting hall or the courthouse. Just beyond it rested a narrow church with a squat steeple and a brass bell in the belfry. The chapel, too, was closed as if Lincoln were no place for law or religion.

Little brown kids playing hide and seek in back of the church spotted Wes and Luther, then scattered like a covey of quail, hiding behind bushes, sheds, and two-wheeled Mexican carts. One daring lad even rushed at the two riders, a pistol-shaped stick in his hand, and fired an imaginary round before retreating to giggle with his playmates. Wes tipped his hat in their direction, and the broad white smiles creasing their bronze faces told of their delight.

Except for the children, the others along the street moved slowly, deliberately, watching Wes and Luther out of the corner of their eyes as if they trusted no one. Mostly the populace was Hispanic, dressed in drab work clothes and tending their gardens or their chickens and goats. Up the road opposite the post office, two hogs nosed under a wobbly wooden fence and nibbled on the garden greens. A pair of squawking chickens, their flightless wings aflutter, darted in front of Wes and Luther, a mongrel dog on their tail and a middle-aged Mexican woman with a switch after him.

Wes, who couldn't remember the last time he had eaten chicken, envied the dog's dinner choice and wished him luck. "Fried chicken would sure taste good, Luther."

"It and a good pint of whiskey," Luther answered.

Wes rode silently on, wondering if this trip to Lincoln might awaken Luther's whiskey cravings. Dammit, Luther had worked hard on the Mirror B and deserved a binge to break the daily tedium. Luther had mentioned digging up the money he thought was hidden by the stream, but Wes offered to pay for his good time if he left the buried tin alone. Wes had to figure out how to inform Luther of his deception, but that wouldn't be easy because of a habit his brother had started. Each day he went without whiskey, Luther dropped a potato size stone over the spot where the tin was buried. To replace the decoy with the real can, Wes would have to rearrange that monument to sobriety. Luther would realize the deception, and hard feelings would ensue.

A pair of riders came from the other end of town, their eyes narrow, their faces littered with whiskers, their gun hands resting near their revolvers, the oiled stocks of their carbines rearing behind their saddles like serpents. Wes returned their silent stares, figuring they were likely the type of men John Chisum said Murphy used to handle his dirty work. The two riders left an unsettled feeling in Wes's stomach and made him thankful he had hired Jace Cousins to watch the Mirror B during his and Luther's absence.

Luther seemed oblivious to the pair as they passed, studying instead the buildings. At one he edged his horse toward the hitching post, looking over his shoulder at his brother. Wes didn't understand until he saw a wooden sign ripped from a crate. The letters crudely burned into the wood spelled out SALOON.

Wes shook his head. "It's not even noon, Luther. Let's have somebody else's cooking for dinner, and then we can hit the saloon and drink all you want."

Luther grumbled and angled his chestnut gelding back toward Wes.

Up ahead, Wes pointed to the Wortley Hotel. "We can take food there."

"I ain't as hungry as I am thirsty," Luther complained.

"The drinks are on me up to two dollars worth, Luther."

They dismounted in front of the Wortley Hotel and tied their mounts. Wes stretched his arms and walked the stiffness out of his legs. Luther only stared, his arms folded across his chest, his boot tapping impatiently on the ground. Wes dug into his pocket and pulled out some cash, handing it to his brother. "For your bottle fever," Wes said.

Luther snapped the bills from Wes's hand like a frog snatching a fly.

"No more this trip," Wes said, figuring his limit would anger Luther, but his brother seemed pleased to be so near quenching his thirst for liquor that nothing else mattered. Wes shifted his gun belt on his waist, his left hand brushing against the Horrell knife. With the set of his holster comfortable against his leg, he stepped toward the Wortley.

Luther fell in behind Wes, but his gaze lingered on the saloon back down the street.

Pushing the door open, Wes paused, remembering his encounter with the Horrells the last time he had stepped through the entryway. Though it was half an hour before noon, the room was crowded and all the tables occupied. At the back table sat L. G. Murphy, dabbing at his red beard with the corner of his napkin. He studied Wes, then his face lit up, and he cut loose a loud laugh that resonated deeply because of his full stomach.

"Wes Bracken," Murphy called out, "come on in. I 'ear the last time ye came to the Wortley to eat ye almost ate some bullets."

Wes studied the room, relieved that he saw no Horrells, but wary of the hard glares of Murphy's allies. No doubt, Murphy was the lead steer in this herd, and all his men turned to stare at Wes. He stepped inside, followed closely by Luther.

Sam Wortley, the proprietor, appeared in the kitchen door, his face reddened from the heat of the stove, glancing from Murphy to Wes. "It'll be a couple minutes before I've got room for both of you."

"Fine," Wes replied, sensing the hard gaze of hard men and noticing the stares of several pausing at his waist.

"Nice looking knife ye've got there," Murphy called out.

Wes realized the men were noting Mart Horrell's knife on his belt. Wes wore it as a badge of survival from his last meeting with the Horrells and a warning to others that he could take care of himself.

Motioning to a single empty chair at his table, Murphy cried, "Ye care to join us, Wes Bracken? The food's on me."

"Not enough room for us both," Wes answered.

"I'll eat with you," Luther said, pushing his way around his brother.

Wes dismissed Luther's choice of lunch companions, knowing his older brother was set on getting to the saloon as soon as possible and saving every penny he could for liquor.

Murphy made a grand gesture of Luther taking a seat beside him. "This is a man that enjoys good company," Murphy announced. "The 'orrells would never 'ave shot at 'im!" Murphy laughed again, delighting in ribbing Wes.

Luther's face reflected a coward's or a drunkard's shame as he sat beside Murphy.

"I 'ear ye ain't much of a shot at anything smaller than a 'orse, and when ye make a kill ye mutilate the saddle. Sounds like ye've got Apache blood in you." Murphy laughed.

His men joined in the conviviality at Wes's expense.

"It's a shame ye won't be joining us, Wes Bracken. I be thinking of selling yer wagon. Don't know that I'll be needing it once my store is built. I'll give ye first offer on it for six hundred dollars."

Wes sensed the anger rising like floodwaters in him. He took a step toward Murphy, then caught himself. Murphy was only baiting him, hoping to create a disturbance that his boys could settle for him.

The proprietor of the Wortley emerged from the kitchen door, balancing four plates on his hands and arms as he weaved among his customers to the table by the window. Wortley delivered the food and a promise. "I'll be back with coffee."

As he passed, Wes grabbed his arm. "You got any chicken today?"

"Nope," Wortley replied, shaking free.

"If I bring you one, will you fry it?"

Wortley nodded. "As long as you can wait until one o'clock when business slows."

"Deal," Wes said, then turned to Luther. "I'll join up with you at the saloon." He spun around and marched out the door, Murphy's laughter following him outside. Wes untied Charlie and led him down the street. Curled up beside a tree, he saw the mongrel that had been chasing the chickens. From the defeated look in the dog's eyes, Wes knew the *señora* had caught up with him before he snatched her hen.

At the first adobe with chickens pecking around it, Wes tied Charlie at the street and advanced to the dwelling. The *señora* with wide hips and a suspicious smile met him at the door. Her nominal English made his request difficult until he pulled a dollar from his pocket. Her eyes widened, and her understanding of English improved dramatically. With words and signals Wes convinced her to sell him a chicken for fifty cents and to kill, gut and pluck it for fifty cents more. Taking the dollar, she held it up to the sun, nodded, then retreated into her abode.

She returned a moment later with a butcher knife and chased a chicken around her place. Next when Wes saw her, she was hanging an old hen by its legs from the low branch of a piñon pine. Then she stretched its neck and, with a swipe of her dagger, decapitated the chicken, its wings flapping wildly as the blood drained into a puddle on the ground. Next, she plucked the feathers, carefully saving them in a basket she had fetched, and finally gutted the bird, displaying the heart and liver in her hand if Wes wanted them. He shook his head, pleasing the *señora*, as she untied the carcass and carried it to him.

Wes grabbed the carcass by its legs, untied Charlie, and returned to the Wortley, going around back and knocking on the door until Wortley stuck his head out. "Here's my lunch; see you in an hour or so," Wes said.

Wortley took the poultry and slammed the door.

With an hour to kill, Wes mounted Charlie and rode west out of town, passing the Murphy store, its imposing walls nearing completion above the scaffolding where two Hispanic men toiled for Murphy. The store looked more like a fortress than an inviting mercantile, and Wes suspected that was no mere coincidence. Murphy focused more on making money than on making friends.

The Rio Bonito valley was wide, the stream to the north of town a glowing ribbon in the midday sun. Behind the Murphy store, a limestone mountain was crowned with a jagged peak and dotted with juniper and piñon pine. The other mountains cradling the valley stood as lesser and gentler companions, none worthy of a limestone crown.

Well beyond Lincoln, he slapped the reins against Charlie and let the stallion run, enjoying the sorrel's powerful strides and the breeze that blew against his face, once almost knocking his hat off. After a couple of miles, he eased back on Charlie and steered him at a canter back toward town.

When he reached the Wortley Hotel, he found the eatery empty of customers and filled with the aroma of frying chicken. Wortley poked his head out the kitchen at the sound of the door, then disappeared when he saw Wes enter. "Be ten or so minutes," Wortley called.

The proprietor returned on schedule, carrying a platter of fried chicken and a bowl of gravy. He augmented that moments later with a plate of cornbread and bowls of hominy and boiled potatoes.

Wes filled the tin plate before him and attacked the food with relish. The first bite was enough to tell him he was about to enjoy the best meal he had eaten since arriving in New Mexico. He lingered over each bite and savored not only its flavor but its aroma as well. When he was done an hour later, he had devoured the meat of the entire chicken, leaving behind only its cleaned bones.

After paying Wortley, he lingered a few minutes at the table, knowing he had several hours to kill before Luther would be ready to go home. Abandoning the hotel, he rode Charlie past the saloon where Luther's horse was tied, as he knew it would be, and then angled off toward the Rio Bonito. He hobbled Charlie and let him graze on the lush grass growing along the stream banks. He pulled his bedroll from Charlie and tossed it in the shade of a wide cottonwood. He found a few twigs that he whittled on for a while, then leaned back on the bedding and took a nap.

Come suppertime, he gathered his bedroll and returned to the Wortley and had a beefsteak, wondering if the beef from which it had been sliced had been stolen from John Chisum. Wortley warned him that Murphy was staying at the Wortley and taking his meals there until his store was finished. Wes knew it was a subtle plea for him to finish his meal and depart before Murphy and trouble arrived. While paying Wortley, Wes heard the bellows that was Murphy approaching, so he slipped into the kitchen and out the back door. Wortley's sigh of relief punctuated his escape.

By now, Wes figured Luther had enjoyed eight hours of liquor, plenty enough. He led Charlie to the saloon, where a tepid yellow light was seeping out into the street. Wes tied Charlie beside Luther's chestnut and entered a room pungent with cigarette smoke, kerosene fumes, and unwashed men. Several looked up from their drinks, pointed his way, and then wetted their lips again.

Before Wes's eyes could adjust to the light and he could spot Luther, he heard him from a back corner. Luther was slobbering drunk and loud enough to be heard in Texas. "I am too," Luther shouted, then slammed his glass into the wooden table, overturning two empty bottles. Luther was sandwiched between two men equally as eloquent from liquor, one with a patch over his eye, the other with a crooked nose from one too many fights and one too few dodges.

"Then why ain't you got more money, if'n you be so rich."

Luther leaned into the table, then pushed himself away abruptly, the chair tipping backward and falling forward with a clunk into the floor. Luther's forward momentum helped him to his feet. He staggered on mushy knees, leaning over the table again and bracing himself with both palms amid the empty bottles and glasses. "I ain't got more money because it's buried." Luther's words echoed like cannon fire around the room. Every conversation halted. "It's buried beneath a pile of stones by the creek."

"Let's go, Luther!" Wes shouted, pushing his way between the tables. "You're so drunk you don't know what you're talking about."

His eyes widening, then narrowing, Luther jerked back his head, then let it tilt forward as his gaze gradually focused on his brother. "Don't know, huh?" Luther took a deep breath.

Wes dodged an outstretched leg in his path, his step accelerating and frightening Luther's two drunk companions. Both wobbled to their feet, prepared to meet the charge.

Luther exhaled, and his lips twisted into a sinister smile. "I know my money's buried under my rock pile by the Ruidoso."

"Come on, Luther, you've had enough to drink."

"And you're the son of a bitch that wouldn't let me have it, my money." Luther swung his arm at Wes as he darted around the table. Eye-patch tripped and fell as Luther's punch made a

147

wide arc through the air, spinning Luther around, disorienting him.

Wes lunged for Luther and caught him in a bear hug. "You gotta sleep it off, Luther."

Luther's arms wriggled beneath Wes's grip, but the liquor had drained his strength and his senses. "Son of a bitch," he mumbled as Wes steered him through the crowd to the door. "I'm gonna dig up my gold when I get home!" he cried.

Behind them, conversations resumed as Wes shoved Luther outside, then clinched him by the scruff of the neck and maneuvered him toward his chestnut. "You're a damn fool, Luther," Wes grumbled, but his brother was oblivious to his words and lectures. At the gelding, Wes lifted Luther's foot and poked his boot into the stirrup. Luther muttered something and did not seem to understand until Wes shoved him against the saddle and boosted him atop his gelding. By instinct Luther held the saddle horn with both hands.

Even in the darkness, Wes could see Luther wobbling atop his chestnut. Wes untied the animal's reins and led him to Charlie, Luther swaying with each step like the day's wash hung out in a breeze. Gingerly, Wes pulled himself aboard his stallion and turned toward home.

The trail out of Lincoln took forever, occasional patches of yellow light dotting the way eastward as they headed for home, their trip made easier by the full moon. They passed the final adobe and rode by the cemetery, a handful of wooden tombstones and tilting crosses just visible in the moonlight. Beyond the graveyard, the eerie noise of screeching crickets and hooting owls serenaded them on their journey. The moonlight helped Wes assist Luther, but he worried the nocturnal glow might make them targets of a Horrell ambush.

Luther sat precariously beside Wes, his lean frame tipping forward, then straightening with a start. He kept dozing off, snoring as his chin dropped toward his chest, then snorting awake when his jaw touched his rough shirt. If they rode long this way, Luther would likely fall off and break his neck. Wes cursed, knowing his bed at home would be more comfortable than a blanket on the ground, but Luther would never make it to the adobe.

Three miles outside of town, Wes angled the horses off the trail, dismounted, and found enough of a clearing for him and Luther to sleep the night. He pulled his brother off and dropped him on the ground like a sack of potatoes. Luther mumbled and snorted, then fell to snoring shortly after he hit the ground. Wes hobbled both horses, pulled down his bedroll, and reclined atop it. He slept in fitful starts, awakened once by a wildcat's scream, then by two foolish riders galloping by in the dark, and several other times by Luther's rough breathing.

Come morning, he helped Luther onto his mount, and they headed east at a canter toward the Mirror B. They rode silently, Wes still tired and Luther looking like he had a headache the size of Lincoln County. As they came within sight of the Mirror B, Wes gave a sigh. All looked well, the horses grazing in the field, smoke rising from the chimney, and Jace Cousins's horse tied out front.

Cousins greeted them at the door, then shook his head at Luther and helped him to his bed. Wes decided to nap, too. Come mid-afternoon, Wes awoke in time to see Luther scurrying out the door. Wes pulled himself up and shook his head. Stepping outside, Wes saw Luther jogging toward the river where he saw Cousins studying the horses. Wes headed for Cousins.

At the Ruidoso, Luther fell to his knees, then dunked his head in the cold water, once, twice, three times, his shouts echoing across the valley. Standing up, he shook water from his head, then angled toward his rock pile where the tin can was buried.

Suddenly, Luther fell to his knees and screamed, pointing toward the horses, then jumped up and ran hell-bent for Wes. Gasping for breath, his eyes wide and wild, Luther grabbed Wes by the arms.

"It's gone," he heaved. "Someone stole my gold, and I know who did it." Luther bolted for Jace Cousins.

CHAPTER 16

Wes sprinted toward Jace Cousins, reaching him just as his brother did. Luther aimed his trigger finger at Jace Cousins, walking in from the horses. "That son of a bitch!" Luther said through gritted teeth. His hand clasped the grip of his pistol and began to pull the weapon from its holster as he took a malicious step toward Cousins.

Before Luther managed another stride, Wes vaulted to him, grabbing his arm and shoving the revolver back into its scabbard. "You're wrong, Luther."

Luther's arm flexed, and Wes's hand tightened like steel around it. Luther's flaming eyes turned from Cousins to Wes. "He stole my gold!"

"You lost it, Luther."

Luther's eyes flared with incredulity. "Me?" He tried to yank the pistol free, but Wes held firm.

"You drank so much in Lincoln, you told the whole saloon where the money was buried."

"It ain't so, Wes. You won't let a man have a drink without blaming him when something goes wrong."

"You shot your drunken mouth off last night, Luther." Wes's hold loosened as he sensed Luther's arm softening. "A couple riders passed us after we bedded down by the trail. Maybe they did it. No one else knew."

Luther's shoulders slumped, and his chin dropped.

Cousins shook his head. "You boys had trouble?"

151

Wes released Luther's arm and turned to Cousins, studying his face intently as he answered with a question. "You see or hear anything yesterday evening by the stream?"

Cousins stroked his cleft chin and eyeballed Wes straight back. "Odd you should ask. Thought I heard something, couldn't say what it was, though it didn't sound right. I had my rifle expecting trouble, figuring someone might try to distract me from your horses so they could move in and take them. I slipped out into the corral with the animals; they were milling and nervous, but they calmed down and nothing ever came of it."

"Hear any riders?" Wes continued.

Cousins nodded. "Thought I did once, but I couldn't say for sure. It ain't my business to ask, but is there trouble I don't know about?"

"Somebody dug up something we had buried," Wes said.

"Come morning, I saw a hole out by that rock pile," Cousins replied.

Wes nodded. "Nothing of value was lost."

"Dammit," Luther interjected, "two hundred dollars of my gold is worth something, even if it's not yours."

Cousins whistled.

Luther's anger flared again, like a pine knot in a dying fire. "How do I know you didn't take it?" Luther advanced toward Cousins, his fingers bunching into fists.

Wes slid in front of Luther, shoving him back. "Get inside, Luther, you've no cause to question Jace here."

"The gold was safe until he came along," Luther spat the words out like poison.

Wes drove his open palms into Luther's shoulders. "Blame your liquored tongue, Luther. Fault yourself, not someone else. Now get in the adobe, or we'll finish our last fight."

Luther kicked at the ground and growled his objections for a moment, then broke away from Wes and stalked off toward the cabin, littering the path with profanities, slamming the door behind him, and, once inside, banging the tin eating utensils and cooking pots in a terrible clatter.

Wes studied the adobe, half fearing Luther might take a shot at Cousins from inside, Wes slid between Cousins and the open window, offering him at least that safety. "Liquor don't take well to Luther."

"I don't either," Cousins replied. "I came on for two dollars. Give me that, and I'll be on my way."

Digging into his pocket, Wes pulled out his dwindling cash and counted out three dollars. "There's an extra dollar," he said, offering the bills to Cousins.

Cousins took the money and pushed it in his pants. "Thanks and good luck to you. You've got a couple fine horses there, and one that'd bring a fine price even though she's not worth a damn."

"The black mare with the narrow head."

Cousins nodded. "Little endurance with such small nostrils. You and me know that, but not everyone. I could sell her for twice what she's worth."

"I'd like to take you up on that, but Luther's my horse trader."

"Just keep him sober or you'll go bust." Cousins laughed and tipped his hat. "I'll be around these parts a while. If you learn of work, remember it in case I run into you again."

"John Chisum always needs good horsemen."

A sly smile worked its way across Cousins's face. "I don't work for big outfits. They hire folks like Jesse Evans." Cousins turned and strode toward the back of the adobe where his gelding was tied.

Wes studied Cousins, his easy gait, the Henry rifle he carried in his hand, his muscled shoulders, his brown hair tumbling in tufts out from beneath his wide-brimmed hat. Something about

153

his relaxed smile told Wes that Cousins was a trustworthy man, despite any trouble he might be running from.

Cousins untied his horse and climbed fluidly into the saddle, its leather neither creaking nor groaning under his weight. He turned the gelding, tipping his hat. "Obliged for the easy money. Which way to Lincoln?"

Pointing at the Lincoln road, Wes cautioned Cousins. "Be careful dealing with L. G. Murphy. He's crooked as a barrel full of rattlesnakes and not nearly as decent."

That sly smile wormed its way across Cousins's face again. "Let me have that black mare of yours, and I'll take Murphy for a few dollars of his own." Cousins slapped the reins against the gelding's neck, and the animal darted toward the Lincoln trail.

Wes watched him ride into the line of trees at the river and disappear around the bend to Lincoln. When Wes turned for the cabin, Luther was standing in the door, his face flushed with anger and his fingers knotted into fists.

"I don't trust him," Luther announced, taking a step toward Wes.

"He doesn't trust you either."

"My money was secure before he arrived."

Wes hit his palm with his right fist and took a deep breath, then let it leak from his lungs. "Your money's still safe, Luther."

Luther's jaw dropped, his eyes widened, and his gaze narrowed with the furrowing of his forehead. "What do you mean?" The menace in his voice was punctuated by the heavy fall of his boots on the ground as he advanced at Wes. "Did you dig up my money?"

Watching Luther approach, Wes paused. Luther should be pleased his money had been hidden from himself, but Wes expected the deception would infuriate his brother, even though Wes's reasoning had proven correct by the events of the last twenty-four hours. "The money never was buried, Luther."

Lifting his fists toward Wes's face, Luther growled. "You spent it, didn't you? I should've finished whipping you when we last fought."

"Get it through your damn head: I didn't spend your money." Wes jutted his chin at his brother, daring him to strike him. "I saved it from yourself."

"You ain't my nursemaid, Wes." Luther drew back his fist.

"Hit me, Luther, and you'll never see the money again."

Luther's lip quivered, and his fists dropped but stayed knotted at his waist. "Give me the money, and you'll never see me again. Wes, I'm done with you, and I'm done with the Mirror B."

Wes felt a pang of conscience, knowing if he turned the money over to Luther, his brother would squander it on liquor and end up with only a terrible headache and a poor memory.

"I'm tired of working for you, Wes. We started out partners, but no more."

A knot bulged in Wes's throat. Luther was family, but even kin could fester on a man and rot a relationship, eating away at the flesh until nothing remained but the bone. Wes could almost hear the rattle of skeletons between them. There was little else to do. Wes nodded. "Sign papers turning your share of the Mirror B over to me. I figure it's an even trade for our wagon and all our tools you squandered here."

Luther shrugged. "I want my gold, Wes. You can have the place, and you don't need no paper to have it."

"No signature, no money, Luther." Wes knew his brother would never reclaim the land, as he was too lazy to work it without supervision. The formality was not to protect him from Luther's claims, but from Lawrence G. Murphy's in case the merchant made a run at title to the property. But Luther would never understand that. "No money without the paper."

Spitting at the ground, Luther shook his head. "Won't even

take my word, will you?"

Wes folded his arms across his chest, saying nothing, just staring into his brother's red and runny eyes.

Luther pounded his palm with his fist a couple times. "I'll sign papers, but I ain't got no pencil or paper."

"I'll fetch you some," Wes answered, stepping around Luther and striding into the house. In his war bag under the bed, Wes kept a ledger and a pencil. His fingers fumbled through his meager belongings—two shirts, a couple pair of work pants, socks that needed mending, a woolen vest, and a box of cartridges—until they grabbed the edge of the ledger and jerked it free. The book, its cover worn from use, was warped from the pencil shoved between the middle pages. Wes dropped the tome on the table, the writing instrument escaping from its prison and rolling along the top. Sliding onto a bench, Wes snapped at the implement before it rolled off the edge. Examining the dull point, Wes jerked the Horrell knife from its scabbard and whittled a workable pencil lead. After sliding the knife in place, he turned to a back page and scribbled out a paragraph that, once signed and dated, would relinquish to Wes any claim Luther had ever had on the Mirror B or the horses. Finishing it, Wes held the ledger up to the light and read over the agreement. It withstood his inspection. "Come here," Wes shouted.

Crowned with a drunkard's arrogance, Luther marched inside, taking a seat opposite Wes at the table. He clasped his hands together and plopped them on the table without ever looking at his brother.

Wes shoved the pencil and ledger at Luther. "Read over it," Wes directed. "We'll work out any problems."

Luther grabbed the book and snatched the pencil. He looked at the document barely long enough to see where to sign, then scrawled his full name beneath his brother's handwriting. He shoved both the ledger and pencil to Wes. "The gold," Luther said, slowly. "I want it now."

"Start a fire," Wes answered.

"No more games, Wes. I want the money!"

"I'll fetch it, but you build the fire or you'll not find the money."

Both angry men stood from their seats, Luther retreating to the corner fireplace and Wes slipping outside and around the back of cabin. Lifting the pole ladder from beside the house, he propped it against the adobe wall. He climbed the ladder, wondering if by chance the tin with the real money might have been stolen. Wes sighed with relief when he saw the can. When his fingers closed around it, he knew by the weight that the coins were still embedded in the candle wax. He descended the ladder. Reaching the ground, Wes kicked the bottom out from under the pole, and it crashed to the ground.

Returning inside, Wes sat the tin at the edge of the small blaze Luther had made. Gradually the milky white of the wax softened into a translucent liquid. As if by magic the gold coins appeared, and Luther's eyes brightened with anticipation. Wes grabbed the hot tin and dumped the hot fluid and coins onto the floor.

Luther's greedy fingers snatched at the gold coins, and he gave a little yelp at the sting of the blistering wax. Each coin he wiped on his britches leg and slipped in his pocket.

Wes wondered how long that money would stay in his pants. How many days before Luther drank it all? Damn the waste! When the inevitable happened, Wes had no intention of taking his brother back.

At that moment, Luther had no thought of returning. His eyes were transfixed on the one remaining coin, his fingernails scraping away the wax that had coagulated on it. "Ha," he hollered, bouncing up from his knees, "this is what I've been waiting for." His gaze fell upon Wes and lingered but an embarrassed moment. He scrambled to his bed, gathered his bedroll, hurriedly tying it together, then tossing it over his shoulder. He grabbed his saddlebags from the bedpost and patted both the pistol at his side and his pants pocket with his money.

His emotions as muddy as a flooding river, Wes watched in silence, experiencing relief, concern, and guilt, all at the same time because Luther was, after all, still family.

"So long, Wes," Luther said, walking around the opposite side of the table from him without so much as a glance.

"Aren't you forgetting something?" Wes said, pointing to the corner where his new carbine leaned against the wall.

Without looking back, Luther shrugged. "You can keep whatever it is."

"Your carbine, dammit. Don't you think you might need it?"

"Not anymore, now that the Horrells shouldn't have anything against me."

Wes shrugged. If nothing else, Luther could always sell the new Winchester and buy himself something to drink when his money ran out, but Luther never thought that far ahead. Wes poured salt on the wound between them. "Without me hiding your money, Luther, you'd have had none."

"No, Wes, I'd have had it long before now."

Wes watched his brother saddle his horse and ride away from the Mirror B.

CHAPTER 17

Even from a distance, Wes recognized the yellow dun and its lanky rider approaching on the road from Lincoln. Jace Cousins sat easy in the saddle, his Henry rifle resting in the crook of his left arm. Tugging his red bandanna from around his neck, Wes leaned on his ax and wiped the sweat from his face. His muscles ached from four straight hours of chopping wood, and he relished an excuse to stop. The wood pile was growing, plenty to cook meals for the rest of the fall and a solid start on a winter supply.

In the three weeks after Luther deserted the Mirror B, Wes found more than enough work to do from dawn until dusk. The filly brimmed with friskiness and danced in the fields all the day giving Wes about the only pleasure he had had except for the good news that Bob Casey's livestock had been recovered by his men and Jesse Evans, who was following John Chisum's orders to the letter and stealing horses with such success from the Apache reservation that an army contingent at Fort Stanton was rumored to be out looking for him.

Wes needed to travel to Casey's place to buy supplies, but with no one to look after the place and the stock, he had been chained to the Mirror B for weeks. For all Luther's problems, Wes missed his companionship, so he was pleased to see Jace Cousins's yellow dun turn off the road toward the Mirror B. Wes retied his bandanna, drew his ax back over his shoulder, and then muscled the sharp blade into a log. The thud echoed

159

down the valley. Wes strode out to meet Cousins, who eased his mount to the hitching post and tossed the reins over it. The gelding, trained as well as it was, stood as steady as if it were tied to a tree.

Cousins seemed to read Wes's mind. "Took me a year to get him to do that, but with a little patience I managed."

"Good to see you, Jace. Heading anywhere in particular?"

Cousins shrugged. "Wherever I can find work. I saw Luther in Lincoln, and the best I can tell, you're gonna need help." Cousins held up his Henry, then tossed it to Wes.

Wes caught the rifle at the breechblock and watched him slide from the saddle.

"You best wear your weapons and keep your Winchester handy, Wes."

"Horrells again?"

"Partly," Cousins nodded, "but mostly it's your brother."

Wes felt his hand tighten around Cousins's Henry repeater. "What's Luther been saying?"

Cousins took his rifle from Wes. "When he's sober, he's telling people how you stole the place from him, robbed him of his rightful share."

"Damn him!"

"Talk is once cold weather hits and the crops are all in, the Horrells and Luther will come a calling to settle old scores," Cousins continued. "A lot more of them than there is of you. I figured you needed help."

"I'd be pleased to have you work with me, but I'm near broke and don't have enough to pay."

Cousins's lips parted in a smile, exposing the gap between his two front teeth. "I'm a horseman, kinda enjoy working with horses, mustanging and breaking animals. Way I figure it, you give me shelter and a little grub to eat, and I can make money trading horses to fatten your pockets and mine."

160

Wes studied Cousins a moment, unsure what to make of this offer. If Cousins was so good a horseman, why didn't he raise horses on his own? He'd make more money that way, without having to split it with someone else. "Generous offer, but a man like you could do better on your own."

Cousins tilted his head, and his grin widened. "Some of us like to be free of hindrances if that day ever comes when we have to leave in a hurry. I don't care to abandon my horses in a lurch if that happens."

"Fair enough," Wes said. "You can toss your bedroll on the spare bed. This'll even the odds against the Horrells and Luther, if he joins up with them."

Offering Wes his hand to close the deal, Cousins spoke again, his face drawn and his words worrisome. "You're gonna face bigger perils than that because L. G. Murphy's decided he's gonna take your place back."

"The Mirror B was never his, and he'll die trying to take it," Wes answered.

"He's as good as dead then, 'cause I know he'll try."

"He'll send others to do his dirty work."

"There's more of them than there are you, that's why you need me."

"Then let's get to work!" Wes said.

Over the coming days, Cousins proved to be a solid worker, but whatever he did, he was never far from his rifle, keeping it propped by the wood pile if he were chopping wood or tied over his shoulder with a leather thong if he were working the fields or feeding the horses. He was a man who didn't say much when he had work to do, and many chores needed handling around the place. Wes wondered what secrets Cousins's past held but figured he'd find out one day, if Jace ever wanted to talk.

In the field, the corn stalks stood taller than a man, and the ears were filling out, promising plenty of corn for winter feed for the animals and for seed in the spring. Occasionally, Wes pulled half a dozen plump ears, and he and Jace roasted them over the fireplace for supper. The alfalfa was green and vigorous, and the horses grazed daily upon it. With plenty to eat, the animals filled out, and their coats were sleek. The filly had the strong, powerful legs of Charlie, her sire, and raced her shadow up and down the field while the other horses foraged or drank cool waters from the Ruidoso.

The essential chores that had to be completed to prepare for fall and winter had mostly been accomplished, though Wes lacked the money to buy the lumber he needed for a barn. And, Wes had failed to think about the importance of a corn crib until one evening when he was herding the horses into the corral and noticed the vibrant green of the corn stalks now showed yellow streaks. He shook his head as he slid the pole gates back in place.

Cousins stood at the corner of the adobe, watching. "Why the long face, Wes?"

"Winter's coming. No barn and no money for lumber. And I just realized, we also could use a corn crib."

Cousins stroked his chin. "Need a little cash," he mused, a touch of larceny in his voice.

"No stealing, Jace, no matter how broke we are."

"Hah, no larceny unless you consider shrewd horse trading stealing," Cousins replied.

"The black mare?" Wes asked.

Cousins nodded. "I figure I can bring us in enough money to build a barn."

Wes shrugged. "How you plan on doing that? Only maybe a handful of men in Lincoln County have cash enough to pay for a horse."

A wide smile erupted on Cousins's face. He licked his lips.

Wes put his hands on his hips and laughed harder than he had since entering New Mexico Territory. "Not Lawrence G. Murphy himself?"

Cousins nodded again. "He's got a place west of Fort Stanton that he prides on running the best horses and cattle in Lincoln County, mostly stolen of course. The black mare's good enough to attract his eye. That's all it'll take."

Wes slapped Jace on the shoulder. "The mare's yours, Jace."

"Give me three days, Wes, and put no stock in anything you might hear I'm saying about you. I gotta set a solid trap if I'm gonna snare old Murphy himself. All I need from you is a signed bill of sale turning the mare over to me for helping you here."

"Good as done," Wes replied, "let's go in and fix supper."

Both men laughed and retired to the house as dusk pulled a blanket of darkness across the land.

Come morning, Cousins saddled his yellow dun and put a halter around the black mare's head. He nodded goodbye to Wes. "Figure out where you want your barn and your corn crib. You'll have your money in three days."

Cousins was wrong. It took four days instead. Late in the afternoon of the fourth day, he came riding down the Lincoln road, his gelding advancing at a canter, the black mare missing. His smile was wide as the sky, and he sat in the saddle as proud as if he were sitting on a throne. Without a word, he rode over to Wes and pulled a folded envelope from his vest pocket. He weighed the envelope in his hand, then tossed it at Wes.

Wes caught it and gauged its thickness between his thumb and forefinger. Cousins had done well. Opening the flap, Wes pulled out a stack of bills.

"You're holding a barn," Cousins said.

Wes counted out the money, then whistled. "A hundred and fifty dollars."

"That's five or six times what the mare's worth, and all thanks to L. G. Murphy."

"How'd you manage, Jace?"

Cousins laughed. "I play a good bluff. Outside Lincoln, I swapped saddles and rode into town on the mare. She danced into Lincoln like the prettiest girl at the dance, tossing her tiny head and prancing like she owned the whole territory. I caught several men's eyes, and I figured I'd spread the word in the saloons what a dumb horse trader you were. I announced I would sell the yellow dun now that I had a real spirited horse."

"Was Luther in town because he knows better?" Wes asked.

"I never saw him. Story has it he's staying with the Horrells. Anyway, I put on a show, riding the mare up and down the street, catching a few eyes, particularly around Murphy's big store. On the second day, L. G. Murphy himself catches me, saying he'd be interested in the dun but would pay a better price for the mare.

"Staring him right in the eye, I laughed and watched him flinch when I told him he didn't have enough money to buy her, and I decided I wasn't selling either horse in Lincoln County. I told him I'd decided to take her to El Paso where I could get two hundred minimum for her." Cousins laughed.

"Murphy stormed away mad but had one of his men keep an eye on me. The next afternoon, I saddled up and rode out west of town like I was going to El Paso. Just as I figured, Murphy sends his henchman to stop me, offering me a hundred dollars for the mare. I decline, countering with a hundred and seventy-five before settling on a hundred and fifty dollars."

Wes laughed. "A man Murphy's size will wind the mare pretty quickly."

"And when word gets around that he got taken, folks'll be laughing at Murphy. 'Course, that won't make him any fonder of you or me."

"But we'll have a barn, Jace. Take your earnings out of the hundred and fifty so I'll know how much money's left for lumber and nails."

Cousins shook his head. "I got paid just outsmarting Murphy himself."

"I still owe you," Wes replied.

"And one day you can pay me."

In three days, Wes made arrangements to borrow Casey's wagon for the journey to Dowlin's Mill. He let Jace make the trip, figuring he would be less likely to encounter trouble from the Horrells than himself. Cousins wound up making two trips for lumber. After three weeks, the duo had erected a sturdy frame next to the corral. Normally, Wes would have built the barn farther from the adobe, but he hoped one day to build a fine wooden house and turn the adobe into a bunkhouse or shed.

About noon one day when they were nailing planks onto the frame for siding, Cousins dropped his hammer and grabbed the Henry rifle he had slung over his back with a leather thong. He pointed the business end of the rifle at three riders approaching from the stream.

Wes pivoted around, his own hand falling to the pistol at his waist. He shook his head and held up his fingers to Jace. "It's okay. He's a friend of mine. His name is Jesse Evans. The other two go by Clem and Ansel."

"I know Jesse," Cousins replied, his voice taut, his fingers still wrapped around the rifle.

As the riders came within thirty feet, Jesse held up his hand, and all three men reined in their mounts. "Well, I'll be damned," Jesse said, "if it ain't Jace Cousins. Long time, no see."

Cousins nodded. "I liked it better that way."

"You didn't come all the way from Texas just to visit me, now did you, Jace?" Jesse smiled wickedly. "Law on your tail again?"

165

Sensing the heating animosities, Wes slipped between the two antagonists. "No trouble, boys. What can I do for you, Jesse?"

Evans answered without taking his eyes off of Cousins. "I came to get my split of those thirteen horses you kept for us."

Wes nodded. "Seven were claimed, and six remain. Take your pick of the ones we brought back. The bay mare and filly are mine as are my stallion and two mules. The yellow dun is Jace's."

"I know his gelding, and I've been expecting to see it for two years," Evans responded.

Wes could sense the mutual animosity and changed the subject. "Chisum making you provide your own horses now?" he asked.

Evans sneered. "John Chisum cut us loose. We stole horses for him, followed his commands, robbed those damn Apaches of as many as we could just like he said. The army gets mad, and then Chisum lets us go, telling the authorities we were acting on our own, not following his orders."

"You leaving Lincoln County?" Wes asked.

"Nope," Evans said. "John Chisum and Lincoln County haven't heard the last of me." Evans paused, his flinty eyes staring at Cousins. "And, you haven't heard the last of me either, Jace Cousins."

Wes gave a sweep of his arm toward the horses grazing in the alfalfa. "Pick out your three horses, Jesse, but don't start any trouble here."

Evans motioned for Clem and Ansel to head for the horses, then he fell in line behind them, Jace Cousins and his Henry rifle following Evans's every move.

"What's that all about?" Wes asked.

"Just bad blood from back in Texas," Cousins replied and said no more.

CHAPTER 18

The warmth of summer gave way to the cool of early autumn along the Rio Ruidoso. The Mirror B hummed with activity as Wes Bracken and Jace Cousins worked from sunrise to sunset. A barn big enough to keep their horses out of the winter winds stood behind the corral, close enough to the adobe for them to keep watch on it. Beyond the new outbuilding a crib framed with leftover lumber and finished with willow sapling sides held several dozen bushels of corn. Inside the cabin, Wes had stored burlap sacks of seed corn for next spring. Wes and Cousins had thrashed cornstalks to feed the horses during the approaching cold and had plowed the field. They had gathered and scattered horse droppings for fertilizer over the fallow field.

All along the Ruidoso and throughout Lincoln County, the farmers and small ranchers worried about winter preparations more than settling their differences. But come winter, when a man had too little constructive to do, those animosities would fester in their minds, giving them an excuse to settle their grievances. Both Wes and Cousins understood they each faced dangers during the frigid months ahead, Wes from the Horrells, Lawrence G. Murphy, Carlos, and possibly even his own brother, as Luther was still reported to be running with the Horrells. For Cousins, past bitterness poisoned him with Jesse Evans, and he had infuriated Murphy when the merchant realized not only had he bought the inferior black mare from Cousins, but also that Cousins still worked with Wes.

Though Wes and Cousins never mentioned the hazards they expected come winter, they discussed plans for the spring, Cousins figuring to go mustanging down south and build up the Mirror B stock, Wes pointing toward a larger corn crop, working the filly, and breeding more horses. Still, both men wore sidearms everywhere, and Wes took to carrying his Winchester like Cousins toted his Henry.

In Lincoln, Lawrence G. Murphy opened his store moving his goods from Fort Stanton to the county seat and tightening his stranglehold on the county economy. Few residents celebrated Murphy's mercantile debut after they saw the prices he was charging. Most had swallowed hard and bought what they had to, often on credit at twelve percent interest, because Murphy provided the only local market for livestock and farm goods, since he held the beef and horse contracts at the fort and reservation now, as well as the flour and hay business. Since few of the smaller ranchers or farmers could afford to freight their crops or drive their cattle out of the region, Murphy ruled the western half of Lincoln County. Wes fumed after Bob Casey informed him that Murphy had parked the Bracken wagon outside the new store and tacked a FOR SALE sign to it. Wes understood that Murphy was thumbing his nose at him for Luther's mistake.

Only John Chisum had the financial wherewithal to stand up to Murphy and to herd cattle to distant markets beyond Murphy's control, but the cattleman only dominated the eastern half of the county. Even so, Chisum had suffered from rustlers, the blame given partly to the Beckwiths and allied Seven Rivers ranchers but mostly to Jesse Evans, who had vowed revenge on Chisum and all his property.

Though Chisum remained his only major threat, Murphy had vowed to get Bob Casey and his store on the Rio Hondo for daring to compete with his own mercantile. Casey's stock of goods never matched Murphy's, but Casey offered the necessities at a decent price that made him a fair profit. Most every honest man, if there were such a thing in Lincoln County, preferred Casey. The men with sordid reputations gathered about Murphy like flies around sugar.

Occasionally, Wes thought of Sarafina, but hard work and time had exorcized the demon of her memory. He had not seen her in months, and by now she must be ripe with child if she had not given birth already. Like Luther, Sarafina seemed distant in his past as so many chores had consumed him since then.

In late November the first hard freeze struck the Hondo valley. The gray clouds rolled in like smoke from the north, their breath spitting droplets of rain and sleet. Wes tugged his coat tight around his neck and held onto his hat as he ran past the corral to check the barn. He lifted the latch and slipped inside among the fidgety horses, including the filly that was whinnying at this, her first winter storm. Wind gusted from over the mountains and whistled through the thin cracks in the barn, splattering spots of moisture against the wood. Though drafty and cold, the barn beat leaving their horses out in the elements. Wes added fodder to their feed trough and broke the thin layer of ice on their water buckets.

After exiting the barn and barring the door, Wes lingered outside, studying the Mirror B, proud of the work he, Cousins, and even Luther had done when he wasn't on liquor. Wes stood satisfied with their accomplishments and confident so much more would come in the spring.

Giving the barn a final glance, Wes trotted back to the house and squeezed through the door, shoving it hard against the wind following him in. He backed up to the corner fireplace and enjoyed the warmth seeping into his coat and pants, and finally into his flesh.

Cousins sat at the table, drinking a cup of coffee, dealing a game of solitaire with a greasy deck of dog-eared cards. "Winter's arrived to stay," he offered, reaching for a candle and a match to fight the encroaching darkness of dusk.

Wes nodded, grabbing a tin and filling it from the blackened coffee pot bubbling over the fireplace coals. "May need more blankets than we've got to stay comfortable tonight."

"It's nights like this when you need a woman to keep you warm," Cousins said, dragging the cards into a single deck and mixing them for another assault on King Sol.

A gust of wind roared over the adobe, rattling the shutters. Wes shivered at the sound, tipping the coffee to his lips, the boiling liquid warming his innards. He took a deep breath. "Snow and ice by morning," he said. "It'll be a long winter. If this keeps up, we'll have plenty of time to talk."

"And not enough to talk about," Cousins answered.

"We'll manage," Wes said, seating himself across the table from Cousins.

Cousins stared hard at Wes and dealt the pasteboards out. "You're welcome to watch, just don't go giving me any advice on how to play my cards. That bothers me."

"It's not those cards I'm interested in seeing," Wes answered, returning Cousins's gaze. "It's the other cards, the ones you're holding close to your chest."

"Can't say I follow you, Wes."

"Somebody dealt a bad hand between you and Jesse Evans, way I see things."

Cousins's eyes narrowed, and he stared beyond Wes somewhere into the past, a place only he could see. Cousins dropped the remaining deck onto the cards he had already dispensed. When he spoke, his words came slowly and deliberately. "Jesse Evans," he said, "will double-cross you quicker than a politician and will turn on you faster than a rattlesnake."

"That's what John Chisum is finding out." Wes sipped coffee and listened.

"Jesse and I grew up together. He was my friend as long as he could use me, and he did." Cousins's eyes seemed to focus on the present now as he studied Wes. "He had me run horses over to the next county, gave me a bill of sale to show he had bought them."

"Stolen?" Wes asked.

Cousins nodded.

Wes cursed.

"I spent two years in prison with a hard lot, and I was lucky an honest sheriff caught me. If cattlemen had, I'd still be hanging from a tree somewhere in Texas. The bill of sale was bogus, and Jesse Evans lied about it on the witness stand. Twenty-four months is a long time to spend behind bars." Cousins laughed. "We had no women to keep us warm in prison."

"My tongue's got a halter on it," Wes said, shaking his head. "You won't have to worry about me telling anyone."

"I'd have never told you if I thought you'd blabber. The day may come when I settle my score with Jesse Evans. When it does, Wes, I'll not be staying around to see what happens. The horses'll be yours."

Wes scratched the stubble on his chin, then rubbed his mustache. "The way Jesse makes enemies, you might have to stand in line to get him."

Shrugging, Cousins picked up the unfinished deck, scraped the scattered cards together, and mixed them again. "I've done my talking for the winter. How about a hand of poker?"

Nodding, Wes pushed himself up from the bench and retreated to a sack of dry beans in the corner near the fireplace. He pulled a handful from the gunnysack and reclaimed his position at the table, dividing the legumes into two piles, shoving one to Cousins and keeping the other for himself. "Loser fixes supper."

Cousins laughed. "If the loser cooks, the winner is the real loser since he'll have to eat it."

Wes grinned, and they played for ninety minutes, Wes finally losing the last of his stake to a full house that beat his two pair. He fried sowbelly, opened a tin of tomatoes, and cooked a half dozen sourdough biscuits.

Outside, the storm vented its fury against the adobe, the ice pellets sounding like gravel thrown against the door. The wind whistled against the shutters, and Wes threw a couple logs on the fire, the flames licking at the wood, then flaring as they took a bite. Wes and Cousins ate their supper, finishing by sopping their biscuits in cane syrup. "All we're missing is fresh churned butter," Cousins said as he worked the last of the syrup's stickiness into his final bite of biscuit.

After eating, they played cards for an hour until the candle burned down. Wes then cracked the door to check the weather. He saw thick clouds and a snow-covered landscape. Cousins added another log to the fireplace, and both men crawled into their cold beds with their clothes on.

"It's nice to think Jesse Evans may be out in this freezing his butt off," Cousins said.

Wes wondered for a while if Luther might be out in this or if he was staying with the Horrells, the damn, drunken fool.

Sleep came but so did the bitter chill as the fire burned down. The cold crept into bed with Wes, stiffening his muscles and corroding his joints until they ached at the slightest movement. Morning dawned as a gentle, diffused light, casting no shadows, like the sun lacked the strength to penetrate the thick cloud cover. Cousins arose first, reviving the embers in the fireplace with a log and starting the coffee. Wes lingered in bed, there not being much they could do this day except tend the horses and tote water from the stream for them.

Cousins opened the door, and the cold rushed inside as Cousins studied the land. "A foot or more of snow and ice, Wes." Cousins slammed the door.

Grumbling as he tossed back the covers, Wes pushed himself up from the bed, pulled on his boots, and limped on stiff joints to the fireplace, giving the crackling fire time to melt his frozen muscles and thaw his frigid joints. "The snow'll be good moisture for the field and pasture," Wes offered.

"What's good for the place and what's good for me are two different things," Cousins grumbled. "It's enough to make me wish I was back in a Texas prison cell."

Wes stretched between yawns. "Plenty of time for poker once I feed and water the horses." He stamped on the floor, trying to generate a little heat for his frigid feet. "A warm prison cell sounds inviting," Wes joked as he pulled on his coat. "A little of your mud ought to help warm me up," he said, pointing at Cousins's coffee pot. His muscles balking against cold's rigidity, Wes eased over to the fire and filled a tin with Arbuckle's best brew. The scalding liquid burned all the way down his gullet. Its warmth felt good, and Wes lingered by its flickering heat, enjoying his coffee. The horses could wait for food and water.

Wes heard the noise, just as he was tipping his tin for the final sip. The coffee, hot though it was, caught in his mouth for a silent moment, burning his tongue. The sound came again, an animal noise, then a braying. Wes's eyes cut a glance at Cousins and saw the surprise on his face. Wes realized he wasn't imagining things and dropped his cup on the table. Both he and Cousins flew into motion, Wes racing to his bed, grabbing his coat, and yanking his revolver from his holster hanging from the bedpost.

From outside, the grating noise cut through the snowy calm again. A donkey brayed. Nearby!

As Wes pulled on his coat and angled for the entry, Cousins

173

grabbed his Henry. Wes flung the door open and darted into the snow, kicking up powdery white crystals with each step. The donkey brayed from somewhere near the barn. As Wes and Cousins rounded the corner of the adobe, they leveled the barrels of their weapons from the waist ready for business.

The burro brayed again, then stopped as Wes and Cousins approached the barn. The donkey's ears flicked toward the two men before the animal with the thick winter coat of matted fur turned away. At that moment, Wes recognized the burro as belonging to Bonifacio Zamora. Wes caught his breath as he saw the streaks of blood, frozen and matted in the donkey's fur around the neck and shoulder. At first Wes thought the animal had been injured, but then he realized the blood could have been from a rider. He spotted in the snow to the west the burro's trail, angling from the road to the barn.

"Trouble at the Zamora place," Wes said, lowering his revolver and clenching his free fist. "I've got to check it out."

"I'll go, too!"

Running to the barn door, Wes shook his head. "You stay here in case someone's planning on stealing the horses. If you hear shooting, that's when to come."

Cousins nodded and spun around toward the adobe. "I'll fetch your holster and Winchester from the cabin."

"Get my hat, too," Wes called as he removed the bar from the barn and flung open the door, the horses dancing nervously at the clatter. Wes tucked his pistol in his coat pocket, then flew into readying Charlie, slipping the bit into his mouth and sliding the bridle over his head. He tossed the cold saddle blanket over Charlie's strong back and muscled the saddle in place, bending beneath the stallion to cinch the saddle down good, yanking once, twice, three times on the leather straps. Standing straight again, he shoved his foot in the stirrup, grabbed the pommel to pull himself aboard. His leg swung over the saddle and in one smooth move, Wes took the reins with his right hand and directed the stallion to the door.

Wes ducked to clear the door and emerged into the white landscape as Cousins ran up, handing him first his buckled holster, which West drooped over his head to let it ride around his neck to save time. After Wes took his hat, Cousins shoved his Winchester in his saddle scabbard.

"Good luck!" Cousins shouted above the howling wind.

"Hiya!" Wes screamed and turned Charlie toward his neighbors' place, touching his heel to the stallion's flank. Charlie reacted instantly, like he had been poked with a firebrand, and raced for the Zamora cabin, kicking up a fog of the fine snow as he darted to the road and headed west up the valley for the two miles between their properties.

The world passed in a giant blur of white, Wes watching out of the corners of his eyes for potential enemies who would be easy to spot on this day because they would stand out so easily against the snow.

Rounding the final curve in the road, Wes raised up in the saddle to see the Zamora place. From a distance, the cabin looked normal, except no smoke trailed from the chimney. It was too cold a day not to have a fire going. Wes's lips tightened.

He turned down the trail that led to the adobe. A knot caught in his throat. The front door was open a third, and the front of the adobe was pockmarked with bullet holes, particularly around the door and the windows.

Drawing nearer, Wes saw a form sprawled just inside the door. At a distance, he could not make out the body. He thought of Sarafina and hoped not.

Halting the stallion at the door, Wes jumped from his saddle and grabbed his Winchester.

A terrifying scream pierced the air, and shivers colder than ice coursed up Wes's back. It was Sarafina, her agony plain by the terror in her voice. She screamed again, mumbling incoherently in Spanish, as Wes stomped to the door, ready to kill her attacker.

He levered a bullet into the chamber of his Winchester, the carbine clicking its metallic tongue and signaling it was ready to spit fire and death.

At the door, Wes recognized the form of Carlos spilled across the doorway. Wes shoved the door, but it failed to budge with Carlos's torso wedging it a third of the way open. Wes kicked Carlos's body, and the youth moaned from his unconscious daze.

Sarafina panted and shrieked.

As Wes threw his shoulder into the door, it budged and gave way. Carlos groaned and gasped.

Sarafina screamed again.

Wes broke into the house, bracing his feet to shoot Sarafina's attacker, but it took a moment for his eyes to adjust to the dimness.

In the far corner, draped across a stack of blankets, lay Sarafina, her legs bare and bent, her eyes wide with terror.

Sarafina was giving birth.

CHAPTER 19

Wes had been prepared for the Horrell brothers, but not for a woman in labor.

"Bonifacio," Sarafina whispered as Wes entered, "what took you so long?"

She was hallucinating. "It's Wes Bracken," he answered, placing his carbine by the door and dragging Carlos away. Next he removed the gun belt from around his neck and buckled it around his waist.

She sobbed, then screamed at the pain, her hips convulsing, her belly quivering beneath her thin blouse with the little one trying to enter the cold world.

Wes propped Carlos against the wall, his hand brushing against the youth's shirt, bloody and stiff with frost.

The dying embers of a fire made hours ago were smoldering in the corner fireplace. Wes grabbed a handful of kindling from beside the hearth and nursed a flame in the hearth. "I'll help you in a minute," he called to Sarafina, embarrassed that in a moment he must face her and the nakedness beneath her waist. "You need warmth."

She cried out again, then gasped and sobbed.

The blaze grew, and Wes fed its meager appetite with larger pieces of yellow pine until the blaze roared and shared its heat with the room.

Wes squatted beside Carlos, grabbing his chin between his fingers and thumb, then shaking his head, the dancing light of the fireplace casting eerie shadows on the wall. Carlos groaned, his eyes flickering open a moment. Blood crusted in Carlos's black hair, and dried rivulets stained his cheek and jaw. A narrow strip of scalp was missing above his ear where a slug had grazed his skull. Wes stroked the youth's neck and his right shoulder, the youth jerking at the touch. Wes unbuttoned the coarse woolen shirt, spotting the purple pucker of a bullet wound. The hole was fringed with caked blood. Wes circled it with his finger, then pressed against the collar bone, still intact. Carlos groaned, his eyes fluttering, shutting, opening again, gradually focusing on Wes.

Carlos cried out, but he spoke in Spanish, and Wes could not fathom if Carlos were thanking or cursing him. "Bonifacio?" Carlos gasped.

Wes shrugged. "I think you'll be okay."

"Bonifacio? Where is he?" Carlos cried.

Shrugging again, Wes rose. "I don't know about Bonifacio, but you must save your strength, while I help your sister."

Carlos nodded and closed his eyes.

Wes mouthed a silent prayer for the youth. He sighed and turned around reluctantly, considering himself a trespasser on Sarafina's privacy.

Sarafina gasped, panted, gasped, panted, seeking breath, her stomach quivering, her waist convulsing, her bent legs tightening, then relaxing.

This differed from watching Luther deliver a foal. Wes felt a knot in his gut that matched the lump in her belly. He moved tentatively toward her, his eyes focused on the birth canal as her body parted, and a patch of slick, black hair appeared, growing larger as the head emerged. Wes dropped to his knees between her legs, cupping his hands at her bottom. "It's coming," he whispered. "Just a little longer," he encouraged her.

After a sharp squeal, Sarafina held her breath and pushed

until her face reddened from the exertion. The baby's head cleared her body, and Wes cradled the tiny head in his palms. "You're almost home," he said, letting his hands glide away from Sarafina's body as the baby inched out. "Now push a little more," he commanded.

Sarafina gasped and shoved with all her might, her fists clinched across her breasts.

The baby emerged with crooked shoulders, then its chest and petite hands, fingers clenched like its mother's. Wes supported the tiny head with one hand and put his other beneath the child's back. Sarafina gasped for a quick breath and thrust again, pushing the baby's waist and buttocks free so that the legs slid easily out. The fragile package, still wet and splotched from birth, rested in Wes's fingers.

Stunned by the cold of the room, the newborn flinched, shivered, then wailed, the unexpected bawl startling Wes, his hands trembling like he might drop a delicate jewel. The howling baby wriggled, and Wes saw between its legs. "A boy," he announced. "It's a boy."

Contentment flooded Sarafina's eyes, and tears streamed down her cheeks. "Now, if only my husband is safe," she cried, her voice hoarse with exhaustion and overcome by fear. Sarafina's whole body convulsed again, and the afterbirth slid from her womb.

The little fellow trembled from the cold and announced his displeasure with a sustained wail. Wes must cover him, but first he had to cut and tie the umbilical cord. He cradled the naked baby between his arm and chest as his left hand worked its way along his belt until he found the Horrell knife. Jerking the weapon from its scabbard, Wes held the shiny blade above the baby's quivering tummy.

Sarafina screamed and tried to push herself up, reaching for Wes, but she was too weak. *"Diablo,"* she spit out.

179

For a moment, Wes did not understand her anger, and he moved the knife close to the newborn's stomach.

Sarafina shouted again, kicking at him with her feet.

"No, no!" Wes replied, horrified that Sarafina thought he might kill her son. "I've got to cut the cord. I must do that, then cover your son with blankets, or he will die of the cold."

As she sank back into her blanket, her last ounce of strength drained from her. She stared through tear-filled eyes at her baby, a son she feared would never rest in his father's arms.

Wes gently positioned the tiny one on the blanket, grasping the sticky umbilical cord between thumb and finger, slicing across it and tying a knot as close as he could manage to the baby's stomach. From a pallet laid out on the floor, Wes jerked a blanket and swathed the baby inside, cradling it in his arms and rocking him tenderly, until its screams turned to soft cries and a sleepy silence. The boy's flesh was the deep brown of fine leather, and his nose was a wriggling button. His right hand knotted into a petite fist and moved to his mouth, his thumb sliding between his dark lips. Shortly, he was making sucking noises.

Wes carried the baby across the room, to the fireplace, holding him by the heat until the blanket felt warm and comfortable. He returned to Sarafina and put the child in his mother's arms for the first time. She kissed his cheek and held him on her bosom, her hand lifting her blouse until her son was at her bare breast. Wes felt his face redden with shame, but Sarafina cared only about her son in her grasp. She pulled her son's thumb from his mouth, and the boy squalled until his lips touched her nipple. Then he was quiet and contented as he suckled his first meal.

The flesh on Sarafina was pimpled with goose bumps, and Wes moved to cover her, but the debris of birth still lay between her legs. Bending over, he gently slid that blanket from beneath her and worked another coverlet under her on the bed of straw. He folded the dirty blanket over itself and tossed it toward the door. Finding more blankets, he tenderly covered the new mother. With averted eyes, he pulled the cloth over the nursing baby at Sarafina's breast. Atop that covering, he piled two more blankets. Sarafina smiled, her lips slowly losing their curve as her head tipped over, and her eyelids slipped shut in exhaustion.

Mother and child would survive, Wes thought, but he was not so sure about Carlos. He had even more doubts about Bonifacio, if he were not already dead. As Wes moved to the fireplace, he saw Carlos's dark eyes watching his every step. Wes tossed more wood on the fire until the flame roared with vigor and spread its warmth across the room.

"Water," Carlos whispered. "Water."

From a rafter, Wes unhooked a goatskin bladder, stiff with the cold, and untied the end. He squeezed the icy liquid into a clay cup, kneeled beside Carlos, and offered it to his mouth. With his left hand, Carlos reached for the cup, wincing at the pain from his right shoulder. Taking the mug from Wes, Carlos lifted it to cracked, chafed lips. He drank greedily.

"More," he said, "more."

Wes obliged for three more cupfuls, which Carlos gulped down, his eyes widening with a lust to strike back at his attackers, if only his wounded body allowed. Wes had seen that smoldering anger before, deep in Carlos's eyes. This time, however, the rage found a new target instead of Wes.

"*Gracias,*" Carlos said, his voice ragged with the hurting that accompanied each breath and movement. "My sister and her little one needed you." He gritted his teeth not just against the physical agony, but also against the anguish of something else. "And I needed you, too," he admitted. "Where's Bonifacio?"

Wes glanced over his shoulder to make sure Sarafina was

asleep. "His donkey strayed up to our place this morning, blood on his back."

Carlos shook his head, and his eyes watered. "He wouldn't let me go to San Patricio. He went for a midwife to help Sarafina. The little one was coming before the snow began. He wanted the whole village to know he would be a father. An old man becomes a father."

"Who did this?" Wes asked. "Do you know?"

Carlos grimaced. "The Texas *diablos,* maybe. Bonifacio is not gone long. We hear gunfire up the road. I see a rider chasing his donkey, then others joined in and attack us."

"The Horrells, you think?"

Carlos nodded. "Bad men. I fired at them, they shot at me, hitting my shoulder. The snows came, and they leave. I don't remember the head wound."

"You defended your sister and new nephew well, Carlos," Wes said, taking count of thirty empty cartridges scattered about the floor.

Biting his lip, Carlos lifted his finger at Wes. "I recognized one man," he said. "It was your brother."

Wes pounded his palm with his right fist. "Dammit, dammit! Luther, why'd you have to take up with the Horrells . . . anybody else but them?"

Carlos spoke next with anguished eyes. "I am sorry to tell you this."

"You need your rest," Wes replied, trusting the wounded boy's words, yet humiliated that his brother might have participated in so cowardly a deed as ambushing Bonifacio Zamora and attacking his meager home. "I must go look for Bonifacio. I'll be back later to care for you and Sarafina. Believe me, I will *not* leave you alone."

Nodding, Carlos pointed to the pallet on the floor near Sarafina. "Help me there so I can protect my sister and nephew."

Wes reached under Carlos's left shoulder and pulled the youth forward, helping him to his feet. Carlos gasped, then gritted his teeth. He moved one step at a time, each ending before the next began, every stride drawing a deep groan.

Moving beside him, Wes noticed that Carlos's knees were mushy, and he feared the youth might fall. But Carlos's pride gave him the resolve to make it across the room. Even in such a short walk, the color had drained from Carlos's face. He eased slowly down on the pallet, Wes bending with him, then covering him with another blanket. Carlos sighed and closed his eyes for the rest he craved.

Wes heard the baby boy feeding at his mother's breast, and he detected the gentle fall of Sarafina's breath. She was sleeping soundly now. Wes guessed she and the newborn would be okay, but if not, Wes realized he wouldn't know what to do about it anyway. He realized one thing, however: that he must find Bonifacio! Wes marched across the room, tossed another log in the fireplace, and stepped back, knowing the fire would last a few hours before someone must attend it again. He dodged the scattered rifle hulls on the floor and yanked his hat down tight. Reaching in his coat pocket, he retrieved his revolver and slid it into his holster, then grabbed his carbine propped up against the wall. Wes cracked the door open just enough for him and as little heat as possible to slip outside.

Untying Charlie, Wes studied the surroundings now; a man couldn't be too careful with folks like the Horrells running roughshod over Lincoln County. Nothing seemed out of the ordinary except the snow, its gentle mounds and roundness taking the hard edges out of the terrain. His right hand sliding into place at the Winchester's trigger, Wes eased around Charlie and mounted the stallion. Bonifacio could be dead anywhere, even ten feet away, and Wes might never find him.

Wes turned back up the trail toward the road, pausing when

he reached it, knowing he should go to the Mirror B and tell Jace Cousins things were as right as they could be with a wounded youth, a birthing woman, and a missing father, but he went instead toward San Patricio.

The snow cushioned each footfall of the stallion, and Wes's eyes looked from side to side of the road, searching for an unnatural shape, a patch of clothing beneath the snow, a shoe sole embedded in a snow bank, anything that would give a clue. He rode a mile down the icy trail, then turned back, figuring the Horrells had ambushed Bonifacio closer to home. Had the ambush been farther from home, the donkey might have returned to the Zamora place instead of running all the way to the Mirror B.

He retraced his route, stopping when Charlie tossed his head. Wes saw it, a hand pointing stiffly from a pile of snow. He had missed the palm and fingers on his previous pass. The hand was wrinkled and brown. Without doubt, Bonifacio was dead. Dismounting, Wes stepped reverently to the white mound and scooped away fists full of snow, uncovering the arm, then shoulder, and finally the face. It was Bonifacio for sure. Frozen into his face was a smile, as if he had known at death he had fathered a son.

CHAPTER 20

The ground was still muddy from the melted snow when they departed to bury Bonifacio Zamora in the San Patricio graveyard. Wes Bracken had borrowed Bob Casey's wagon and paid for a pine box to hold Zamora's remains. When the weather broke three days after his death, Wes and Jace Cousins loaded Zamora's coffin in the wagon. As Cousins mounted his dun, Wes helped Sarafina and her baby up into the bench seat, then offered to help Carlos get in the back. But the youth, his right arm in a sling, brooded now, hating all white men, even Wes who had saved him from freezing to death on his cabin floor. Carlos had struggled into the back of the wagon beside the coffin, the clenched fist of his left hand resting on Zamora's casket.

The ride toward San Patricio was a somber one, Wes riding with the Winchester resting across his thighs, and Jace Cousins scouting ahead with his Henry at the ready. Except for the occasional whimpers of the baby boy, no one made a noise. Sarafina rode with a stiff lip and an unwavering gaze down the road, her grief equal doses of remorse and anger as they neared the grave site. Wooden crosses and stone cairns dotted the San Patricio cemetery, the burial sites immaculate from regular care, some with borders of limestone rocks, others with primitive tree-branch fences around them as if the deceased, even in death were staking a claim, however tenuous, to their own piece of Lincoln County soil.

Locals had dug a grave, and Wes directed the wagon to its

185

side. San Patricio was a small village with a smattering of adobes, huts, and *jacales* surrounded by fallow fields. A small store that traded with the Hispanic locals and a cantina that served the thirsty of any race as long as they had money to pay or goods to barter were the only buildings of trade. An adobe building plastered with white lime and topped with a carved cross stood near the graveyard away from the other structures. The chapel was hardly large enough to hold more than a dozen people, fewer than rested in the adjacent cemetery.

As Wes pulled the team up beside the muddy grave, he noticed the dwellings of San Patricio offering up their humble residents, who marched toward the grave site, men with hats in their hands, women with eyes averted, and children awed by the silence of death. Wes helped Sarafina and her son from the wagon, then met Cousins at the tailgate, where Carlos attempted to unload the coffin with his one good hand.

"We'll get it for you," Wes said, patting Carlos on his uninjured shoulder.

Mumbling something in Spanish, the angry youth jerked his arm away and marched to join his sister. Wes and Cousins placed their rifles on the wagon bed, slid the coffin out between them, and easily carried it to the grave, Zamora having been a frail man in life. They lowered the casket beside the hole that would be his final resting place while the citizens of San Patricio circled it, fifty people total. Wes stepped toward the wagon, but Cousins shook his head. "I'll move it. You stay with these people."

Cousins slipped through the circle of mourners and bounded up into the seat, turning the team around and driving them twenty yards away before tying the reins and setting the brake. Climbing over into the back, Cousins retrieved his Henry rifle and stood guard, scanning the valley in all directions for trouble.

Wes took off his hat and waited as the people of San Patricio crowded in on the coffin, though none of them joined Sarafina, nor offered her condolences. Three young women approached Carlos, the gentle smiles on their lips and in their eyes suggesting their awe of word he had held off the Horrells when they attacked his cabin. Brave youths like him would make strong husbands. The bravest of the trio gently touched his wounded shoulder, and Carlos jerked back, startling the girl. She screamed, drawing the disapproving stares of her elders and the titters of her two rivals for Carlos's affection. Carlos grinned that he had fooled her.

For an awkward instant, no one knew what to do, and Wes detected hardness in Sarafina's eyes, as she rocked the baby in her arms and stared from person to person in the crowd. Her eyes were as black as the mourning dress she wore. After a moment, an elderly man stepped forward to take charge. He spoke in Spanish, his words a mystery to Wes, who studied Sarafina and her ironclad emotion. She did not reach out for condolences as the old man gave the eulogy, and no one offered her any sympathy.

The tone of the leader's voice changed, and around Wes every head bowed to pray, except Sarafina's. Defiance was embedded in her gaze as she looked unbowed at the crowd. Her eyes met Wes's, and, for an instant, hers thawed before moving their gaze to the next person and resuming her icy glare.

When the prayer ended, the mourners lifted their heads, looking at one another, but not at Sarafina. Men replaced their hats, and a quartet of the town's elders moved to the grave and picked up two horsehair lariats and slid them under the casket. With the ends of the ropes, the men lifted the coffin over the pit and lowered it into the earth. Bonifacio's son cried in Sarafina's arms. After the pine box settled into the grave, two men pulled the ropes free while the other pair grabbed shovels from the mound beside the hole. Heavy with moisture, the dirt clung to the spades as the men tried to cover the coffin.

Rocking her crying son, Sarafina watched the four bury her husband. She stood alone from the crowd, no other woman approaching to offer condolences. As the grave filled, the observers seeped away back to the village, not a person offering a sympathetic word to Sarafina. Except for the three young women clinging around Carlos, it was as if the villagers didn't recognize Bonifacio's family as existing at all. A stern matron walked past Carlos, calling out in Spanish to his three admirers. The grins on the young women's faces disappeared at her strict command. Though one of them winked at Carlos, even she spun around and marched silently with the other pair to their dwellings.

Except for the four men who alternated with the two shovels to fill the grave, everyone else was walking back home, speaking in whispers as if they did not care for Sarafina to overhear a single word emanating from their mouths.

The baby's crying had turned to whimpering, and Wes knew he must be hungry. Stepping beside Sarafina, Wes motioned with his arm toward the wagon. "You can rest there and feed your son," he offered.

"No!" Her reply was emphatic and laced with bitterness. "Not until my husband is buried."

Wes stepped away and glanced over his shoulder at Cousins, still standing guard nearby. By his shrug, Wes knew Cousins was as puzzled as himself about this cold, uncaring funeral.

Carlos walked to the wagon and returned in a moment with a wooden cross, Bonifacio's named burned into it. Sliding between Wes and Sarafina, Carlos held the cross at his side, like a cane. Wes observed fatigue in Carlos's eyes and in his face. It would be weeks before Carlos regained full strength, but his wounded arm remained limber, and the bullet graze across his head had scabbed over without festering. When Carlos moved, he groaned at a shooting pain that periodically stabbed his shoulder. The bullet may well have lodged in his shoulder blade, for it left no exit wound. That slug might plague him the rest of his life, but at least he still had a life, Wes thought.

The four village men finally mounded the plot over and tipped their hats to Sarafina as they marched single file past her. Not one man spoke a word to her.

"*Gracias,*" she said as they tramped silently to San Patricio.

Carlos eased to the grave and pushed the cross into the soft earth. With only one able hand, he could not force his weight equally on the marker, and when he stepped away, the cross angled toward the southern line of mountains cradling the valley.

Wes stepped to straighten it and earned Carlos's Spanish curses.

"*Silencio,*" Sarafina commanded. "*Señor* Bracken is our friend."

"Your *amigo,* not mine," Carlos shot back, angling to the wagon. "He likes you for a woman, not a friend."

Sarafina pointed a quivering finger at Carlos. "And what is wrong with that? It pleased you when the three *señoritas* flattered you."

"He's not our kind!" Carlos yelled.

"Maybe he's better!" Sarafina shouted back, startling the baby. "You saw how our kind ignored us. They showed no respect for Bonifacio." The baby wailed, and Sarafina rocked him in her arms. "He makes me so mad, Carlos does. He is so stubborn."

Wes wriggled the cross until it was upright and stamped his boot on the ground around the base of the grave marker. When he turned about, Sarafina stared at him, tears overflowing on her cheeks, the first grief Wes had observed in her.

"I should not have buried him here," she sobbed. "He

189

deserved better than San Patricio."

Stepping beside her, Wes motioned to the wagon. "I'll take you home." He took her arm and walked by her side.

Sarafina moved closer against him, leaning on his shoulder. "People will talk," she said. "San Patricio has always hated me. They refused to let me marry Bonifacio in the church."

Wes felt the ice in Carlos's frigid gaze as they stepped to the wagon, but Sarafina stood defiant, and she tossed her head at Carlos and held her nose in the air. Wes helped her place her foot on a wheel spoke and gave her a boost up toward the seat.

Behind him, Wes heard the creak of leather as Jace Cousins pulled himself into the saddle of his dun. As Wes took his place behind the team and picked up the leather lines, Cousins rode over, handing him his Winchester from the back. "You never know when you might need this."

Wes nodded, looking over his shoulder at Carlos, who was propped against the sideboard as far away from Wes as he could get and still be in the wagon.

"Friendly little village, isn't it?" Cousins scratched his chin, patting the barrel of his Henry where it rested across his saddle. "Prison was friendlier." He rattled his reins against the dun's neck, and the gelding turned around and loped toward the Mirror B.

Wes released the brake. "Giddy up," he called, and Bob Casey's team tugged the wagon for home.

Sarafina pulled the black shawl from her head and draped it over her fretting baby. With the cloth screening her bosom from Wes, she prepared to nurse her son. The young one was hungry. Shortly, Wes heard his suckling noises even over the clatter of the wagon chains and wheels.

"You dislike San Patricio," Wes said, guiding the team around the eroded spots and holes that might jar the wagon and interrupt the little one's meal.

Preoccupied with the baby, Sarafina ignored his question for awhile. Eventually, she spoke. "The day will never come when I shall love San Patricio or its people."

"Odd that you would bury your husband there."

"Bonifacio liked San Patricio, wanted to live there, but the people did not want me. The people refused us a church wedding."

"But why?"

Sarafina sighed and shifted the baby to her other side. She stalled, but Wes allowed her whatever time she needed because he sensed she was struggling with both words and emotions. When Sarafina spoke, her answer resounded with anger and disappointment. "Among our kind, none are wealthy in this valley. As a young man, Bonifacio worked hard and spent little, saving his money for something important, though he did not know what it might be. Families in the village with young daughters thought he would make a good husband, one with both substance and many years behind him so he would die soon and leave their daughters an inheritance."

Her voice broke, and Wes watched her out of the corner of his eyes. She dabbed at tears on her cheek, then tossed her hair back and looked straight ahead through moist eyes.

"You don't have to go on," Wes offered.

"No, you don't," Carlos scolded from the back.

Shaking her head, Sarafina continued. "Apaches killed my parents and stole Carlos and me when I had just become a woman. The Apache men used me as they pleased, and they beat Carlos until he almost died. Bonifacio was a kind man, and he knew how the Apaches treated me. He sent word through a friendly Apache that he desired to buy the both of us for a hundred and forty dollars, much of the money he had worked a lifetime to save. He saw how shamed I was and how the men and women of San Patricio scorned me. As I had no folks and

no one that cared for me other than Carlos, the man all the villagers wanted their daughters to marry asked me to be his wife.
He was not the husband I would have picked before the Apaches
came, but I said yes, and I came to love him. Bonifacio did not
care that the Indians had used me, and he was gentle, not pushing himself on me as a younger man might and as the young
men in the village tried to."

Sarafina dabbed at the corners of her eyes. " '*Para gato viejo,
raton tierno,*' they said about us. It means 'for an old cat, a tender
mouse.' And they, all wanting their daughters to be the mouse,
despised me and refused us a marriage in the chapel. So we had
no wedding, and one day he hoped we could be married in a
proper church with a priest. I wanted that very much, but no
priest served our section of Lincoln County then. What money
remained of his savings, he spent on the place away from these
mean people." She paused and tended her son, then resumed.

"My husband was an old man, but a proud one. That is why
he rode to San Patricio for the midwife, so he could announce
that, ancient as he was, he could father a child and that I had
been his wife in all ways."

Taking the baby from her breast and covering herself, Sarafina made cooing noises at her son, then lifted the bundle in the
woolen blanket to her shoulder and patted his back until he
burped.

Never had she been stronger as a woman than now, and never
had she looked more attractive to Wes than at that moment of
confession. Ahead Wes saw the Zamora adobe, and he was glad.
Her husband still fresh in his grave, and he thinking of her this
way.

Sarafina cradled the infant in one arm and worked the shawl
over her head again. "Now you tell me something, Wes
Bracken," she said.

Wes nodded. "Okay."

"I have known you to be an honest and a decent man"— Sarafina began, then paused,—"but I have never seen you smile. Hard men do not smile, but you are not a hard man."

Wes sensed Sarafina's gaze boring into him.

"In the late war, I got a rifle butt in the mouth." He turned his head and stared straight into her eyes. He offered a narrow grin, enough to expose his upper front teeth, one wickedly chipped and discolored. It pleased Wes that Sarafina displayed no shock in her eyes.

As Wes directed the team off the main road and toward the Zamora cabin, Cousins passed on his yellow dun. "I'll ride ahead and check the place."

Wes nodded. "I'll be there shortly."

Sarafina leaned against Wes's shoulder and continued. "Your smile is honest; your tooth does not matter so much as that." She lifted her head and smiled at him as she reached for his cheek. Her thumb and forefinger pinched at something at the corner of his eye. "An eyelash," she said, as Wes pulled up the team in front of the cabin door.

From the back, Wes heard Carlos jump out of the wagon and thump into the soft soil. In an instant Carlos shoved the door open and slammed it behind him.

Wes tied the team lines and set the brake lever, then moved to get down.

"Not yet," Sarafina said, holding her hand toward Wes.

He saw his eyelash in the middle of her thumb.

"Place your thumb against mine," she instructed. "An eyelash brings good luck. If you make a wish, it will come true."

Sarafina closed her eyelids, her lips mouthing her desire. As she opened her eyes, she pulled her thumb away from his, then inspected their thumbs. The eyelash had disappeared.

Wes shook his head. "Such odd superstitions. Wishes don't come true like that," he said, his face breaking into a grin.

"Yes, they do," she insisted. "I wished to see you smile again, and you did."

Wes only shrugged, then dismounted and went around the wagon to help her down.

Sarafina handed the baby to Wes, who held it in one arm and offered his other to her. With his hand for a brace, Sarafina climbed down and stood beside him, her dark eyes staring straight into his. She took her son back.

"With winter coming, you have a few months before you need to consider what you'll do with this place in the spring. I'll check on you periodically."

"Gracias," Sarafina answered.

"If there's anything I can do for you, please let me know."

"One thing," she said, her eyes never wavering from his. "In Lincoln, they always hold a dance before Christmas. There will be talk, but I would like you to take me."

Wes smiled. "I'd be honored to accompany you."

CHAPTER 21

"At the dance tonight," Sarafina said, "some will say I am a shameful woman. Others may believe you killed Bonifacio."

Wes listened as he maneuvered the team down the long street that was Lincoln. The December air was crisp with winter, the harsh chill hiding in the deep shadows and waiting for the sun to drop behind the mountains. Then a bone-numbing cold would permeate everything.

Carlos, riding in the back of Casey's loaned wagon, hawked and spat on the street. "They won't like him because he's not our kind. He's bad luck."

"Bad luck? You're lucky to even be coming to the dance," his sister shot back. "He saved your life and borrowed this wagon to bring us to Lincoln. You're too weak to ride and still have any strength to dance. You say nothing more ill of him."

Carlos grumbled in Spanish, his clenched fist pounding against the sideboard.

From the basket in her lap, the baby cried out. Anger rose in Sarafina's voice. "See what you've done, Carlos? You've startled Luis."

Carlos scowled.

Several Hispanic men and women stopped to stare as Wes drove by. Others pointed and whispered to each other. Two young females with black hair and alluring eyes waved at Carlos and giggled.

"Stop the wagon," Carlos commanded.

Wes obliged, giving him time to crawl out, then rattling the lines and proceeding.

Sarafina shook her head. "Don't mind him," she apologized. "No people have been his type since the Apaches took us."

Around one building, a throng of Hispanic men, women and children gathered. Catching her breath, Sarafina jostled the basket in her lap, drawing another cry from Luis. "They will not like it, but I must stop at the Montaño Store."

Wes guided the wagon to the south side of the street, pulling to a stop in front of an adobe building.

Sarafina pointed to a larger adobe building up ahead. "The dance will be there. I shall meet you at the front in two hours, but I must let them insult me now so we can attend without trouble."

Wes moved to set the brake and climb down to assist, but Sarafina grabbed his arm.

"No," she said. "It is best I get down alone."

In front of the Montaño Store, people shook their heads as if Sarafina's appearance with Wes confirmed vicious rumors spread about her husband's death.

Handing Wes the baby basket, Sarafina stood up, brushing the trail dust from her coat, then straightening the veil around her face. Scooting to the edge of her seat, she lifted a leg over the sideboard and stepped on the wheel spoke. Holding the side of the bench, she lowered her other leg and hopped to the ground. Her head held high, she reached to Wes, who handed her the basket with Luis. She patted the cloth cover over her son and strode toward the door, a path among the Hispanics clearing before her, but not a word of condolence for her dead husband or a word of congratulation on a new son greeted her. Sarafina disappeared inside the store, and the observers looked up at Wes, their eyes filled with suspicion about him and the Winchester resting across his thighs.

Tipping his hat toward the silent gathering, Wes jostled the lines and the team jerked the wagon ahead. On the street many people congregated, mostly Hispanic families who had come for miles for the Christmas celebration. Musicians, including the best violinists from throughout southeastern New Mexico Territory, had descended on Lincoln to play in the dance. Blackie Davison, a sergeant with the black cavalry at Fort Stanton and possibly the most skilled fiddle player in the Southwest, was rumored to be attending as well.

The team continued west to the opposite end of town, Wes searching for the Horrells. He expected to see Luther's horse outside the adobe saloon down the street. By now, Luther might have sold his gelding for whiskey money. A single gray pony was hitched to a rail by the establishment, but it was surely not his brother's, as Luther despised grays, at least when he was sober. Who knew what he liked when drunk?

Up ahead around a slight curve in the road, Wes saw the imposing structure of Murphy's store. The two-story adobe building wore the fresh badges of wealth in Lincoln County— wooden shingles, sparkling glass windows, and paint. The porch, balcony, exterior stairs, every door and window frame, and all the wooden trim wore two coats of expensive white paint. Murphy had spared no expense to display his wealth and dominance over the region. Most galling to Wes, however, the wagon that had once belonged to him and Luther now parked at the far corner of the store. Wes clenched his jaw when he saw the FOR SALE signboard nailed to the side of his former wagon. Wes halted the borrowed team in front of the Wortley Hotel and coughed out the bad thoughts of Murphy as he jumped from the wagon with his carbine. As crowded as town was, Wes figured the hotel would be full, but it was worth a check to prevent a long ride home after the dance or an overnight stay in the back of the wagon on such a cold night. Sam Wortley stood behind the registration desk as Wes pushed the door open and strode in. Wortley nodded, eyed the carbine, and scratched his head. "You expecting trouble, Wes?"

"I never know what's waiting for me inside your place, Sam."

The proprietor laughed. His hands grabbing the edge of the counter, Wortley leaned forward. "You wouldn't need a room, would you?"

"Two, if you've got them."

"God bless you, Wes Bracken. As big a crowd as there is in town for the *baile,* you'd think I'd be full, but Mexicans seldom stay with me—can't afford it. And damn Lawrence G. Murphy, the old cuss, has turned on me! The sordid commerce he once sent me now bunks in his new store. My business ain't been good since his place opened." Wortley turned the register around and pushed the pen and inkwell at Bracken. "Two rooms is it? You and who else?"

"Sarafina Zamora."

Wortley whistled, his eyes narrowing. "Bad stories going around about her husband's death. Some say you killed him, and some are arguing the Horrells murdered him."

"The stories and the truth aren't always the same, Sam." Wes took the pen, dipped it in ink, signed his name. Again he wet the writing implement with ink, then danced it across the next line, leaving Sarafina's name in a bold cursive. Shoving the pen back in the inkwell, Wes eyed the proprietor. "Now about those stories, does Luther figure in any of them?"

Wortley licked his lips and nodded. "Some say he rode with the Horrells when Zamora was killed. Could be true, as I have seen him with the Horrell brothers when he's not drinking at Murphy's store."

Wes sighed. "He was never the same after the war."

Wortley shrugged. "Not just that, but Lincoln County brings out the worst in a man."

Wes visited with the proprietor and arranged for him to take a dozen tins of peaches and two bread loaves to the dance hall as Sarafina's contribution to the food table. With carbine in hand, Wes retreated outside and left it in the wagon as he unhooked the team and drove them into the Wortley corral, where he finished un-harnessing them. After draping the rigging over the top rail in the wooden fence, Wes retrieved his Winchester and started back toward Wortley's for his room, but he stopped cold in his tracks. In front of Murphy's store, he saw a familiar chestnut gelding hitched to the rack along with a dozen other horses. It was Luther's mount.

Cursing to himself, Wes headed toward the largest building in Lincoln County. His strides were long and purposeful. He could feel the anger rising within him, like steam in a boiler. Carbine in his left hand, he stepped onto the painted porch and pushed open a thick wooden door, a blast of heat striking him as he entered. Murphy could afford to keep his place hotter than anyone else in town.

His eyes adjusted to the dimness, and he saw three men glaring at him. Behind them stood shelves well stocked with canned goods and boxes of supplies. By the back counter, bloated sacks of flour, sugar, and coffee leaned against one another like drunken soldiers. The smell of new leather, kerosene, and cheap tobacco mingled into a perfume no other store in Lincoln County could afford.

From a room to his right, Wes heard the noise of men drinking. He stamped across the wooden floor to the doorway, then entered brashly, realizing it intemperate of him to barge into a place where the Horrells might be. A dozen rugged men froze in their chairs, studying Wes as he returned their stares, quickly noting that none were Horrells. Behind the bar stood Lawrence Murphy himself, a contemptuous smile cracking his face. In the opposite corner alone at a table sat Luther, his only companion a bottle. Of the men in the saloon, only Luther seemed oblivious to Wes's arrival.

"Afternoon, Wes Bracken," mocked Murphy. "Ye come to town to bushwhack more old greasers at the dance tonight?"

Wes leveled his Winchester at Murphy, then swung it around to his henchmen reaching for their guns at the table nearest the door. "Easy and nobody gets hurt."

At Wes's voice, Luther lifted his head. As his eyes focused on his brother, a trace of a smile glimmered across his face, then disappeared as he lifted a bottle to his lips.

Wes backed against the wall by the door so none of Murphy's men could slip behind him. "Come on, Luther, let's go outside for some fresh air."

Luther broke his mouth from the bottle and tilted his head as if getting a bearing on his brother. "Sure thing, Wes," Luther said. He lifted the liquor container by its neck. "Can I take this with me, Murphy?"

"Sure, me boy," the Irishman called in mockery again.

"No, Luther, leave the whiskey," Wes interrupted. "Come alone. Now!"

Luther struggled to his feet, taking a last draft on the liquid and slamming the bottle into the table. He stumbled forward, his slender body leaning ahead as his legs gathered momentum and finally caught up, his neck jerking. His glassy eyes focusing on the Winchester leveled toward Murphy and the other men, Luther shook his head. "No need for your gun, Wes. These boys are Luther's friends."

Wes waved the weapon. "They're not my friends, Luther. We'll talk on the street."

"Sure, Wes, whatever you say," Luther answered as he stumbled by Wes into the adjoining room.

Murphy laughed at Luther's ungraceful exit. "Didn't ye 'ear yer brother? We're 'is friends." Murphy's laugh resonated through the saloon, and he stuck his thumbs through his suspenders, rocking on his heels for a moment.

Wes glanced into the adjoining room. Seeing Luther had made it to the front door, Wes eased away from the wall and backed out the doorway. As Luther opened the front door, Wes bolted into the opening, grabbed Luther's arm, and jerked him outside. "Come on, dammit!"

Luther lurched ahead, stumbling off the porch and staggering into the street. Wes darted up the dusty trail and stopped behind the wagon that had once belonged to the Bracken brothers.

Out in the street, Luther turned in a slow circle, his muddled mind unable to comprehend where his younger brother had gone.

"Over here, Luther, behind our wagon," Wes called.

Luther lifted his hand and shaded his eyes from something known only to him. "Where'd you go, Wes?"

Detecting no danger from the Murphy store, Wes exposed himself around the end of the cart and motioned him over. "Luther."

Finally, Luther nodded, his face widening into a smile exaggerated by liquor. He lurched forward, his gaze alternating between Wes and the ground. Reaching the wagon, he grabbed the sideboard and eased himself to Wes, his overdrawn smile unyielding. "I'm glad to see you, Wes."

Wes shook his head in disgust.

"Can you loan me a few dollars, can you, Wes?" Luther smiled so widely, it looked as if his lips had been pried open.

The liquor heavy on his breath sickened Wes. "No money, Luther."

The grin melted away like a snowball on a hot stove. In an instant, only the bitter dregs of disappointment lingered on his lips. "I'm your brother, Wes. Just a little to tide me over."

"Until when? Never, Luther, because liquor's got a hold on you."

Doubling his fist, Luther shook it in Wes's face. "Some brother you are."

Taking a step toward his brother, Wes shoved his finger in Luther's nose. "You want cash, I'll pay you some, if you answer a couple questions. Okay?"

Luther cocked his head and licked his lips, his fist falling to his side. "Sure, Wes, whatever you want to know." A nauseating smile snaked back across his face.

"Did you have anything to do with the killing of Bonifacio Zamora?"

The grin froze, then turned sickly, his lips tight with guilt, his glassy eyes widening in silent shame.

"Did you?" Wes grabbed a handful of his coat and pulled his brother toward him. "Did you? There's five dollars in this for you."

Luther swallowed hard and caught his breath, nodding slowly, gritting his teeth as if he expected his younger brother to punch him.

Wes shook his hand free of Luther's lapels.

"They were coming after you, Wes, and ran into that greaser. It saved your life, Wes, because the storm hit when we attacked the house. We turned back."

"You're no different from the Horrells, Luther, and I'll treat you as such the next time I run into you."

Luther's lower lip quivered. "I'm your kin, Wes, your brother!"

"No more by my book, Luther."

Luther's head fell, and he stared at his boots. "What about my five dollars?"

"You cost me and the Mirror B more than that, like this wagon," Wes said, slamming his fist against the side. So I'll hang onto my money to cover part of what you owe me."

"It's not fair, Wes!"

"Was killing Bonifacio fair?"

"They did it . . . my friends, not me!"

Wes nodded. "If they're such friends, get your five bucks from them."

Luther jerked his head up, his eyes flaring with anger. "You despise my friends, and you hate me drinking a little now and again."

"No money, Luther."

"Well, by damn, Wesley Bracken, I'll see the Horrells. They treat me better than my own brother."

"You do that Luther. And next time you run into me, be ready to defend yourself."

Luther spun around, almost losing his balance before leaning against the wagon. He steadied himself and moved toward the Murphy store, stopping at his gelding by the hitching post. Luther fumbled with the reins to his chestnut, finally unwrapping them from the pole. He labored to get his foot into the stirrup, then hauled himself aboard and galloped out of town. Wes watched him depart, then checked the Murphy store for signs of danger before returning to the Wortley.

CHAPTER 22

Wes Bracken looked in the mirror, his hand stroking his freshly shaved chin, his hat pulled down over his forehead, the stiff collar of his shirt poking its way through the neck of his coat. He took a deep breath, looking around his Wortley room, then tugged the handle of the door that opened out onto the street of Lincoln. Stepping outside, he glanced at the Murphy store, but things were quiet there. Bracken patted the lump that was his pistol at his waist beneath his coat, then turned eastward, his wide stride carrying him to the dance site. He was as uncertain of how the Hispanics would accept him as he was of what he would do when next he ran into Luther.

Hispanic couples strolled the street toward the adobe building while matrons dressed in black followed as chaperones. Families moved in clumps, carrying babies and victuals to the destination. The sun had fallen behind the mountains, leaving Lincoln shivering in the winter chill. Along with the cold, excitement was thick in the air, the anticipation of food and dance with friends strong. Wes studied the people, feeling himself a stranger amongst them, wishing Sarafina would appear by his side. Odd that a man who had faced regiments of Yankee soldiers without flinching during the War Between the States had now caught the jitters, he thought.

As he approached the building, he saw Sarafina emerge from the door, a smile wide across her face. She reached for his hand as a disapproving matron strode by, her nose held high. "You look troubled, so you should smile," Sarafina said, patting his hand.

"I've a room for you and Luis at the Wortley."

"*Gracias*," she said. "I've never slept in a fine hotel. Do they have feather beds?"

Wes nodded and smiled when she turned her dark eyes toward his.

"I shall enjoy that, and Luis will too."

Taking her arm in his, Wes guided her to the door. He took off his hat, holding it over his chest as he ducked beneath the low entryway typical of adobe dwellings, then stepped down to the recessed dirt floor. Around the walls, people lounged on benches or stood in clumps gossiping with their neighbors. At the far end of the room, Wes saw ten musicians, comparing fiddles, or tuning their guitars. A black soldier in a fresh sergeant's uniform, his face as dark as coal and his teeth as white as pearls, strolled among them. At the side three long but narrow tables overflowed with food, including Wortley's delivery of two bread loaves and a dozen tins of peaches, their open lids saluting diners.

A few men stared at Wes as he escorted Sarafina across the straw-strewn floor to a basket on a bench by the window. Sarafina pulled back the blanket from the basket and uncovered the angelic face of a drowsy Luis. After picking up the basket and sitting in its place on the bench, she lowered the bundle to her lap, rocking her legs gently and drawing a smile from her son. The old ladies studied Sarafina with disapproving sneers that she ignored.

Wes looked around, studying the assembly. Except for one white man near the musicians, the group was entirely Hispanic. The Anglo caught Wes's eye and started across the room. "Who is that man?" Wes asked Sarafina, nodding in the stranger's direction.

"The deputy sheriff," she answered, her voice free of worry. "His wife is one of us, so he understands my kind."

The room was warm, and Wes unbuttoned his coat as the deputy approached. Tugging his coat off, Wes noticed two men pointing at him. The lawman stepped before Wes, an easy smile across his face, his hand extended.

"You must be Wes Bracken," he said as he grabbed Wes's hand and pumped it warmly. "I'm Joe Haskins. I'm deputy sheriff for Lincoln County."

Wes nodded, uncomfortable that so many men were staring at them. "Am I in trouble with the law, deputy?"

"These are good people," Haskins answered, "but they're nervous with you wearing a gun to their dance." With his free hand, the deputy pointed to a row of pegs embedded in the wall by the door. "Hang your gun belt there and cover it with your coat. It'll make folks breathe a little easier."

"Obliged," Wes said, pulling his fingers from Haskins's and unbuckling his gun belt. As he did, the Mexicans who had been staring turned back to their own business.

The deputy accompanied Wes to the door, watching him hang up his weapon and coat. His hand closed around Wes's arm before he could return to Sarafina. "Let me ask you a question, Wes. Do you have any idea who killed Bonifacio Zamora?"

Wes nodded. "Ideas? Yes, but no proof."

"The Horrells?"

"That's my feeling, them and my brother."

Haskins whistled and his hand fell away from Wes's arm. "Maybe that explains the rumor that you were responsible. Gossip has it you want to make Sarafina your bride."

Wes shrugged, uncertain what to say.

"Sarafina's a fine-looking Mexican gal, like my wife." Haskins pointed to a bench by the wall, where a woman with raven hair, black eyes, and a slender figure sat watching the fiddlers tuning, stroking, and plucking their instruments. "These people are good, peaceful folks that don't like the violence Texans have brought into our valleys. These intruders are terrifying folks. Some say they're worse than the Apaches."

"I'm a guest, not a troublemaker," replied Wes, studying Haskins's sharp blue eyes, muscled shoulders over a slender frame, and weather-beaten face with hardened visage.

"I'm pleased to hear that because I know you'll respect them and their customs," Haskins nodded.

"As long as I know about them," Wes answered.

Folks still crowded in the door, passing Wes and Haskins on their way to greet friends. At the front, a musician tapped his bow against the back of his fiddle. He spoke in Spanish, and the crowd applauded.

"That's the *maestro de baile,* who announces when it's time to dance," Haskins translated as the musicians broke into a song. About the room, young men and women hurried to the floor, drawing the disapproving glares of many matrons. Wes saw Carlos step to the center of the room, holding hands with a smitten young maiden. As Carlos waltzed with his partner, Wes noticed an occasional grimace, likely from the pain of the bullet still encased in his shoulder.

"Many Mexicans around here distrust you," Haskins told Wes. "Sarafina's a headstrong woman, and they don't appreciate that. I believe she was devoted to Bonifacio. No doubt that brown bean of a baby is his and not yours, but there's questions in some minds. You bringing her to the dance so soon after Bonifacio's death has strengthened their opinions. They've heard you were involved in killing the Mes brothers. Even if the Mes boys were thieves, they deserved a trial, so these folks fear you're no different than the others from Texas."

"I passed through Texas here, but I'm from Arkansas," Wes responded.

"And, they know your brother's a drunk."

Wes shrugged. "I can't change that, though I've tried."

"But you can make it worse," Haskins said. "Word is you're an honest man who'll stand up to anyone from the Mes Brothers to L. G. Murphy, but that doesn't square with Zamora's death and you swooping in on Sarafina like a sparrow on a June bug. What's between you and Sarafina is your business, but don't forget that your neighbors gossip."

"You saying don't dance with her?"

Haskins stroked his chin. "No, just don't dance more than a couple times at first and then wait until later when folks are distracted by food or conversation or exhaustion. Everybody's watching the two of you. Lincoln County needs good honest men, Wes, so all I'm asking is that you make it easy on yourself by earning these people's respect."

"I'm obliged for the advice," Wes said, looking toward Sarafina, who sat on the bench, the basket with Luis in her lap, her legs swaying to the beat of the music.

Haskins grinned. "Remember my advice is only worth as much as you paid for it." He laughed and shook Wes's hand. "Good luck to you." The deputy eased his way past the pool of dancers until he reached his wife. In a moment, Haskins was dancing with her around the floor.

Wes settled into the seat by Sarafina. Luis was cooing at her, his big black eyes seeming to dance to the music, unlike any noise he had ever heard before. Sarafina beamed at Wes, her lips upturned with joy, a smile that confused Wes. Was it the pleasure of a mother holding her son or the desire of a woman pleased with her suitor? The answer perplexed Wes, and he fidgeted, his fingers strumming against his leg.

"I want to dance," Sarafina said.

Mulling Haskins's advice, Wes replied. "After the others have cleared out a little."

"Soon," Sarafina answered.

"When it is time, I will ask you," he told her.

The smile faded from Sarafina's face, then reappeared like the sun from behind a cloud, when her gaze fell upon Luis.

For more than an hour, Sarafina and Wes sat side by side, watching the dancers and the musicians. As the celebration continued, Wes noticed that fewer people cast suspicious glances his way, their distrust slowly diminishing with each new song or dance. Waltzes, polkas, schottisches, and a step Sarafina called the "varsouviana" were the most popular.

Outside the darkness was total, and the cold was complete, everyone crowding into the building as much for the warmth as the fun. Two corner fireplaces crackled, while lit lamps around the room provided a golden halo above the dancers. Overhead a crude wooden chandelier served as the roost for a dozen candles, their tiny flames flickering to the music.

In the second hour of the dance, the black sergeant in the cavalry uniform stepped away from the Mexican musicians and hopped up onto a bench. He held out his arms toward the revelers, in one hand a worn fiddle and in the other a bow. A Spanish musician grinned, then introduced Blackie Davison in Spanish. Wes understood the name, but nothing else until the ensuing applause and whistles.

Davison bowed before his audience, lifted his head, stuck the fiddle under his chin, drew back his bow, aimed for the strings, and shoved his bow toward them, the whole crowd leaning in, awaiting the first note of his music. The fiddler lifted the bowstrings without striking a string, and the crowd sighed in disappointment. The sergeant laughed, his white teeth showing like perfect pearls between his pink lips, and the audience cackled, too, at his joke. Before their snickering finished, Davison attacked his fiddle, a tune springing like magic from his fingers and the instrument. Instantly, Wes recognized "Listen to the Mockingbird," Davison's nimble fingers and quick bow mimicking the songbird with the melody. The observers clapped their approval, then stopped when they realized the applause interfered with their enjoyment of his artistry. Not a person danced, everyone's eyes riveted on him as he swayed on the bench, his head dipping low, then rising sharply, the fiddle slipping from his jaw and down his arm until he cradled the chin rest in the crook of his elbow, never missing a note, the music resonating like the joy around the room.

"He's good," Sarafina whispered to Wes as Davison finished the song with the softness of a baby's breath. The room exploded in applause and cheers. The fiddler tipped his kepi with his bow hand, relishing the clapping as much as the audience had enjoyed his music. A master of the fiddle and of a crowd, Davison tugged his cap back on his head and spread his arms for silence. Tucking the instrument under his chin and lifting the bowstrings, he made a gobbling noise with his mouth and jumped from the bench to the floor, his fiddle starting a breakneck rendition of "Turkey in the Straw." As he played, he danced a jig around the room, the observers scattering from his path so they would not hinder his virtuosity. He danced to Sarafina and Wes, spotting the basket with Luis, and dipping low over it, Luis cackling his approval at the music before the sergeant frolicked away. Even the matrons that previously had only frowned for fear of otherwise endorsing the affections of the unmarried couples in the room smiled at Davison.

The fiddler bounded around the dance floor, his own music invigorating him as much as the audience. Even Wes grinned, though he noticed a few revelers pointing at his chipped tooth. Davison danced to the front of the room as he finished that song and stepped up on the platform with the other musicians and played with them a song that Wes did not recognize.

"*Jalisco,*" Sarafina whispered to him, her hand slipping over his and squeezing it. "After this, the dance is even more fun."

The song was a favorite fiddle tune of all the Hispanics as they swayed to the melody. Though Davison's manner was more subdued now that he was playing with other musicians, his artistry over the fiddle strings could be detected above the other players' noble efforts. When the song ended, the other fiddlers pointed their bows at Davison, who bowed to the applause, then turned around and shook the hand of every musician with him on the platform, their smiles as broad as his.

As the clapping died, the *maestro de baile* joined the musicians and loudly announced, *"Valse chiquiao."* The unmarried girls giggled, and their boyfriends grimaced to one another.

"This is great fun," Sarafina whispered.

The dancers evacuated the center of floor, and someone placed a chair in the middle of the human circle. The maestro clapped his hands and called out the name of a young lady. She stepped forward, dragging her boyfriend by the hand. Taking the seat, the young woman fluttered her eyelashes at the boy, and everyone laughed, except her suitor.

The young man walked around the chair, staring helplessly at the crowd and then back at his girl. Her lips were tight in mock seriousness, but her face glowed when her suitor spoke.

Sarafina leaned toward Wes and whispered. "He must coax her from the chair with pretty words and compliments. The dancing cannot start again until the lady arises and until the *maestro de baile* agrees her suitor has said things worthy of her leaving her seat and the dance resuming."

The young man's words drew giggles from the crowd and evoked a smile from his partner. She held her nose high and shook her head as her beau begged her to stand with him. He lowered his head and sank to his knees, his arms outstretched toward her, imploring her to rise from the chair. She feinted a couple times, tickling everyone but her suitor, then arose to his relief and the applause of everyone.

"The *maestro de baile* never lets the dance begin after the first couple," Sarafina told Wes. "Sometimes it takes several couples."

As the applause died down, the *maestro de baile* studied the couple and the crowd. "No!" he said to a chorus of groans, then a ripple of anticipation as another courting pair stood to be embarrassed before their friends.

"See, I told you," she said.

The process was repeated a second, third, and fourth time, the maestro always refusing to let the dance continue. He called a young lady and then Carlos's name. Sarafina giggled. "Carlos will hate this."

Wes stood for a better view, watching a reluctant Carlos being pushed toward the chair, the pretty young woman who was his dancing partner aglow with a smile. Carlos clasped his hands at his waist, his gaze staring at the ground instead of her. When he spoke, the Spanish came out in fits and starts, lacking the fluid consistency of those who had preceded him. Lifting her delicate hands, his girl gestured for him to continue. Carlos stuttered, then shouted something Wes could not understand. Around him people laughed, though his partner reddened in embarrassment, and Sarafina shook her head and lowered it into her hand. "Carlos is so shy," she said. Finally, the girl stood up and marched to Carlos. He took her hand, bowed his head, and tried to disappear among the spectators. The maestro refused to permit more dancing until the next young man succeeded where others had failed, and the music and festivities resumed.

Wes looked into Sarafina's dark eyes, filled with anticipation. "If Luis is asleep," he whispered, "we can dance now." He stood up.

"Gracias," she said, "he will be fine here." Gently placing the basket where Wes had sat, she arose and took his hand as the

musicians started a waltz.

Together they joined other dancers, stepping into one another's arms and into the flow of the music. Even though he held her at arm's length, that circumspection could not prevent the stares of the prudish matrons lining the walls with folded arms and scowls on their wrinkled faces. Sarafina, by the slight hesitation in each step, felt their hard gazes, but her equally strong will countered their disapproval.

Wes recognized the tune as "After the Ball," and above all the fiddles he recognized that of the soldier Davison for its sharp precision.

As the song ended, Sarafina curtsied to Wes, who bowed just as the door flew open. A woman screamed. Wes glanced at the commotion, his hand falling instinctively to his waist for his pistol. His fingers came up empty, then he remembered hanging his gun belt on a peg by the door.

A shot exploded in the room.

Wes jumped for Sarafina, pushing her to the floor, flinging himself atop of her.

Women and children screamed as adults tripped over themselves hiding.

One, two, three more shots punctured the air, the smell of black powder engulfing the dance floor. People gasped and shrieked. Near the entry, Wes saw a man clutching a bloody spot on his shirt.

"Luis!" screamed Sarafina, clawing from under Wes and crawling over people toward her son. Wes jumped up, shoved her back to the floor, and clambered over the thrashing forms between him and the bench. All around men were blowing out the lamps, and the room dimmed, lit only by the flickering candles on the chandelier and by the flames in the two corner fireplaces. Wes darted to the wall where Luis had rested. The bench, though, was overturned, and nothing looked the same. A

213

baby's wailing rose above the commotion.

Three more shots, one after another, flared from the entryway to be answered by more screams and the loud wail of Luis. Wes clambered for the basket. Just as he reached for it, two more explosions spit lead from the door, and the basket jerked and tumbled beyond Wes's grasp.

"Luis!" Sarafina screamed.

Wes glanced at the door, seeing the profile of two men with pistols in their hands. He looked over his shoulder in time to see Sarafina jump up from the tangle of arms and legs that moments before had been dancers.

"Get down, Sarafina, now!" Wes shouted as he grabbed the basket and pulled it into him, but the basket was empty. He heard a whimper nearby, then a scream as his hand fell against a bundle on the ground. It was Luis.

Wes jerked the baby to him, flinching at the touch because the wrap covering him was soaked, Wes fearing from blood. The baby screamed uncontrollably as Wes screened him from the men at the door.

Two more shots flashed and thundered into the smoke-filled room, now acrid with the bitter aroma of gunpowder. "Let's get out of here," a voice called, followed by the heavy fall of boots outside.

Before anyone else stood up, Sarafina ran to Wes's side, clutching her son's damp bundle. In the dimness, she unwrapped him and celebrated. "He's only wet himself," she cried. "He's okay." Then she sobbed.

Wes pounced to his feet and scampered over the cowering forms toward the door. Knocking his coat from the peg, he jerked his gun belt free and strapped it on. At the exit, he met Haskins tugging his scabbard in place. Together they dashed outside. Fifty yards down the street, two men turned and fired at them.

"You sons 'a bitches!" Wes cried out. He grabbed his pistol and took aim. "You'll die tonight!" he screamed.

CHAPTER 23

"Over there!" Haskins shouted, waving his gun at a darkened adobe building. Haskins fired, a spark flickering where the lead glanced off the corner of the structure. "Damn," he cursed.

In the darkness, Wes discerned two figures darting from the side of one structure to the next. "Fire at them, Joe!" he hollered. "Keep 'em busy, and I'll get ahead of 'em."

Wes bolted down the street. Behind him he heard the wails of grieving women and the shouts of angry men streaming out of the meeting house. Wes sprinted ahead, his heart pounding, his breath heaving with anger. If he failed to cut the two assailants off, they might find shelter in Murphy's store.

Haskins fired twice and issued commands for the mob to stay put. "Wes Bracken's trying to cut them off. Don't shoot him."

Wes heard shots popping from the street, followed by two answering blasts from behind the string of buildings lining the road. All the gunfire came from his rear. He had outrun the assailants.

"You're mine now," Wes grunted to himself. Ahead he spotted the Wortley Hotel and beyond it, the Murphy store. He angled off the road for the corral at the hotel, then worked himself behind the nearest structure. His breath heaved; his gun quivered in his hand. Then he advanced, his gun hand steadying with each step. By a tree he spooked two tied horses. They stamped their feet, whinnying and tossing their heads at the gunfire behind them. Odd place to tie horses this time of night unless the assailants had left them there for their escape. Wes's left hand fell to his waist and returned with the knife he had taken from the Horrells. One horse shied away from him, but the second seemed calmed by his approach. In the darkness, Wes could not make out their color for sure, but the profile of the even-tempered horse looked familiar.

"Dammit," Wes spit, "Luther's horse!" With a savage swing of his knife, he sliced the reins free, and the horse trotted across the street, turned, and stared. Wes cut the tether of the second horse, which ran toward the Rio Bonito.

The shouts of the mob drew closer, and Wes detected the noise of pounding boots approaching. He braced his feet and lifted his revolver.

"The horses, dammit, where are they?" came a voice Wes recognized as Luther's.

"We're dead!" yelled the man at his side.

"Dammit to hell!" Luther cried in disgust, stopping in his tracks and grabbing the arm of his accomplice. "Who's that?" He pointed to Wes.

"Drop your guns, Luther, and whoever's with you!" Wes shouted.

"Who is it?" the stranger yelled.

"My brother!"

"What? I thought you plugged him at the dance hall?"

Luther coughed. "So did I."

With Haskins leading the approaching mob of a dozen men, the deputy called out, "Easy men, we have them surrounded. You okay, Wes?"

"Careful, Joe, they've still got their guns."

"Drop 'em boys, this is the law speaking."

For a moment, all was calm. Then, Luther's pal jerked his gun up.

Wes fired his revolver, the pistol jolting and bucking in his fingers. The stranger screamed, grabbing his hand just as the deputy fired. The assassin staggered forward, then dropped to the ground.

Luther tossed his gun away and bolted for the stream. Wes spun around and shot at a shadow. The specter stumbled, grabbing his arm and tumbling into the bushes. "I winged him!" Wes yelled as the others in the mob cut loose a volley. The ambusher jumped up, then scooted for the Rio Bonito.

"Dammit!" cried Haskins. "He's getting away."

"Maybe not," Wes called out. "I'm sure I nicked him. Come sunrise, we'll find out."

Haskins marched to the body at the edge of the street as Wes joined him. The deputy kicked him over with his boot. "One dead here," Haskins called out. "Somebody get a lamp and we'll identify him."

As a volunteer darted away for a light, another rushed up. "Joe," he said, "there's four dead back at the dance."

"Dammit," Haskins said. "Is my wife okay?"

The messenger shrugged. "I don't know. As far as I could see, all the dead are men."

The volunteer returned with a lantern, and the circle of men around the body parted to let him through, the yellow light illuminating the face of the deceased. Wes recognized him as one of the Horrells.

Haskins coughed. "Ben Horrell."

Wes squatted by the corpse, studying the chest wound near the heart. That was Haskins's shot. He had aimed for the gut, hitting instead his revolver. Horrell's gun hand was missing his ring finger, the wound at the knuckle still oozing liquid.

"You have an idea of who the other one was?" Haskins asked.

Licking his lips, Wes stood up and turned his back to the deputy. "I've got my suspicions."

"One of the Horrells?"

Wes nodded. "You might say that."

From the back of the crowd, a husky voice issued orders. "Get out of my way, fellows. This is the sheriff."

"Damn," Haskins said under his breath.

A big man with a booming voice and a broad nose, the sheriff shouldered his way into the circle of light. "What's going on, Haskins?" the sheriff demanded. "I was at Murphy's place, and I hear there's been a shooting."

"One dead here and possibly another downed by the river," Haskins answered. "Up at the meeting hall, there's four dead, so I've been told."

"This one's a white man, looks like one of the Horrells. What about those at the meeting hall? They all Mexicans?" the sheriff asked.

"From what I know, Ham."

"Good, it could've been worse." The sheriff shoved his revolver back in his holster.

Haskins flinched at his boss's comment.

Wes stood up and slid the knife back in its scabbard.

The sheriff looked from the body to the blade to Wes and back to the dead man's hand. "Damn, fellow, no need to cut off his finger. You got Apache blood in you?"

Haskins interrupted. "Wes Bracken, meet Ham Mills, sheriff of Lincoln County."

Rocking on his feet, the sheriff folded his arms across his chest and studied Wes. "So you're the one that pulled a rifle on L. G. Murphy this afternoon? That's not a smart thing to do in these parts. You best keep to killing Horrells and Mexicans, instead of threatening upstanding citizens like Mr. Murphy."

Wes felt his temper flaring, but he took a deep breath and calmly reloaded his revolver before sliding it back in its holster. As he heard the distant noise of a galloping horse, he wondered if it were Luther escaping to tell the other Horrells of brother Ben's fate.

"Any more problems with L. G. Murphy," Mills said, pointing his finger like a gun at Wes's nose, "and you'll be answering to the law in Lincoln County. You understand that, Bracken?"

Wes nodded. "Seems the law and Murphy are the same in this county."

Mills grinned. "You ain't as dumb as you look."

Tipping his hat, Wes moved past the sheriff and headed for the road.

The sheriff laughed in Wes's wake and turned to Haskins. "Why don't you go tend to that Mexican wife of yours, Joe, and I'll handle things around here." The sheriff laughed again.

Haskins strode away angry, his indignant stride soon bringing him abreast of Wes. Haskins cursed. "Ham only does Murphy's bidding. The law be damned."

Wes spat on the ground. "Why're you willing to work for him?"

"A man's got to make a living somehow," Haskins answered, his words remorseful.

Up the street, Wes saw lamps burning in front of the dance hall and women walking away, their heads buried in their hands, their small children hanging onto their legs and tugging at their skirts. For the first time since leaving the building, Wes acknowledged the cold and shivered.

As he neared the hall, he grimaced at the sobs of loved ones grieving over their dead. The wails of fear that had pierced the air when he left had turned into the gentle weeping of helplessness with the realization that nothing would revive their beloved. He pushed his way through the door, the deputy following behind him. A woman rushed by Wes and grabbed Haskins, hugging him tightly and sobbing something in Spanish. Wes recognized the woman as Haskins's wife.

By the wall lay the bodies of four men, their clothes bloodied, their expressions frozen in death. In the back corner by a fireplace Wes spotted Sarafina, nursing Luis. Beside the door, Wes bent and picked up his coat from the floor, slipping it on as he marched to Sarafina. Her eyes brimmed with tears and relief. She pressed Luis closer to her breast.

"I'm so happy you are unhurt," she said, her voice breaking into gentle sobs.

"Then why cry?"

Sarafina shook her head. "The old women, they blame you and me for this misery. They say none of this would have happened had we not danced with Bonifacio still warm in the grave." Tears streamed down her face.

Wes sighed. Maybe he was to blame. Luther had ridden away from their afternoon encounter with a vengeful fire burning in him. Wes joined Sarafina on the bench and wrapped his arm over her shoulder. She leaned her head against him. "Is Carlos okay?" Wes asked.

Nodding, she wept. "He went with the men and probably blames us, too."

"We can't worry about what the others say or think. Aren't some of these the same ones that wouldn't let you wed in the chapel in San Patricio?"

Her chin bobbed gently. "It's true."

"Then they've never cared for you." Wes lowered his arm from around her back and softly nudged her away.

Standing, he took a deep breath, then walked across the room to the bodies. At each corpse, he offered his condolences to the surrounding family members, uncertain if any of them understood his words. The women resented him, but the men nodded knowingly.

Retreating to the door, Wes found his crumpled hat and picked it up, punching it back into as good a shape as was possible for a piece of felt trampled by dozens of terrified feet. When Wes turned around, he observed Sarafina buttoning her blouse, then wrapping Luis in his covers. She put the boy softly into the basket and stood up, bending for her coat, which had fallen behind the bench. She was putting on her wrap as Wes reached her.

"You can get a good night's sleep in a feather bed at the Wortley."

"I am tired." Sarafina picked up the bundle that was her son, and Wes slid his arm inside hers and escorted her outside. She faltered on mushy knees the first couple steps before finding a reserve of strength or pride that would not let her fall before the other women.

An elderly Hispanic man moved ahead of them to the door, holding it open for them and extending his hand to Wes. *"Gracias, muchas gracias,"* he said.

Outside, many other men who had given chase to the assailants stood in a knot in their path. They murmured among themselves until they saw Wes Bracken. The clump of men broke into two strands lining the path. As Wes approached, the men extended their hands. "I don't understand," he told Sarafina.

"They are offering thanks for shooting the attackers. White men seldom help our people," she answered.

Wes shook each proffered hand, including that of Carlos, who stood at the end of the line.

Sarafina stopped by her brother and stared at him. "See, he is our kind, honest and decent." She marched ahead for the street.

Wes escorted her and the baby to their hotel room door, then retired to his adjoining room. He slept fitfully, so he was up and dressed before dawn. As new light framed the mountains to the east, Wes cradled his Winchester in his arm and walked toward the Rio Bonito to find Luther. Deputy Joe Haskins joined him.

By the tree where Ben Horrell had died, they spread out and

marched toward the stream, finding occasional droplets of dried blood, but nothing more. Luther had escaped. Wes vowed to kill him the next time he encountered him.

"The Mexican men respect what you did last night, Wes. They say you are a good man," Haskins said.

"That's not what the women say."

Haskins laughed. "They gossip too much." He stopped and put his hands on his hips, staring along the banks of the Rio Bonito. "I didn't expect to find anybody because word of the shooting got to the Horrells quick last night. Somebody told them because they rode into town well before dawn to get Ben's body. I figure they'll be back for me and for you."

Wes nodded. "They've been after me a good while. I'll get by."

"I'm on their list now," Haskins said, "thanks to Sheriff Ham Mills. He announced it was me or you that killed Ben. They vowed to get us both."

"Can't you talk the sheriff into arresting them for Bonifacio Zamora's murder?"

Haskins laughed. "Ham Mills only does what Murphy says, and Murphy don't care a whit about Mexicans. They don't give him any business."

"Someday, somewhere, somebody needs to take Lawrence G. Murphy down a notch, Joe."

"Right now, Wes, I'm more worried about the Horrells than Murphy."

CHAPTER 24

Come afternoon, Wes gathered his belongings from his room at the Wortley, grabbed his Winchester, and emerged from the hotel, leaving everything in the wagon except for the carbine, which he carried to the corral and propped against the fence while he harnessed the team.

Carlos skulked about the back of the pen, watching Wes but not offering to help. Out of the corner of his eye, Wes could see Carlos stalking around, a pistol in his hand, his eyes alert to everything. Wes decided Carlos was standing guard over him, but what had brought this change? Knowing Carlos, Wes figured it best to ignore him rather than thank him for his concern.

With the mules in the harness, Wes fetched his carbine leaning against a post and greeted Carlos, who was shoving his pistol in his waistband. The youth took the Winchester from him, saying, "You'll have your hands full." He waved the weapon toward the wagon. "Once you hitch the team, I'll return your carbine."

Wes nodded. "Get the gate, Carlos." Wes retrieved the reins and shook them against the rumps of the mules. The pair danced ahead to the jingle of trace chains and the creak of worn leather. Once the mules and Wes cleared the gate, Carlos latched it and trotted beside Wes, his gaze taking in the whole of the quiet street but returning regularly to the Murphy store.

At the rig, Wes backed the team up straddling the wagon tongue, then hooked each singletree to the doubletree. "Easy, boys," he said, as he tied the lines and checked the set of the brake. "I'm ready to leave whenever Sarafina is."

"I'll get her," Carlos said, offering Wes the carbine.

Wes waved it away. "You keep it for a while."

Carlos answered with a sly grin and marched over to Sarafina's door, rapping proudly on the frame. In a moment Sarafina, bundled up against the frigid air, opened the door, carrying the basket with Luis. She pointed to a gunnysack with her belongings inside, and Carlos fetched it. Sarafina eyed the Winchester, saying something in Spanish that Wes could not make out, but Carlos strode by his sister, toting her possessions to the wagon.

"Featherbeds are wonderful," she beamed. "And for you to buy us lunch at Wortley's was a treat. Never have I eaten a hotel meal before." She wore a somber smile, her pleasure at her new experiences dampened by the memory of the previous night's tragedy.

Wes took Luis from her and rocked the basket gently with one hand while he offered the other to help Sarafina climb into the seat. Wes transferred the baby carrier to Sarafina, then checked the harnesses a final time. "You ready, Carlos?"

"*Sí*," Carlos answered, climbing over the tailgate into the back, then standing in the wagon bed and offering Wes his Winchester.

"Hang onto it for a spell, Carlos. I'll have my hands full with the team."

A smile flicked across Carlos's face as he dropped to his knees atop a folded blanket. His eyes studied the town diligently, looking for trouble.

Wes didn't expect any encounters on this day. The Horrells were probably burying their own dead, but they would seek vengeance before long. Wes knew that as certain as the sun would set tonight and rise again in the morning.

Hauling himself into his seat, Wes untied the lines to Casey's borrowed rig and released the brakes, shaking the reins as he did. Easily, he swung the team into a big arc across the road and turned the wagon back for home, glad to be putting distance between himself and Murphy's store.

Unlike the frosty stares offered by the Hispanics upon their arrival, the men out on the street nodded or touched their hats as Wes passed. The few women braving the cold remained reserved.

When they cleared Lincoln, Wes breathed easier. At least the reminders of last night were gone, he thought, until he reached the cemetery, just east of town. Four new graves were being dug for the victims at the dance. Damn Luther for all the misery he brought those families.

Once beyond the graveyard, the journey passed without incident. Reaching Mirror B property at the confluence of the Ruidoso and the Bonito, Wes saw Jace Cousins out feeding the horses. Wes whistled and waved. Cousins removed his hat and shook it over his head in response. Wes turned the wagon up the valley toward the Zamora place. Drawing closer, he issued instructions to Sarafina and Carlos.

"The Horrells will come after me. You must both be careful. They could bother you as well. Remain inside as much as possible."

Pulling up in front of their adobe, Wes felt Sarafina leaning to him. As she saw Carlos distracted in getting out of the wagon, she arose slightly and pecked him on the cheek. *"Gracias,"* she said, "for taking me, and letting me stay and eat in the hotel, and, most of all, for protecting Luis during the shooting."

Wes nodded as Carlos stepped around to his side and handed Wes his carbine.

"The Horrells shouldn't bother you, Carlos, but promise me you won't start any trouble of your own. Stay near your place and watch out for Sarafina and Luis. Things will heat up before they cool down," Wes continued, "but come spring we'll have taken care of the Horrells."

Carlos nodded.

Sarafina grabbed Wes's arm as he lowered the carbine across his knees. "You must promise us you *will* be careful." Her voice bespoke concern, and her eyes brimmed with worry.

"With Jace Cousins around, I've got help. He's a good man with a rifle."

Carlos circled the wagon and took the basket with Luis from Sarafina and carried his nephew inside. Luis squalled, and Carlos retreated to Sarafina, a bewildered look upon his face.

Sarafina laughed. "Help me down, Carlos, and I will tend Luis if you'll build a fire."

After assisting Sarafina from her seat, Carlos gathered their belongings from the back and trailed her inside the adobe. *"Adios!"* Carlos called over his shoulder as Wes turned the wagon around and started the team down the trail for the Mirror B.

Shortly, Wes was pulling the rig in front of his adobe as Cousins walked up. "I hear there was trouble in Lincoln? Is it true several were killed?"

Standing up and stretching, his Winchester in his hand, Wes jumped to the ground, landing with perfect balance. "Four killed at the dance. A deputy and I killed one of the Horrells. The other gunman got away."

"Another Horrell?"

"No, Luther."

Cousins whistled.

Wes marched inside, leaving his Winchester on the table and pouring a cup of coffee from the pot Cousins always kept going. Cousins followed him, pulling up a chair and taking a seat, gathering the worn cards from his last game of solitaire.

"It was quiet around here."

Wes shook his head. "It won't be for long. Things are coming to a head with the Horrells and the whole county."

"It's just as well that we get it settled before spring when there's work to be done," Cousins answered. "This'll just be another winter chore for us."

Wes nodded, then finished his coffee. "I'd best return Casey's wagon to the mill and buy more ammunition while I'm there. We'll need it before this hand's been played."

Cousins scratched his chin and grinned. "When the shooting starts, I might have a chance to settle things with Jesse Evans."

Wes slapped his empty tin on the table and pushed himself up and toward the door. "I'll saddle Charlie and return Casey's wagon."

Cousins yawned. "Get us more coffee while you're that direction."

After rigging Charlie, Wes tied the reins to the back of the wagon and started for Casey's. The ride was uncomfortable, the wind picking up and turning the chill prickly. The frigid air seeped into his clothes, stinging the muscle all the way to the bone. He was glad when the mill appeared off the road.

Casey shouted at him from the door as soon as he approached. "Come in and give me your news." Poking his head outside, Casey issued a shrill whistle. The high-pitched signal brought one of his hired hands running in from the barn.

"Yes, sir," the hand said.

"Take care of my wagon and team," Casey ordered.

Wes untied Charlie's reins and looped them over the hitching post. "I need ammunition and coffee," Wes announced, stepping inside the warmth of Casey's store.

Mrs. Casey was reading stories to the kids, all huddled by the stove. She looked up and paused, a smile working its way across her face. "Glad you weren't hurt, Wes."

"Every time I borrow your husband's wagon I run into

trouble. Maybe he should quit loaning it to me."

Casey laughed and swatted Wes on the back. "You're the least of my troubles. L. G. Murphy's still displeased I'm hanging onto this store. He wants all the business for himself, no matter that folks in the Hondo Valley have to ride a dozen or more miles just to let him overcharge them. He'll hold it against me that I sell you any coffee or ammunition. Five pounds of Arbuckle's and a couple boxes of rifle bullets, will that do?"

"It should on the coffee, but four cartons of ammo."

"Now," Casey said, pulling the cartridges containers from behind the counter and then working on the coffee, "tell me what happened at the dance."

Wes explained the events in Lincoln, except for Luther's role in it, and, though Mrs. Casey kept reading a story to her children, she paused often to hear the details of the murders.

Casey shook his head. "What's Lincoln County coming to?"

"War, Bob. Until the Horrells are killed or driven out, this violence will continue."

"Aye, it's true," Casey answered, "but the Horrells are not the biggest problem. It's that thief Murphy, trying to squeeze out of every honest man in the region what little money he has."

"The Horrells must go first, Bob. We can't worry about Murphy if we've got to look over our backs every minute we're doing our chores or living our lives."

"I suppose you're right, but the Horrells are small potatoes stacked up against Murphy," Casey argued.

"They may be small, but they're mean, the Horrells are. As for Murphy, he's on our side for the time being. As soon as we drive the Horrell brothers out, he'll try to take over their place and what improvements they've made without lifting a finger to do the work. He sells another sucker a quitclaim deed and profits even more."

"Damn him," Casey exclaimed.

"Hush, Bob, such language in front of the children," his wife scolded.

Wes picked up the cartons of ammunition and slipped them in his coat pockets. He stared at Mrs. Casey and could see the strain in her tight lips and her worried eyes.

"You best keep the children close by the house for the next few weeks, ma'am."

She nodded and tried to continue her story but grew distracted. "Why don't you children go to the kitchen stove. There should be enough leftover biscuits for you each to have one."

Frightened as well, the kids clung to their mother's security.

"Go on, now," she said, until they reluctantly obeyed. "I don't know if it's worth it, trying to stay here."

"Now, kitten, this is fine land," Casey said.

She shook her head. "No, this is mean land, not worth fighting over. It may kill us all before it's done."

"Then it's good land for a man to be buried in," Casey replied.

"Not for a father with growing kids," she shot back.

She was right, Wes thought as he took his coffee from Casey and started for the door.

"This is not your fight, Bob, so stay clear and keep your family away, too." Pushing his way outside, Wes packed the coffee in his saddlebags, mounted Charlie, and headed for the Mirror B with plenty on his mind. For the first time since arriving in Lincoln County, Wes admitted to himself the violence he had left Arkansas to escape was just as bad in New Mexico Territory. When he had abandoned the Arkansas turmoil, he had vowed never to run away again. He still meant it.

CHAPTER 25

"Get out here, Wes, hurry!" Jace Cousins yelled.

This sounded like trouble, Cousins not being one to spook. Wes tossed his fork in a puddle of beans in his tin plate and grabbed his Winchester from the corner. Disregarding his coat, he rushed outside, his carbine leveled at the hip, ready to meet the unknown.

Cousins pointed up the road. Some thirty riders, most carrying rifles, were watering their horses and staring at the Mirror B.

"The Horrells don't have that many friends in New Mexico Territory," Wes said, lowering his weapon. "Could be Murphy's men or even Chisum's."

As he studied the horsemen, he noted more Hispanics than whites, but the two men who separated themselves from the others and trotted toward the Mirror B were Anglos. Wes recognized them, the bigger one being Ham Mills, the sheriff of Lincoln County, and the other Deputy Joe Haskins.

"Must be a posse, Jace. That's lawmen approaching. There's been trouble somewhere." Wes retreated inside to retrieve his coat. As he was buttoning it and stepping back outside, Mills and Haskins drew up their mounts in front of Cousins.

"Afternoon, gents," Mills said.

Wes and Cousins nodded, both preferring to let the sheriff do the talking.

"Word's reached us the Horrells have killed a couple

Mexicans near their place. We're rounding up men to check it out, bring the killers in, if that's what it takes. We figured you boys'd make good hands in that."

"This on the square, Sheriff?" Wes asked, looking at Haskins. The deputy nodded.

"I'm here, ain't I!" Mills bellowed. "That's all you need to know. You in or not?"

"We're in."

"Then get saddled, and let's go," Mills commanded. "When we finish watering our horses, we'll head on. You can catch up with us." The sheriff jerked his mount around. "You coming with me, Joe?"

"In a minute," Haskins replied.

Mills spurred his horse and rejoined the others. Wes and Cousins scurried back in the adobe, each stuffing a box of cartridges in their coat pocket. Wes scooped a couple more bites of beans from his plate, then grabbed his hat and ran outside, tugging it in place with his right hand while holding his carbine in his left.

Haskins sat easy on his gelding, fixing a smoke as the two men bolted for the barn. They scrambled to saddle their mounts, each moving with fluid precision, neither wasting a movement nor prolonging a task. Once Charlie was rigged, Wes shoved his Winchester in the scabbard, watching Cousins mount with his Henry in hand.

Wes climbed atop his stallion and turned him around, admiring for a moment the filly that was growing by the day. She would be a fine dame for Mirror B horses. Charlie pranced outside, Cousins's mount following. Once both animals cleared the door, Cousins pushed it shut and barred it.

By the stream a few riders still watered their mounts, so Wes rode to Haskins. "What do you make of this?"

The deputy shrugged. "Mills doesn't do much that Murphy

doesn't know about. I can't figure his motive here. We didn't send out a posse when the Horrells murdered Zamora. The sheriff rarely sends out posses for Mexican murderers, but two Mexicans are reported dead up the road."

Wes spat a sour taste from his mouth. "Could it be Murphy wants to claim the Horrell place now with spring nearing? It'd be there for the taking if the Horrells abandoned it. Murphy could sell another quitclaim deed on it, defraud some new fool looking for a fresh start here."

"That could be it, Wes."

The posse started at a canter, and Wes, Cousins, and the deputy angled across the Mirror B to intersect them at the road.

"Murphy's always got an angle in Lincoln County affairs," Haskins called matter of factly. "It's enough to make a fellow want to puke." Haskins nudged his mount ahead and led Wes and Cousins to the posse members as they resumed their journey.

The day hung like a gray shroud over them, an occasional mist heightening the cold. The posse rode past the Zamora place, Carlos emerging, his rifle in his hand. Wes was glad to see him, since it indicated all was okay. Next, they advanced through San Patricio, its streets abandoned and its residents watching through the cracks of shuttered windows. The village had been shot up by the Horrells before, and any group of riders sent folks scurrying for the safety of their homes.

Beyond San Patricio, the trail shadowed the Rio Ruidoso, its waters shivering like the men with the chill of winter. They had seven miles to ride before they reached the Horrell place when Haskins maneuvered his horse beside Wes's.

"I've been thinking," the deputy called. "I figure you're right about this posse."

Wes shrugged. "If we get the Horrells, we'll have to admit we were wrong. If we don't, we'll all be suspicious."

The deputy pointed back over his shoulder to the Mexican riders following them. "They wanted you with them, Wes."

"What?"

"After your fight at the dance, they trusted you to defend them. Mills wanted them to ride in his posse, but they refused unless you and I went along."

Wes tugged his hat tighter on his head to withstand the gust that blew into his face. "I'm flattered." Wes pointed to Mills in the lead. "Does the sheriff usually take Mexicans along in posses?"

"Nope," Haskins answered.

"I think that just answered our question. He may be putting on a show for Murphy, the Horrells, and our Mexican friends."

Within a mile of the Horrell place, the sheriff held up his hand, and the posse slowed to a walk. "We'll go easy from here," Mills ordered.

Wes, Cousins, and Haskins worked their way through the riders between them and the sheriff.

"What's the plan?" Wes asked the leader.

"I'll tell you when the time's right," Mills bellowed.

"That time's nearing," Wes said, studying the trail up ahead, then cursing in disgust. "Rumor was right. The Horrells killed two more." Wes pointed down the road. Two bodies were splayed across the trail.

Wes touched Charlie's flank with his boot heel, and the horse danced ahead, reaching the victims before Haskins and Cousins, the sheriff riding up with the others.

Reining up on Charlie, Wes slid from his saddle and landed between the two bodies, both Hispanic men, both without a gun belt or any other indication they had been armed.

Mills rode up to Wes, examining the deceased from his mount. "What's two more Mexicans?" he said under his breath.

Behind Mills, Wes saw Haskins's face grimace, and his hand slide to his pistol. Cousins grabbed the deputy's fingers before Haskins acted rashly. Quickly, Wes remounted and slipped Charlie between the deputy and the sheriff.

"Haskins," Mills shouted, "have two of your boys see if they can identify the dead and bury them."

The deputy assigned two men to deliver the bodies to San Patricio and notify their kin for a proper burial. Haskins turned to Wes. "Those are men with families. Maybe it'll keep them out of danger when we reach the Horrells."

The sheriff guided his nervous horse between the bodies while the rest of the posse made a wide swath around them, a nominal gesture of respect but the best they could offer. The posse continued up the valley, except for the two members dispatched to deliver the deceased.

When the riders came within sight of the Horrell place, smoke was rising lazily from the chimney. Wes drew up Charlie and studied the layout. No one seemed on guard. With a little luck, the posse might get close enough to surprise the Horrells and avoid a prolonged siege.

Around him men checked the loads in their guns, all except the sheriff. Wes nudged Charlie toward Mills. "If we advance quietly, we might surprise them, make it easier on everyone."

"I'm in charge, Bracken," he answered, his voice a mite loud by Wes's reckoning, especially so close to their quarry. "Circle the place," Mills ordered the others. "Listen to my commands, and don't shoot until I give the order."

The riders fanned out around the place, though it was not encircled before Mills took a deep breath, then yelled at the house. "You Horrells, come out. This is Sheriff Mills here to arrest you."

"You idiot!" Wes shouted. "They'll not surrender to you or anyone else."

235

Mills's face turned red, and he cursed Wes. "We don't want any folks hurt."

"Especially the Horrells? Is that it, Sheriff? What's your orders from Murphy?"

"Don't be riding me, Bracken. I can have you arrested."

"You need to remember this, Sheriff. You could get shot by accident out here, and not a man in Lincoln would know who killed you. Not only that, none of the men here would point a finger at the murderer."

"That a threat, Bracken?"

"Just a fact, sheriff."

Mills's face flushed, and his eyes bulged for an instant. He shook his fist at Wes just as a shout came from inside the cabin.

"What you fellows want?"

Wes recognized the voice as that of stiff-necked Mart Horrell.

"We came to arrest you for killing two Mexicans we found down the road."

A taunting laugh preceded Mart's reply. "Why don't you fellows come on in and take us?" One by one rifle barrels appeared out of gun ports around the house. "We got women and children in here," Mart called back.

Mills leaned forward in his saddle. "Send them out, and *we'll* take care of them."

"Hell, sheriff, they'd sooner die with us than trust you to tend them."

Mills cupped his hand over his mouth. "You might ought to ask them about that."

Horrell laughed. "I did, and this is their answer." Two rifles exploded from the gun ports.

Wes turned Charlie in a tight circle and darted for cover along with Cousins and the deputy. Two bullets whizzed overhead, and the sheriff, paralyzed for an instant, jerked his horse around and stampeded for the rocks by the road. "Damn 'em!" Mills shouted.

The surrounding trees and boulders exploded with the posse's gunfire, dust flying around the gun ports as lead slugs struck the adobe walls.

Mills jumped from his horse, jerking his carbine from the saddle boot and emptying it at the house and its shuttered windows. His mount trotted off the road. "Damn," he said, "somebody catch my horse."

Haskins started after the animal. Wes studied the house a moment, motioning for Cousins to follow Haskins. "He may need help." Wes grinned and nudged Charlie, the horse bolting after the deputy with Cousins behind him on his yellow dun.

A quarter mile away, the three riders caught the sheriff's frightened mount. As the animal slowed, Haskins reached over from his saddle and grabbed the bridle, easing the spooked horse into a canter and gradually a walk.

The deputy grabbed his pocket for his tobacco pouch and cigarette makings. "Damn fool sheriff," he cursed. "He don't care to arrest them. He's just putting on a show."

Wes nodded. "He's following Murphy's orders, like the rest of Lincoln County."

Haskins flared a match at the tip of his cigarette and blew out a cloud of smoke when the flame took hold.

Cousins pointed toward the house. "No sense in wasting our ammunition, the way the Horrells are forted up. Come night, though, we might move in, fire the roof."

Wes shrugged. "We might smoke them out, if we could plug up the chimney, but why risk lives for this sham?"

"Fact is," Haskins said, "there are ways we could get them out, if the sheriff genuinely desired to arrest them. If not, we'll know this was all an act to benefit Murphy."

The gunfire continued sporadically and ineffectively. After Haskins finished his smoke, the three men returned to the posse and tied their horses out of sight of the Horrell place. They darted along the slope to the rocks hiding Mills. Around the sheriff's boots lay dozens of hulls.

"You get paid by the shells you shoot, Sheriff?" Wes asked.

Mills growled. "Didn't take three of you to fetch my horse."

"Just as well do something constructive as waste our ammunition," Wes said.

"I'm trying to do a job, Bracken."

"For who, Sheriff?"

Mills grumbled and spent another load of bullets at the house.

"We figure come dark, we can fire the place or smoke them out," Wes suggested.

The sheriff turned around and shook his fist at Wes. "No, we're not burning down the place, not with women and children inside."

"We don't know that," Wes shot back.

"I won't take any chances. If we haven't gotten them by nightfall, we're pulling out."

"Damn, sheriff, we might as well leave right now and save our ammunition," Wes replied.

Mills turned his contempt toward the Horrell abode and emptied another load of lead into the adobe walls, a process he repeated periodically for the next three hours. As the light diffused by the clouds faded, Mills ordered everyone to pull out without so much as drawing a drop of Horrell blood or losing a drop of their own.

The posse retreated down the road, joined in San Patricio by the two men who had delivered the two slain men to their families. The posse headed sullenly toward Lincoln, Haskins riding alongside Wes Bracken.

"You were right, Wes," Haskins said, resignation in his voice. "This was a sham. Murphy's manipulating Ham Mills and the law for a reason I can't put my finger on."

CHAPTER 26

The filly's ears flicked as she danced nervously around the corral, kicking up her hooves and tossing her head. Wes glanced at the Winchester propped up against a fence post, then turned about and studied the Mirror B. Nothing appeared amiss, so he attributed the filly's fidgetiness to being separated from her mother, still shut up in the barn. Then from the east, Wes heard a galloping horse approaching. Wes grabbed his Winchester, his fingers sliding smoothly into the trigger guard and lever.

When the horseman appeared through a break in the trees along the river, Wes relaxed his hold on the Winchester and jogged to the cabin. He recognized Bob Casey, riding stiffly in the saddle, only his arms limber as they bounced with every footfall of the charging steed. Hitting the stream crossing, the horse kicked up a brief curtain of water and emerged in stride, angling across Mirror B land straight for Wes.

Flecked with sweat from the ride, the spotted sorrel eased off its long stride as Casey pulled back on the reins, but the animal had galloped too hard for too long to slow so easily. When it looked like the sorrel might barrel into Wes, Casey yanked the reins, the sorrel's head lifting and shaking as the animal halted not twenty feet from Wes and the cabin.

Behind him, Wes heard the door to the adobe swing open as Jace Cousins pushed his way out. In an instant, Cousins was beside him, Henry rifle in hand.

"Bad night in Lincoln," Casey announced, his voice as wild

as his eyes. "Assassins took deputy Haskins from his bed and killed him in front of his wife."

Wes gritted his teeth. The news struck him hard. "Dammit. The Horrells?"

Casey nodded as he caught his breath. "That's what everybody thinks, suspecting it's for the deputy's hand in killing Ben Horrell after the Christmas dance."

"What about my brother? He involved?" Wes stepped toward Casey, his hands tightening around his carbine.

"Nobody knows for certain, Wes, though most suspect it."

The taste in his mouth grew bitter. Wes knew he should have killed Luther before now, but it was hard to kill your own kin.

"What's the sheriff doing?" Cousins asked.

Casey shrugged. "Talking with Murphy, best as everyone can tell."

Cousins lowered his rifle and scratched his head. "It makes little sense why Murphy doesn't send the law against those fellows, if he's after their place."

"Word has it the Horrells have sent their women and young 'uns back to Texas for a while until they're through killing. And, Wes,"—Casey let his name hang in the air, staring hard at the head of the Mirror B—"rumor is that you're next on their list."

Wes grinned. "Don't you fellows understand? Murphy's not after just the Horrell place. He wants the Mirror B and Casey's place, too. Murphy sent the sheriff against the Horrell place last time for show, but he won't send the law after the Horrells again until after they've killed me and maybe even Bob."

"I'll be damned!" Cousins kicked at the ground.

"That Irish son of a bitch," Casey added.

They stared at one another in silence, nodding their heads as they realized they must act against the Texas *diablos* and Murphy.

"There's a time to stand," Wes said, "and this is it."

Cousins nodded and licked his lips. "Then let's get to it."

Casey stared, looking beyond Wes at something more distant. He bit his lip. Wes detected in Casey's eyes fear not for himself as much as his family's safety. A married man had more considerations than just horses and buildings like Wes and Cousins.

"Little to do about Murphy right now," Wes said, "but we've got to get to the Horrells and Luther. Drive them out of Lincoln County if we can or kill them if we can't."

"And soon," Cousins interjected.

Casey leaned forward and patted the neck of his mount, not so much Wes thought to comfort his horse as to screen his worried eyes.

"Bob, you fort up your family in your store and keep them there. Anybody going down the valley will pass your place. You watch who passes and when," Wes instructed.

Casey sat up straight in the saddle, relief washing over his face. "Besides that, I'll provide all the supplies you can use."

Wes nodded. "Men are what we need, but I can count on the fingers of one hand those I can trust in Lincoln County, and it's the three of us."

"What about John Chisum?" Casey asked. "He's got plenty of men."

"This isn't his battle. He's got fights of his own," Wes replied, rubbing his chin. "You go down the list: Chisum, Murphy, Jesse Evans, the Beckwiths, and the small ranchers from Seven Rivers—all of them've got a stake in Lincoln County, but only Murphy and the Mexicans have any interest in seeing the Horrells out. I don't want to side with Murphy, and the Mexicans aren't likely to join any Anglos."

Casey cleared his throat and straightened in the saddle. "You'll need me."

Shaking his head, Wes answered. "Not as much as your family needs you. Give us two days to figure out a plan, Bob, then Jace and I'll inform you what to do."

"You fellas sure?"

Cousins stepped toward Casey. "Absolutely."

"Keep us posted on any movements," Wes instructed. "Don't travel yourself, but send one of your hands."

Casey touched the brim of his hat. "Will do." He twisted around and pointed to his saddlebags. "I brought you something that'll come in handy, if you'll get it."

Wes stepped to the leather pouch and untied the flap. Lifting the cover, he slipped his fingers inside and pulled out a carton of rifle ammunition.

"There's six boxes for you and Jace," Casey said. "I figure you'll need plenty of bullets in days ahead."

One by one, Wes removed the cartons and handed them to Cousins. "You saved enough for yourself, Bob, didn't you?"

Casey nodded as Wes closed his saddlebag and stepped back.

Casey pulled the reins and turned his mount around for home. "Tell me when you need me," he said, "and I'll ride with you." Casey slapped the neck of his horse with the end of his reins and headed down the valley.

With a sly grin worming its way across his face, Cousins turned to Wes. "We don't need two days to figure out what to do. We both know we'll move tonight. You didn't want to risk Casey getting hurt, now did you?"

Stroking his chin, Wes nodded. "No sense in endangering Casey, since he's got a family to raise. Come nightfall, I figure we should ride over to the Horrell place and give them a dose of their own medicine."

"No point in waiting for them to make their play against us," Cousins replied.

Wes studied the sun a moment. "Five hours until dusk. Let's

oil our guns, put a little food in our bellies, and get our horses ready to ride after dark."

From the west, the bright sunlight angled down the Ruidoso valley. The air was crisp but still, and the valley was quiet, the earth hibernating as another winter day came to a close. The adobe was warm with the heat from the corner fireplace.

Wes fidgeted by the window, keeping watch on the road, while Cousins snapped cards onto the table during another game of solitaire. Cousins was a good man and ally with a rifle, but there were still four Horrells left to face plus whatever riffraff had fallen in with them, aimless men like his brother. Damn Luther. Damn his drinking.

From the west, Wes thought he heard a galloping horse, but perhaps it was his nerves because the sound ended as faintly as it had begun. The heel of his hand rested on the butt of the pistol at his side, his fingers tapping the holster. No time is longer nor more frustrating than waiting time because it passes drop by drop through a man's anxieties. At least after sundown, Wes and Cousins would be doing something rather than lingering around waiting for the Horrells to ambush them.

Wes looked over his shoulder at Cousins gathering up the cards after a losing hand at solitaire. When Wes turned back to the trail, he spotted a lone rider sitting on his horse, staring at the adobe. Wes grabbed his Winchester propped against the wall by a front window. By the scrape of the bench against the hard-packed floor, Wes knew Cousins had recognized the possibility of trouble. In an instant, Cousins stood opposite the door at the other window, easing his gun barrel through the shutters.

"Well, I'll be damned," Cousins said.

Gradually, Wes realized the import of the exclamation as he recognized the rider on the chestnut mount.

It was Luther!

Wes shoved his rifle barrel outside, taking aim at Luther. With his thumb, he toyed with the hammer on the Winchester and steadied his elbow against the window sill.

His brother advanced tentatively, lifting his reins high to show he was not holding a carbine nor reaching for the pistol at his side.

Wes's index finger brushed against the trigger. He sighted in on Luther's chest, taking aim at his brother's heart. Damn you, Luther, Wes thought as his brother drew closer. Damn if Luther didn't need killing for his part in the Horrells' foul deeds, but damn if it wasn't hard to shoot your own brother.

Fearlessly, Luther rode forward, his chestnut aimed straight at Wes's window. Luther could not help but see the gun barrel, and still he pushed ahead.

Without a doubt, Wes could—and should—kill him now, as his older sibling was that close, and Wes's Winchester was sighted on his chest. Slowly, Wes's finger took out the slack between the trigger and his brother's death, until Wes felt a gentle touch upon his shoulder.

"Don't do it, Wes. This is something you shouldn't carry on your conscience," Cousins said softly. "Ask him what he wants."

His finger sliding away from the trigger, Wes lifted his cheek from the carbine, then raised the weapon skyward and jerked it back inside. "Thanks, Jace," Wes whispered and stepped to the door. "I'll see what he's after. You stay inside in case it's a trick."

Cousins took a position at his window as Wes opened the door and strode outside, looking carefully along the road for any ambushers. Wes cradled his Winchester in the crook of his elbow and stared with hardened eyes at his brother.

Within thirty feet of the adobe, Luther pulled up and let his hand fall to the saddle horn, his fingers twitching nervously. The chestnut was lathered and, like Luther, looked overworked and underfed.

"You're not welcome here, Luther. You best ride on." Wes wanted his words to have a hard bite to them, but they came out softer than he preferred. He pitied Luther, but he couldn't keep giving him another chance after the bottle took the last one away.

Luther stared with hollow eyes, his tongue licking his lips between the shag of an untrimmed beard. "I'm your brother, Wes."

"If I've got a brother, it's Jace, not you anymore."

Luther flinched, a grimace staining his face. He looked from Wes to the saddle horn and back. He sat silent and still.

Wes could not read his brother. Maybe there was hurt in his eyes or perhaps it was just liquor. The chestnut, lathered from a hard ride, blew a couple times, and Luther looked up from his saddle, his eyes barely visible beneath the brim of his stained hat.

Shaking his head, he whispered. "I'm sorry, Wes, I'm sorry."

"That don't bring back the dead. Zamora, the four at the dance, Haskins, and how many others, Luther, how many?"

His brother shrugged. "I was liquored up, Wes. I didn't realize what I was doing. I'm sorry, I tell you." Anger tinged his words.

"I swore I'd kill you the next time we met, Luther. If it hadn't been for Jace, you'd be dead now. When I encounter you again, Jace might not be around."

Biting his lip, Luther nodded. "You won't see me again. I'm leaving Lincoln County. So are the Horrells!"

"Is this some kind of trick, Luther?"

"No, dammit!" he shouted. "They've already sent their women and children across the Texas border." He paused, his next words coming awkwardly from his lips. "They plan on killing you before they leave. I owed it to you to let you know. They think you're the one that started all their troubles and killed

245

Ben Horrell."

As Wes stared at Luther, his face puckered in contempt. "You have no debt with me, just the families of the folks you helped kill. I should've shot you long before now, Luther. It would have saved the blood of so many others."

Luther's face turned ashen. "I'm going home, Wes, back to Arkansas." Luther extended his hand and nudged his chestnut toward Wes. "A handshake and I'll be gone."

His teeth clenched, Wes refused. "Your hand's dipped in too much innocent blood, Luther. Get off my place."

Luther's eyes widened. "It was my place, too. I found it for us."

"Put your horse to moving."

"We're brothers, Wes. Please!" His words rang desperate. "The same blood runs in our veins."

"Yours is cold blood, Luther." Wes stared for a moment into his brother's begging eyes, then turned and stepped away.

"Please, Wes, just a handshake. I'm sorry for what I've done. It wasn't me, but the liquor acting."

"You chose whiskey above me, above our place, above decency, above even yourself, Luther. Now, go."

Wes kept walking toward the door where Cousins had moved, furious that Luther had shamed himself and the Bracken name. "Damn you to hell, Luther Bracken," Wes called out over his shoulder. He heard his brother sobbing, but all the tears he shed were but a trickle to the river of grief he and the Horrells had rained on Lincoln County. By rights, Wes thought he should go ahead and kill Luther, family or not.

"A handshake is all I ask," Luther pleaded.

Wes stopped two feet from the door, shaking his head and not even looking at his brother. "No, dammit!" His voice, gritty with disdain, silenced Luther.

A gunshot, strangely distant, went off behind Wes. Then

another and another.

Wes flinched and leveled his Winchester at his waist to kill his brother, but before he could turn around and shoot, Cousins jumped from the cabin, grabbed Wes's arm, and jerked him inside.

As Cousins swung the door closed, Wes cursed Luther. Cousins bounded to the window, pointing his Henry down the valley. "It's the Horrells!" he shouted at Wes.

"Dammit," Wes cursed. "Luther set me up."

"I don't know, Wes," Cousins answered, nodding outside. "He's still here."

Wes jumped to the adjacent window and leveled his Winchester, aiming to kill Luther.

His brother struggled to control his flailing horse. "They tricked me, Wes, they did!" he cried as he fought his frightened mount.

Wes drew a bead on his brother's heart as shots rang out from across the road.

"I didn't know they followed me, Wes. Tell me you believe me, please." Luther gasped, then opened his mouth to say something. Instead of words, a trickle of blood seeped out one corner of his lips and down his chin. Luther released the reins and slid slowly from the saddle. The chestnut, nervous between his dying legs, bolted away, and Luther collapsed to earth, Wes spotting a growing red stain in the back of his brother's coat.

Terrified by the gunshots, the gelding dashed toward Casey's Mill as the shooting increased from both the road and the Rio Ruidoso. The Horrells had taken up good positions because they were hard to spot in the dwindling light. Cousins and Wes fired a couple shots each to answer the attackers but realized any more would be a waste of ammunition. Wes moved from his position just as a bullet grazed the corner, splintering a shutter.

247

He slipped to the rear window, where he watched but saw nothing.

"Come dark," Wes called to Cousins, "we'll slip out the rear to the barn and get our horses. We can make a run for it then."

Before Cousins could answer, Wes detected a scratching, then a thumping on the door.

"It's cold out, Wes," Luther rasped, his voice wheezing like a torn bellows. "Please let me in. And, shake my hand, please."

Wes stood motionless. He ignored the plea.

"For God's sake, Wes, he's your brother," Cousins implored.

Shaking his head, Wes turned back to the window and fired a shot toward the mountains behind the house. He heard the door swing open and knew Cousins was pulling Luther inside. Wes turned to see Cousins slamming the door again and barring it, as a fusillade of bullets struck the front of the adobe.

Cousins squatted over Luther, then grabbed his hand. Luther's eyes seemed to find Cousins's face, and his bloody lips parted in a narrow grimace of a smile.

"Thank you, Wes," Luther rasped. "I didn't mean no—" Luther's head drooped to his side, and his sentence went unfinished forever.

CHAPTER 27

As Luther's hand slid from his grasp, Cousins looked up, his eyes bearing in on Wes, his gaze unflinching even when a bullet pinged off the adobe wall. "Sorry about your brother, Wes."

Wes sensed Cousins's solemn look before he pulled his rifle from the window and stared at Luther on the floor. A strange peace was etched in the curve of Luther's lips and the lines of his face.

"Damn sorry about your brother," Cousins repeated.

"He brought it on himself," Wes answered as a bullet thudded into the window frame nearby. "And us!" Wes ducked behind the wall, reloaded his carbine, and jumped back in front of the opening, emptying the Winchester quickly, firing without seeing his attackers or caring. Sliding from the shutters, he leaned against the adobe wall, feeling recklessness rising in his blood as he shoved bullets into the Winchester.

Cousins dragged Luther away from the door, releasing him between the two beds and reaching for his blanket.

"Cover him with mine," Wes ordered. "He's my brother."

Nodding, Cousins tugged Wes's spread from atop the bed and draped it over Luther's body, dragging the corner slowly over his head and tucking the woolen material under his sides. Crouching, Cousins picked up his Henry and scampered from window to window, checking for approaching assailants. As he passed one opening, a bullet whistled past his ear, thudding into the opposite wall near the shelf of tin dishes. "They're still out there, Wes," he said, his understatement drawing a nod from his partner.

Wes squeezed off a shot toward the gathering darkness, his jaw clenched. He glimpsed Cousins staring hard into him, but he had nothing to offer. What could he say about his dead brother that would be true? He was sorry, but he wasn't, Luther bringing his death upon himself by throwing in with the Horrells. Now, Wes was the last of the Bracken line. If he died, he hoped he departed with more honor than his brother.

"I figure," Cousins said, "Luther was telling the truth. The Horrells double-crossed him."

"All I know is we're in a tight spot, Jace. They can slip up on us once it's dark."

Cousins shoved his Henry out the window and fired at a speck of movement along the river. "Or, we can slip away. Our horses are saddled in the barn."

A ribbon of darkness seeped into the valley, Wes and Cousins moving from window to window to ensure no one was sneaking up on them until it was dark enough to dash for the barn. Occasionally, they glimpsed a form moving among the trees, a form too shadowy to know if it were real or just their imagination from staring too hard for too long. The shots came sporadically, plowing into the adobe walls, doing little more than reminding Wes and Cousins they had vicious visitors. Wes caught the flash of a gun muzzle and instantly emptied his Winchester at the location. No noise answered Wes's gunshots. Nothing but silence floated on the air until a gunshot from the rear of the house resounded.

Wes backed away from his window and patted his coat pocket. "Looks like we'll be using the cartridges Casey brought us."

Cousins lifted his Henry to his shoulder, held it a moment, pointed toward the road, then lowered it again. "We need to make our move before too long. We don't want to give them too much time to work their way closer."

Nodding, Wes thumbed a cartridge into his Winchester. He turned to answer Cousins but held his words at the sound of six, seven, maybe eight rapid shots, echoing through the valley. These rifle retorts differed from the sporadic gunfire up until then. "What do you make of that?" Wes whispered.

"They've got more men coming in."

Wes shrugged as he heard the attackers yelling to each other in the trees by the river.

More shots followed, Wes spotting the flashes of a distant rifle, a third of the way up the mountain behind the house.

"Dammit!" cried an attacker. "Let's get out of here."

Cousins laughed. "Maybe we've got allies on the mountain."

"But who?" Wes asked.

The far gun fired again and again until Wes heard galloping horse hooves from the road and along the stream. He saw a couple dark shadows riding eastward.

"Casey," Cousins offered. "Bless his soul!"

Wes shrugged. "He couldn't have heard the gunfire at his place. Too far." Then, he leaned his carbine against the wall. "Could be a trick."

"The Horrells ain't that smart."

Both men laughed, then Wes squatted beside Luther's body and stroked his brother's arm protruding from under the blanket. "I wish it had worked out better for us, Luther." He took his dead brother's hand and bowed his head, his lips mouthing a silent prayer. He patted the cold hand and tenderly lowered it to the floor, covering it with the blanket. "If you had just known men as good as you knew horses, Luther, it'd been okay."

"Shhhh," Cousins whispered, waving a hand at Wes. "You hear that?"

"What?" Wes answered.

Cousins shook his arm at Wes, then cupped his fingers to his ear.

Faintly, a howl cut across the valley, indecipherable at first, then coming like the wail of a dead man, Wes just able to make out the noise as words but unable to understand them.

"*Hola, amigos,*" came the cry, intermittently across the valley, slowly growing louder and nearer.

"Mexican talk," Cousins said. " 'Friends, hello, friends.' "

Finally, the voice clicked in Wes's mind. With the next shout from outside, he recognized the caller for certain. "I'll be damned," Wes spit out, "it's Carlos."

"He's welcome by me," Cousins laughed.

Wes pushed himself away from his brother's body and lifted his Winchester. Stepping to the door and cracking it, he shouted, "Carlos, is that you?"

"*Sí, están bien?*" His voice now came loud and confident, carrying well in the cool night air as he crossed the Ruidoso.

"Stay put, Jace," Wes called, "in case there's a problem. Carlos can be hot headed and unpredictable."

Gradually, a shape emerged from the trees, Carlos taking form as he drew closer to the barn and then the adobe. From inside the barn, the horses stamped and snorted their fear.

"*Gracias, Carlos, muchas gracias,*" Wes called out, stepping to greet him with a handshake. "We were in a tight spot. Sarafina, is she okay? And Luis?"

Carlos stood before him, and even in the dark his smile was visible. "*Sí, están bien!*" His voice brimmed with pride. "I heard gunshots and came after I hid Sarafina and Luis across the river in a cave."

"Did you recognize the attackers?"

"*Sí,* the Horrells." He spat the name out like poison. "When they first galloped by, I think trouble. They are mean men. Then I hear the shots and know they are attacking you."

Cousins slipped out from the adobe. Startled, Carlos swung his carbine in his direction, then lowered it when he realized his mistake.

"Where's your mount, Carlos, and I'll put him in the barn?" Cousins offered.

Shaking his head, Carlos waved his Winchester toward home. "I ran here on foot."

"Are you certain your sister and Luis are okay?" Wes asked.

"*Sí*, I am sure."

"The coffee pot's on the stove, Carlos; have a cup." Turning to Cousins, Wes pointed to the barn. "Get your horse, Jace, and see if you can find Luther's chestnut. Carlos can have it and his rigging." Turning his back on Cousins, Wes announced, "I've a chore to attend myself."

Carlos stepped inside the door, then retreated, swiping his hat off his head and holding it over his heart. "Who is dead?"

"My brother." His words came out cold.

"The one that rides with the Horrells?"

Wes nodded, stepping past Carlos into the dimness of the cabin. Wes tossed his Winchester on the bed, knelt down, and slid his arms under Luther's back and legs. As Wes stood with his load, Luther fell limp, his arm flopping down and swinging awkwardly with each step Wes took toward the door.

"Sarafina told you the cabin was bad luck," Carlos said as Wes marched by.

Wes answered, "Bad men and bad liquor, Carlos, not bad luck." He headed to the Ruidoso, where he would bury Luther by the stream. If Luther grew thirsty now, he would find the sweet waters of the Ruidoso nearby. The ravages of whiskey had taken their toll on Luther's body. It was frail, not the strapping, hard-muscled form Wes remembered. Wes approached the river and a tall cottonwood tree, its limbs reaching like spindly arms to accept Luther. When Wes stopped, his boots stumbled over a slew of fist-sized rocks scattered like marbles on the earth. As Wes lowered Luther to the ground, he realized he stood where he had buried the tin can. He would bury Luther there as well. The stones his older brother had picked up would join others in his cairn.

Wes turned around and aimed for the barn but stopped when he spotted Cousins riding his way, a shovel in his hand.

Cousins reached him in a minute and extended the implement. "I thought you might want this, Wes. I'll be glad to help, once I round up Luther's horse, but I figured you'd prefer to handle this yourself."

Wes nodded as he accepted the proffered shovel and Cousins's words. Though the moon was dim, it cast enough light for Wes to see what he was doing. A shovel at a time, the grave grew, the soft earth easy digging unless a tree root got in the way. For an hour, Wes worked on the grave, finally getting the narrow hole waist deep. He stuck the shovel in the dark mound by the hole and climbed out, kneeling over Luther, working the blanket around his face and tucking it under his arms and legs. Gently, Wes picked up his brother for the last time and eased him feet first into the pit, finally lowering his head into the cold earth that would be Luther's pillow for eternity.

Removing his hat, Wes looked from the grave to the stars above, tiny beacons of hope in the night sky. "Luther, may you have the peace you could never find after the war. Amen." That said, Wes replaced his headgear, took the shovel, and tossed dirt over his brother. It went quickly, like a thousand other chores Wes had done in his life. When the dirt was mounded over, Wes promised himself on another day, when he had more time, he would collect stones to cover the grave, and he would make a cross to mark the spot.

As he carried the shovel back to the adobe, he spotted three saddled horses tied in front of the place. Cousins had recovered Luther's chestnut, and Carlos would now have his own mount.

A faint glow seeped out the open door. As Wes approached, he observed a single candle on the table, a tiny flame holding its own against the darkness. A lamp would have lit the whole room, but a candle was safer in case the Horrells returned.

From a dim edge of the candle's illumination, Cousins pointed toward the stove as Wes propped the shovel against the door frame and strode inside. "There's salt pork in the skillet and coffee on the fire, Wes. We've had our share."

Wes waved the offer away. "Let's check on your sister and the baby, Carlos. Then Jace and I'll settle our score with the Horrells come morning."

Gulping down their final sips of coffee, Cousins and Carlos grabbed their weapons. "Your Winchester is in your saddle boot, Wes," Cousins told him as they stepped outside and closed the door.

The three men stretched against the night's brisk air, then climbed one after the other atop their mounts and headed west along the Ruidoso, instead of the road, where assassins might wait, finally angling up to the Zamora cabin from the back, studying it, before Cousins advanced alone to check it out in case the Horrells had forted up there. Cousins eased up to the adobe and disappeared inside for a moment. His shadowy form emerged shortly, waving his hand over his head that all was clear.

"Your sister, Carlos, where is she?" Wes asked as Cousins returned.

"Half way up the mountain is a cave," Carlos answered. "But we must leave the horses. The ground is too rough."

As Cousins approached, Wes dismounted, signaling for Carlos to do the same. Then Wes tossed Charlie's reins to Cousins. "Keep our horses until we return."

Together Carlos and Wes ascended the mountain, stumbling among the rocks and juniper stumps and dodging cholla bushes. As Wes climbed, the cold air burned his lungs, and his ears felt brittle from the chill.

Finally, Carlos pointed to a dark splotch beneath an overhang. "There," he said to Wes. "Sarafina, Sarafina," he called softly at the hole.

As Wes approached, he noticed the faint glow of a candle from inside. The slit of an opening admitted Carlos and then Wes after a narrow squeeze. On the cave floor, a nub of a candle burned. By the back wall, Wes spotted Sarafina curled up under two wool blankets with her son.

"Sarafina," Carlos said, stamping his feet.

She stirred, her eyes emerging from behind pinched eyelids. A smile worked its way across her lips, and she pushed the covers away from herself, careful to keep Luis covered, his tiny breath rasping with each draft through his nose.

"I am so happy you're both safe," she answered, her voice quivering as she stood. She strode to Carlos and hugged him and kissed his cheek, then stepped to Wes, throwing her arms around him. "Thank God you are well, Wes Bracken."

Surprised this emotion was for him, Wes turned his head to Carlos. Instead of a snarl on Carlos's lips, Wes noticed a wisp of a smile, which was as much as Wes knew he would ever get from Carlos. But the smile was sincere, seeping all the way into his eyes. Wes wrapped his arms around Sarafina's delicate back. Even over the mustiness of the cave, he smelled the sweetness of her hair and enjoyed it as much as the soft curves of her flesh pushing against his chest. With his trigger finger, he found her chin and lifted her face until he looked straight into her dark eyes. They brimmed with tears.

"It pleases me you are uninjured," she managed, her voice cracking.

Wes raised her chin a tad more until his lips met hers. He kissed her like he had never kissed a woman before. And, Sarafina drew him even closer.

Chapter 28

Carlos averted his eyes from Sarafina and Wes, then turned to face the curved walls of the cave. When Wes glimpsed Carlos, the youth acted more embarrassed than angered, but Wes could never be sure, not with the youth's volatile temperament.

Wes pried himself from Sarafina's lips, though he longed to linger in her embrace. He held her at arm's length and smiled, his lips slowly opening and exposing his chipped front tooth. Sarafina answered his smile with hers.

"Thank you for sending Carlos," Wes offered. "He helped Jace and me out of a spot."

"It was Carlos. I feared him leaving me and Luis, but he said we owed it to you." Her eyes avoided his, and her head slipped down.

Placing his finger beneath her chin, he softly lifted her face to meet his. "We're all scared. When this is finished, life will be easier on us all."

"For some, but I shall have no one to watch over me and my young son."

"You don't know the future."

She shrugged. "I told you the cabin was cursed."

"The Horrells brought bad luck, not my house."

Carlos turned toward his sister. "And now the Texas *diablos* have killed his brother."

Even in the dim light of the flickering candle, Wes saw shock in Sarafina's eyes. "It could have been you," she gasped.

"It still might be," he answered. "Jace and I are riding out tonight. We're tired of the fear in everyone. We'll rid Lincoln County of the Horrells or—" He left the sentence unfinished, but by the horror magnified in her face, Wes realized she understood the alternative.

Carlos stepped behind his sister and stared over her shoulder at Wes. "There are more of them than you. I'll help."

His hands sliding from Sarafina, Wes shook his head. "You must stay with Sarafina and protect her and your nephew, should the Horrells return."

"But why? She is protected here."

Wes saw in Carlos's scowl the hot temper that had gotten him in so much trouble. "You're her last family. I don't want to risk you."

"You cannot stop me from following you," he challenged, his chin thrust forward.

"We will not advance if you do trail us," Wes shot back.

Carlos said something undecipherable in Spanish, likely curses because Sarafina flinched at the words. Now, Wes thought, Carlos was his usual self.

Then the fire disappeared from his eyes, like it had been doused with water. "I will not follow, but promise me you will not attack them until sunrise."

Wes shrugged. "The longer we wait, the farther they may be from us. You want them dead or gone, just like I do."

Sarafina turned to Carlos, speaking rapidly in Spanish, her tone troubled, then softening. Carlos answered in Spanish. She nodded and explained to Wes. "Carlos says you are hardheaded, but you should listen to his wishes. Show him you believe him to be a man by delaying the attack," she pleaded. "It would do little harm to agree, and it would demonstrate your respect for him."

Stroking his mustache, Wes nodded. "I'll try as long as it

doesn't endanger Jace and me."

"That's agreeable. Neither Carlos nor I would want you harmed."

Wes took Sarafina's hand and squeezed it. "Jace and I are heading to the Horrell place to see if they've abandoned it. Last I saw they were riding east toward Casey's Mill. Stay hidden until you hear from us."

Sarafina moved closer to him. Standing on her tiptoes, she pecked Wes on the cheek. "God bless you."

Turning from Sarafina, he extended his hand to Carlos. "Thanks for coming to help tonight, Carlos."

The youth's grip was strong, and his handshake was as steady as his eyes. He said nothing, but Wes knew Carlos had matured enough to be considered a man, but he would only be recognized as an adult if he could control his emotions, for they ran too hot through his veins.

Wes turned to the cave's mouth and squeezed outside into the cool air. It embarrassed him to have kept Jace waiting so long with the horses. In a moment, Carlos emerged from the cave behind him. "I must tend my horse," Carlos whispered, his words carrying on the brisk air. They descended the slope together.

At the foot of the mountain, Wes crossed the Ruidoso and saw the darkened forms of the three horses grazing among the cottonwood trees. Wes noticed Cousins stirring from under a tree and stretching his arms.

"Are Sarafina and the baby okay?" Cousins asked softly as Wes approached.

"Fine, just scared."

Cousins pointed behind Wes. "You didn't invite Carlos to accompany us to the Horrell place, did you?"

"No, sir! He's coming to take care of his horse. Promised he wouldn't follow us if we waited to chase the Horrells until sunrise."

"Odd request," Cousins answered. "It might put more distance between us and them."

"I went along with it, figuring that was easier than reining him in. He's hot-headed and too impatient to listen to reason sometimes."

Wes and Cousins sauntered over to their mounts, lifting their forelegs and un-hobbling them. They were in their saddles by the time Carlos mounted.

"Adios, Carlos," Wes said.

"Be careful," Carlos answered.

The partners turned their horses west toward the Horrell place and slapped their reins against the animals' necks. At a canter, they left Carlos behind, riding a half mile and reining up to listen, in case Carlos had followed them in spite of his promise.

First, they heard silence, then the sound of galloping hooves down the road.

"I knew we couldn't trust him," Cousins said.

Wes felt his face burn with anger.

"Damn fool," Cousins continued, "riding that hard'll wake up the whole county, Horrells and everybody else."

But instead of growing louder, the pounding hoofbeats grew fainter and evaporated into the distance. Carlos was heading east rather than following them.

"What do you make of that, Jace?" Wes asked, uncertain what to think. "Surely he's not going after the Horrells alone?"

"Don't make sense to me, but we could be here all night trying to figure it out."

Wes tugged his hat tight against his forehead. "Let's ride."

The Horrell place stood silent and foreboding when they

reached it. Wes and Cousins tied their horses a hundred yards away from the house, unlimbered their long guns, and filled their pockets with cartridges.

They advanced, their eyes straining for any sign of movement, their hands tightly gripping their weapons, ready to fire at any threat. The corrals were empty, and their wagons were gone. Unless the men had taken their horses inside with them, they were not around.

Wes and Cousins clung to the trees along the Ruidoso as long as they could for cover, then split up and advanced on the house, stride for stride. A dying breath of night blew through the valley. The front door moved a fraction, moaning on dry wooden hinges. Wes tensed before realizing it was only the breeze.

To the east, a thread of pink wormed its way over the mountains, and the sky was changing for the approach of day. Cousins slipped to the far side of the house, both men advancing wordlessly. Cousins eased out of sight around the dwelling, then moments later reappeared on the other side. Wes reached the door and jabbed at it with the barrel of his carbine, the door swinging harmlessly in, its wooden hinges screeching with thirst. Wes stepped in, swinging his carbine in an arc that covered the whole room, in case someone should be awaiting him. Even in the dim light he could see an emptiness littered by overturned furniture. Further, it was as cold inside as out. It had been hours if not days since someone had built a fire in the dwelling.

Wes lowered the carbine to his side and turned around to face Cousins. "Nobody here. Best I can tell, it's been a while at that."

"Word they sent their women and children back to Texas must be true." Cousins spat at the house. "I don't figure they'll return here."

"But I doubt we've seen the last of them," Wes answered.

"We might as well head back to the Mirror B."

They walked silently to their tied horses and mounted. Wes shoved his carbine in his saddle boot, then stretched and yawned. The exhaustion from a full day without sleep nagged his body. He tried to shake the muddle out of his mind, recalling his time in the Confederate army when he had gone days without catching any more shuteye than he could get on the periodic breaks they took on the march. He glanced at Cousins, who appeared none the worse for the night's ride.

Wes jostled the reins, and Charlie turned toward home. He accepted Cousins's suggestion that they ride off the trail and let each other bed down for a spell. Wes fell to sleep almost as soon as he threw his bedroll on the ground and himself upon his blankets. Even though the nap was brief, he felt better when Cousins nudged him it was his turn. Wes arose and rolled up his bedding, strapping it on Charlie. By the heavy fall of Cousins's breath, Wes realized he had been more tired than he had appeared. After what Wes estimated as a half hour, he woke Cousins, and the two headed back to the Mirror B.

By noon, they were hungry and slumped over in their saddles, ready for the miserable day to end. At the sound of galloping hoofbeats, both men snapped to attention. Initially, the noise was hard to place, a slight rumble, like a stampede. Then it grew, coming from the east. Wes pointed at the dust cloud a mile away and headed toward them. It sounded like a dozen or more men. If it wasn't the Horrells, it was likely one of Murphy's gangs.

Wes and Cousins jerked their long guns from their saddle scabbards and aimed their horses for a ravine that cut through the mountain looming beside the trail. It would suffice to screen them from the approaching riders, though not to protect them from bullets.

The sound drew closer as Wes and Cousins reined up in the

ravine. Wes turned Charlie about and eased the horse to a point where he could see the bend in the trail around a hillock. The hills screened the horsemen from him and Cousins.

When they galloped around the bend, Wes caught his breath at the sight. Atop the chestnut gelding rode Carlos. Behind followed thirty others. "I'll be damned, Jace. It's Carlos."

Wes rode out onto the trail, and Cousins joined him. Carlos reined up his horse and screamed at the other men. Wes saw a wide grin on his face.

"We told that kid not to bother us," Cousins said.

Wes laughed. "I didn't know he had that many friends."

When Carlos reached them, he yanked off his hat, swept it across his chest, and bowed to Wes and Cousins.

"Thought we told you not to follow us," Wes joked.

Carlos answered with a sheepish grin, shrugging. "I wanted to reach you before sunrise to attack the Horrell place, but it took longer than I guessed to round up men to help. Did you attack the Horrells at sunrise?"

"We didn't find them," Wes replied, shoving his carbine back in his saddle boot. "They've abandoned their place."

"I know. I alerted the valley of the trouble, and Bob Casey said they had been in to drink last night. They planned to attack the Mirror B again this afternoon, then make a run for Texas. We want to help them along."

Wes nodded. "We best get going."

Holding up his hand, Carlos answered emphatically. "Let them attack. More of our people are at your place."

Wes looked from face to face. Thirty Mexican men, some old and even a pair that seemed younger than Carlos, smiled back. They all carried guns—not new guns, but single-shot rifles, occasional shotguns, and an odd assortment of handguns—but weapons nonetheless.

"Thanks for coming to ride with us," Wes said, nodding to

the men. *"Gracias, gracias."*

Members of the posse nodded and touched their hats in respect.

"In all of Lincoln County," Carlos said, "you are the only white man they now trust."

CHAPTER 29

At the Zamora place, the band split up, half climbing the mountains that clung to the northern side of the trail and the rest crossing the Ruidoso and ascending the facing peaks to the south. Wes rode with Carlos to the north, sending Cousins with the others.

"If they attack the adobe, we'll ambush the ambushers. Stay hidden, and don't shoot until you're close enough to hit what you're aiming at," Wes instructed as Cousins headed for his position. Cousins had a good head for these things, but the Hispanics who accompanied him were peaceful folks, not accustomed to this kind of business.

Wes wanted to check on Sarafina but realized it best not to tip off the others to where she was. The fewer folks that knew about the cave, the more secure it would remain.

Carlos rode proudly beside Wes on Luther's chestnut. Occasionally, he grimaced as if the shoulder wound he had taken when the Horrells killed Bonifacio still bothered him. His dark eyes were afire, and he sat erect in his saddle, as if proud to have galvanized so many of the Hispanics into a fighting force.

They angled up the slopes, then moved east, keeping an eye on the road for the Horrells and on their allies making their way along the mountains on the opposite side of the Ruidoso.

Shortly, the mountain curved back away from the stream, and Wes saw the Mirror B, quiet and tranquil, nothing unusual except two strange horses tied to the hitching post in front of

266

the house. Though his view took in the whole place where the Rio Bonito and Rio Ruidoso converged, Wes's gaze returned to a spot by the river, a site where fresh-turned dirt marked Luther's grave. Damn him for taking up with the Horrells, damn him for clinging to the bottle, and damn him most of all for getting himself killed.

Shaking his head at the bittersweet memory, Wes asked Carlos, "Whose horses?"

Carlos grinned at Wes. "More of our men. Three are armed in your house. Three more are out at the barn. We herded your stock, including the filly, up to Casey's Mill for safety."

"You've thought it all out, Carlos."

Nodding, Carlos pointed east along the course of the Rio Ruidoso. "Our people all along the way today know to expect trouble. In every house where men remain, they are waiting with guns. The Horrells will not find a friend in the entire county."

The band of men had reached the point of the mountain from which they could look both ways down the Rio Bonito valley stretching back toward Lincoln and along the Ruidoso valley. Wes directed the Mexicans to hide their horses and take positions behind the scrub juniper and piñon pine. Wes dismounted as Carlos ordered one of his men to hobble Charlie for him. Wes grabbed his canteen and took a swig of the cool water. The liquid felt good going down his throat, but his stomach craved food even more.

Behind a broad juniper bush, Wes sat down in the shade and shivered. He relished the sun's warmth almost as much as he desired food, and he envied those men on the southern mountains. There when they hid behind the bushes, they would at least be in the sun. But when this dance of death started, Wes figured he would be nearer to the Horrells and closer to avenging Luther's demise.

Carlos plopped a leather bag beside Wes. "There's food inside. Eat and get some sleep if you can. We know you've been up all night."

"*Gracias*," Wes replied, his fingers attacking the thongs around the bag. He pushed his hand into the pouch and pulled out a stack of tortillas. He gobbled them down, enjoying their blandness all the way from his mouth to his stomach.

Wes reclined on the hard earth splattered with rocks that would have made rest impossible had he not been exhausted. He was quickly and deeply asleep, lost in the comfortable cradle of welcome rest. He did not know how long the hand had shaken his shoulder, but when he snapped out of his deep sleep, Carlos was leaning over him.

"They have come," Carlos whispered.

As Wes sat up, he glanced at the sun. It was late afternoon, maybe two hours before the sun would fall behind the mountains. Carlos pointed to the southeast, and Wes followed the youth's finger, until he spotted nine riders approaching not along the road, but on the opposite side of the stream. Wes recognized four as the Horrells. At first, the other five were unfamiliar, likely part of the outlaw backwash that the lawless tides from Texas kept pushing into New Mexico Territory. Then Wes cursed. One of the riders was Jesse Evans. His compatriots Clem and Ansel rode with him, just as they had in the Organ Mountains at the killing of the Mes brothers. Back then those three and Wes had scared the Horrells away after encountering them on the road home. Then Jesse had been an ally against the Horrells, but now he had thrown in with the enemy. Nothing in Lincoln County surprised him anymore. This would give Cousins his chance to settle his score with Evans.

All around him, Wes saw the Hispanics leaning forward, staring at the men who had caused so much terror in the county. A couple made moves to stand up for a better view. "Stay down,"

Wes called softly, motioning for them to stay down. "They'll likely circle the house and start shooting. Keep hidden until then."

As Wes had predicted, the riders broke into two groups, one clinging to the cover of the trees along the Ruidoso, the other moving north toward the road and the base of the mountain where Wes and his half hid. Wes smiled at his luck. The Horrell brothers were coming to his side of the valley, likely because they wanted to be near the road to make their escape. Wes wondered if Cousins had recognized Jesse Evans across the river.

When the Horrells took their positions, the quiet of the valley was interrupted by the explosion of their weapons. Instantly, they were answered by the weapons emerging from the cabin and the barn. The dance had begun!

"Listen," Wes called to those around him. "While they're occupied with the cabin, we can slip up on them. Take your mounts down easy with no unnecessary noise. Don't shoot until you get close enough to plug them or they'll escape."

Carlos repeated the instructions in Spanish, and they nodded their understanding.

"Let's go," Wes commanded. The men scampered from their hiding spots to their horses. Quickly, they mounted with guns in their hands and looks of uncertainty on their faces. This was a new experience for them, but the doubt in their eyes was countered by the determined clench of their jaws. "Remember, nobody shoots until we're spotted or I fire."

Wes unhobbled Charlie and pulled himself atop the stallion, yanking his Winchester from its scabbard in one smooth motion. When he nodded, the men advanced down the mountainside, their faces tense with uncertainty. Across the valley, Wes watched Cousins marshaling his forces as well and moving cautiously down the slope.

The gunfire was steady below them and a haze of gunpowder hovered in places around the rocks and trees where the Horrells had taken their positions.

Beside Wes rode Carlos. A wild look upon his face, Carlos licked his lips and squeezed the carbine until his knuckles were white.

"Easy, Carlos," Wes encouraged. "We're in this together."

Carlos grunted an answer as the men advanced halfway down the slope, the horses gathering momentum for the surprise that should end the Horrells' reign of terror and trap them all in the jaws of death. Across the valley, Wes watched Cousins's volunteers advancing as well.

Two thirds of the way down the mountain, the noise of the horse hooves was picking up, and still the Horrells were preoccupied with the adobe and the barn. And all of Wes's allies seemed to have held their excitement in check. Like Wes, Carlos could see one of the Horrells firing away at the cabin from behind a rock.

A hundred yards from this nearest Horrell, Carlos's chestnut leaped over a small piñon bush. Carlos shouted in surprise. The nearest Horrell spun around to check on the noise. Wes recognized Mart Horrell.

Without orders, Carlos fired his carbine.

Wes cursed as all around him guns exploded, too far away to threaten the attackers.

Mart Horrell scrambled for his horse, grabbing its reins and issuing the alarm to the others. "Ambush, ambush!" he screamed. The warning echoed through the valley. Instantly, Wes saw gang members bolting from their hiding spots atop horses and galloping east toward Casey's Mill. From the opposite mountainside, firing erupted as well, and Wes watched Jesse Evans dash from behind a cottonwood tree, grab at his bucking horse, and clamber into his stirrups and saddle. The gray gelding galloped across the Mirror B fields, taking the shortest possible course for the road. Wes lifted his Winchester to his shoulder and squeezed off a futile shot, knowing the thief was too far away for the bullet to do damage. Even so, it felt good to shoot at him.

Four other men on horses raced after Jesse. As they crossed the Mirror B, three men scrambled from the house and two more from the barn, emptying their weapons at them without visible effect.

Damn it, Wes thought. From the looks of things the Horrells and their accomplices were escaping without so much as a scratch. If only Carlos hadn't fired and alerted them. If only they could have gotten closer before the shooting started.

The men at the house jumped on their horses, joining Cousins's riders as they passed. Almost forty against nine, Wes thought. The odds were on his side, but these Hispanics weren't hardened killers like their prey. These were decent men, driven by thoughts of safety for their families and for their valley.

When Charlie hit the road, Wes slapped the reins against his neck, and the stallion raced past all others. Even so, he was at least two hundred yards behind the thieves, and none of the Hispanics rode horses that could keep up with Charlie. Wes watched the four Horrells converge with Jesse Evans's men, and they galloped ahead. Cousins's men reached the road ahead of Wes, but Charlie quickly passed them and with effort caught up with Cousins.

"What happened?" Cousins screamed. "I almost had Jesse."

"Carlos fired too early."

"Damn!" Cousins yelled, glancing over his shoulder at the riders following him. "Their horses'll never catch the Horrells." Straightening in the saddle, Cousins pressed the butt of his Henry against his shoulder and squeezed off a shot at a fleeing Jesse Evans.

"Let's keep on their tails," Wes yelled over the thunder of the hoofbeats. "We can drive them out of the valley by dark."

They galloped ahead, their horses drawing away from all but Carlos's chestnut among their allies but not gaining on the killers.

When the trail curved clear of the river and Wes could see Casey's Mill up ahead, he cringed when he saw the Horrells aim their horses toward the store. Then came gunshots, and Wes's first thought was for the Casey children. Another barrage of gunfire exploded, and the Horrells whipped their mounts and dashed down the road. As he neared the mill building, Wes spotted smoking rifle barrels sticking from the portholes and windows.

As Charlie spurted ahead, Casey and his hands rushed from the mill, raising their rifles over their head. They shouted encouragement as Wes and Cousins galloped by. Moments later, Wes heard another cheer as the others passed.

The chase continued for miles. Three times the Horrells slowed to stop at adobes to make a stand, and each time gunfire answered them from the Mexican homes. On each occasion they raced on, every time their horses slowing further from exhaustion. Carlos had done his job well in notifying the valley. Refuge would be scarce in Lincoln County for the Horrells.

The trail would ultimately reach John Chisum's place by the Pecos River, but Wes knew Jesse Evans was no longer welcomed by his former employer. Chisum ran the ranch with an iron hand, and Wes doubted the crusty cowman would like problems of the valley intruding on his empire.

Around them, the valley narrowed, and the mountains became hills. Above them, the sky darkened, and the riders dimmed in the distance as they cleared the basin and emerged onto the plains, dotted with cattle.

Wes and Cousins pushed their horses as hard as possible to

keep them in sight as dusk draped darkness across the land. They gained enough to observe three killers split off from the main bunch and head south, skirting the mountains. As night closed in on them, Wes and Cousins slowed. No sense riding into an ambush, now that the Horrells under cover of night could wait for them beside the road and bushwhack them.

Finally, both Wes and Cousins pulled their horses to a stop, letting them blow. Both men drank water from their canteens. Cousins took a swig, then plugged his. "I reckon Jesse Evans was among that trio that cut out south. I figure he was scared to cross Chisum land. I'll head that way and see if I can settle with Jesse."

Wes nodded. "I thought you would. Remember, you're always welcome at the Mirror B."

Cousins laughed. "If there are no witnesses when I'm done, I may show up and make you a decent worker for a change."

"I'd even take you on as a partner."

Cousins grabbed Wes's hand and shook it vigorously. "First things first, Wes. Good luck to you." Then Cousins rattled his reins and sent his gelding southward. Man and beast disappeared into the darkness. Wes had lost sense of time, and it was several minutes before he heard another horse approaching from the valley.

"Carlos," he yelled, "take it easy." Wes heard the horse slow to a trot.

The Mexican youth materialized out of the night. When he called to Wes, panic tinged his voice. "You're not giving up, are you?"

As Carlos stopped opposite him, Wes shook his head. "Darkness gives them the advantage. They could be laying for us now anywhere along the trail. Our horses need the rest, so we'll pick up the trail at daylight."

Carlos growled his disapproval, then was instantly silent.

Preston Lewis

"Jace, is he all right?"

"We think Jesse Evans and two others split from the rest. Cousins went after them."

"Three against one."

"Yep," Wes answered, "that should be even odds."

274

CHAPTER 30

Everyone slept fretfully, knowing the Texas *diablos* remained out there somewhere and might double back and attack. Wes assigned watch to five shifts of four men each and took the first shift, the one he considered the most likely for the Horrells to make a play. When they didn't, he retired to his bedroll and slept as well as a man can on an empty stomach in a cold camp.

Come dawn, the men arose and saddled, climbing atop their mounts as wearily as corpses returning from the dead. Wes rode around, giving encouragement, looking into eyes hollow with hunger and exhaustion, watching faces drawn with anxiety and covered with dust. Carlos, too, wandered among the Mexicans, answering with animation the pointed questions several asked.

"Let's go," Wes yelled out, "the morning's a wasting." He aimed Charlie east toward the Pecos River and John Chisum's headquarters.

Carlos took a place beside Wes. "Many worry about their families," he confided to Wes. "They fear the *diablos* circled back overnight and might threaten their wives and children."

"Can't say it couldn't happen, but I doubt it. The Horrells evacuated their women and children two weeks ago. I doubt they'll return, not after the send-off your people gave them."

Carlos shrugged. "You know their kind better than we do."

"Tell any of them that want to go back they are welcome to," Wes answered, "but remind them if the Horrells got behind us it won't be too healthy for anyone to run into them alone."

Carlos considered the risk. "I'll tell them we'll stick together."

"Then let's spread out for about a hundred yards apart and see if we can find a trail where they cut off from the road," Wes suggested.

Carlos swiveled about in his saddle and issued the command to his people.

The men advanced at a lope, not pushing their horses after such a hard ride the day before. By mid-morning they had seen no sign of the Horrells, nor any sign of them having left the trail. Above them a cloudless sky offered the full sun to thaw the stiffness out of their joints from a frigid night on frosty ground.

Carlos dug into the bag hanging off his saddle horn and offered Wes half of the tortillas he had. Wes accepted and devoured them. Stuffing the last bite in his mouth, he wiped his sleeve across his lips. That was when he saw the riders approaching, a couple miles ahead on the trail. There were a dozen of them, and they appeared to be in no hurry.

Carlos spotted them, pointing excitedly with the tortilla in his gun hand. "The Horrells?"

"Easy, Carlos, they wouldn't approach this many horsemen straight on. It's bound to be Chisum's hands." A murmur spread among the other riders, and Wes glanced back over his shoulder. "Tell your people not to pull guns or make any threatening moves unless I give the command."

Carlos's men tightened their ranks, moving closer to Wes and Carlos, so they might hear any order he gave.

The men ahead drew closer, their pace as steady as the passing of time. Wes eased Charlie into a walk, and the men behind him slowed their mounts. When only a quarter of a mile separated the two groups, Wes thought he recognized one horseman as John Chisum. When the distance separating them was halved, Wes confirmed the big rancher's identity.

"Tell your men to go easy as that's Mr. John Chisum himself and a handful of his men."

"Some say he's a bad man," Carlos replied.

"You're listening to the wrong people," Wes answered, holding up his hand for the Mexicans to stop. "Carlos, you and I will ride out to visit. He'll know where the Horrells are. Tell the rest of your people to wait here."

Carlos yelled out his command in Spanish, and the old men and boys nodded they understood. Carlos reached to pull the carbine from its scabbard.

"Leave your gun alone, Carlos, or you stay with the others," Wes said, nudging Charlie ahead.

His fingers slid away from the carbine, and Carlos eased his chestnut up beside Wes. Both advanced at a lope, Chisum riding ahead of his hands for a distance, then pulling up and allowing Wes and Carlos to reach him the same time as his own men caught up. Wes studied Chisum's cowboys, all lean with serious and narrow eyes.

"Morning, Mr. Chisum. I'm Wes Bracken; we met last year at Casey's Mill."

"I remember you, Mr. Bracken," Chisum said, his angular face not showing any emotion. "Didn't realize you would be with these Mexicans."

Wes saw Carlos flinch. "They're good people, Mr. Chisum, and this one beside me's one of the best. Carlos, my neighbor, pulled me out of a tight spot with the Horrell brothers."

Chisum lowered his reins and rested both hands on his saddle horn, his dark eyes penetrating Wes as if he could see clear through to a man's soul. Chisum shook his head. "The Horrell boys are as ugly a bunch as I've ever seen, but they ain't done a damn thing to me and my spread, far as I can tell."

"You don't know all, sir. Until we chased them from the valley, Jesse Evans was riding with them."

277

The rancher laughed. "Seems I remember you riding with him on at least one occasion."

Wes tugged at the corner of his mustache. "At least I didn't hire him."

"I fired him after I found out he was stealing from me, too," Chisum replied, pursing his lips. "But Jesse Evans is not the issue here. I'll be plain and blunt about it."

"Go ahead," Wes answered.

"They are at my place, three with gun wounds. None serious, but a mite uncomfortable to ride with. They've done nothing to me, and I don't want them murdered on my land, as it'll just give the law or Lawrence G. Murphy an excuse to meddle into how I run my business."

Carlos spoke in Spanish, and Chisum's gaze turned icy as it locked on the youth.

Chisum spat at the foot of Carlos's chestnut. "I understand your language, boy, and you better learn to hold your tongue until you've heard my offer."

Easing Charlie closer to Carlos and his mount, Wes grabbed the youth's arm and shook it. "Just listen."

Turning to Wes, Chisum continued. "They've caused problems back in the valley for sure, likely murdering folks, and you want to be rid of them. I understand that, but I don't want this to cause me any worries. The deal is, you let them ride off my land back into Texas with no more trouble. In return, they stay out of New Mexico Territory from now on."

"Can you make them live up to the deal?" Wes asked.

"Not in all of New Mexico, but they'll be marked outlaws if they cross my land to reach the Hondo valley. No sense risking more of your men. If fighting starts on my place, the only side my hands take is mine. Several of you are apt to get hurt, since most of you don't look like fighting men."

Thrusting his chin forward, Carlos challenged the cattle king.

278

"They're brave."

Chisum drew a slow breath, then exhaled his frustration. "Boy, I didn't say they were cowards. I said they don't look like fighting men. There are many hard cases in New Mexico, men weaned on the glass nipple of a whiskey bottle. These men may be decent, but I wouldn't throw my lot in with them in a big fight. *Comprende?*"

Carlos stared silently at the cattleman, not moving a muscle, though Wes thought he saw a quiver of his lip for an instant.

Wes released Carlos's arm. "Go explain the offer to your people. I'll accept their decision."

"And, boy," Chisum said, "if the Horrells return to Lincoln County, I'll send my fighting men to drive them off for you."

Carlos jerked the bridle on his horse, spinning the animal around and heading for the others.

"They'll be fools not to take my proposal," Chisum laughed. "The Horrells won't be back. They're scared. Seems every place they tried to make a stand in the valley, people were shooting at them."

"A dose of their own medicine."

The rancher straightened up in his saddle and grinned. "Well, sir, it cured them of New Mexico. And I'll have my hands escort them to the Texas border to guarantee the cure sticks."

Carlos returned, his mood subdued. Without looking at Chisum, he spoke. "They agree, and thank you." Carlos turned his horse to rejoin the others. Except for Carlos, all the Mexicans looked relieved, as much from knowing the Horrells hadn't circled back and endangered their families as from realizing their fighting was done.

"The valley is grateful and indebted to you, Mr. Chisum."

"Someday you can help me rid the county of Murphy. He's a bigger snake than all the Horrells put together," Chisum replied. "Once you send your men home, Mr. Bracken, you're welcome to come to my place for food."

Wes looked back over his shoulder, all the men staring at him, waiting for his answer. Turning back to Chisum, Wes lifted his hat and ran his fingers through his hair. "Obliged, Mr. Chisum, but these are my neighbors. I'll be riding home to the valley with them."

Chisum tipped his hat. "Remember you've always got a friend out here on the prairie." Turning to his cowhands, Chisum issued orders. "We've work to do." The Chisum hands turned their horses toward the east and ranch headquarters. They galloped away, Chisum in the lead, a veil of dust trailing them across the flat expanse.

Carlos eased his chestnut beside Wes. "We were prepared to fight." His voice carried a sharp edge as if he felt his men still had something to prove.

Snugging his hat, Wes stared at Carlos. "Sure they were, Carlos, but there'll be more fights before Lincoln County is a place where everyone will feel safe."

"It true what Chisum says about L. G. Murphy being a threat?"

Wes nodded. "The Horrells are rattlesnakes, but Murphy's a bigger one and more dangerous because he's missing his rattle. He strikes with little warning."

Carlos grumbled, "He has cheated my people."

"He's cheated everyone, including me," Wes replied, turning his horse toward home. "As long as he can intimidate people and get away with it, he will continue."

Carlos turned to the men and spoke in Spanish. As the men nodded in unison, Carlos twisted around to Wes. "They say they'll take on Murphy, if you will lead them."

Wes faced the men, who halted in a semi-circle in front of him. His gaze moved from face to face, taking in the solemn stares and determined mouths. Wes smiled at them and nodded.

"His men are killers, more dangerous than all of us in a fight, but if we can give a show of strength, we may scare him a tad and keep him off of us."

Motioning for the men to move in around him, they crowded together as he outlined a plan. It was a simple strategy, yet a bold one, for only Chisum had ever challenged Murphy in Lincoln County, and then only on the prairies. In the mountains and valleys, Murphy still ruled. Carlos translated Wes's plan for those who did not comprehend English. One by one, each man nodded agreement, each having had a bad experience with the arrogant Irishman and his store. They answered Carlos in Spanish.

When Carlos turned to him, Wes knew the answer even before the youth could open his mouth. "Everyone will help, and others may want to join in."

Smiling again, Wes maneuvered Charlie by each mount, shaking the hand of its rider. "We can whip him if we stick together." When he had shaken the hand of each man, he stood in his stirrups and pointed toward the mountains, standing like giant purple tombstones to the west. "Let's ride for home. Remember, we meet in Lincoln in four days."

With that, the men returned to the valley and their homes. Wes stopped at the Casey store and explained the outcome, confident that the Horrells would never return to Lincoln County. After a filling meal with the Caseys, he reclaimed his horses and mules from the Casey corral and started the trek the rest of the way home, even if it was to an empty cabin.

After he had penned and fed his stock, he retreated to his cabin, first starting a fire to warm up the place and then gathering from the floor the rifle hulls that had been expended in the battle with the Horrells. When he sat down at the table, he spotted a covered bowl filled with tortillas, a gift he suspected from Sarafina. He smiled.

CHAPTER 31

The day he was to ride to Lincoln, Wes awoke early and tended the horses. He had hoped to learn something of Jace Cousins's luck with Jesse Evans and his gunmen, but every evening had ended in disappointment, and Wes wondered if Cousins would ever return.

In the barn, he saddled Charlie and harnessed the two plow animals. As Wes planned to reclaim the Bracken wagon that Murphy had swindled from Luther, he would need the mules. Then he returned to the adobe and ate the remaining tortillas Sarafina had left for him, wishing he had squeezed in a visit over the last three days to check on her and Luis. Or, better yet, that she had come to see him, though it was best this way in case things in Lincoln went awry.

The sun had just cleared the mountains to the east when Wes flushed the two harnessed mules from the barn and led Charlie outside. After mounting and taking a deep breath of brisk morning air, Wes started down the road to the county seat. He hoped the Hispanics remained as firm and committed to the showdown with Murphy as he did.

His doubts dissolved when he spied a couple men who had ridden with him against the Horrell brothers ease onto the trail behind him. Up ahead, rode three more. They all were riding to Lincoln. He felt foolish for having ever doubted their word. They were following his instructions well, neither gaining on him from behind nor losing ground up ahead. If too many armed Mexicans came to Lincoln together, Murphy and his cronies would realize that trouble was brewing. Wes had instructed them to trickle into town during the night and in ones and twos during the day. They had followed his directions perfectly, and Wes expected to see dozens more in town.

The sun had passed its peak when Wes herded the mules around the last bend in the road before Lincoln. The community smelled of piñon smoke, which lay like a gray veil over adobe buildings. At the edge of town, Wes recognized a familiar chestnut tied to a tree and watched Carlos jump from a low limb to the ground. He untied the gelding and led him out to the street before pulling himself into the saddle. Signaling with his arm, he leaned down, pulling his carbine from out of its scabbard. Carlos maneuvered his horse in front of the mules, and they stopped, one tossing his head at the youth.

Wes reined up opposite Carlos, and the two riders who had followed him since leaving the Mirror B passed, both nodding from beneath their wide hats. Wes dragged his revolver from his holster, checking the load. "Is my wagon still at Murphy's store?" he asked as he spun the cylinder on his revolver.

"*Sí*," Carlos answered, "where it always is. The men, they are ready, many more than rode against the Horrells."

Shoving his pistol back in the holster, Wes asked, "And Sarafina, is she okay?"

Carlos nodded, his lips curling upward in a smile. "She is doing good. She said she would pray all day for me."

Wes pursed his lips. "That is good."

"And for you," Carlos continued. "Sarafina is praying for Wes Bracken as well."

"Then we've nothing to worry about," he replied. "Let's attend our business." He touched the flank of his horse with his boot heel and started toward the other end of town.

Carlos turned his chestnut in beside Wes and swatted his hat at the mules. They jumped ahead, their harnesses creaking.

"Remember, Carlos, no one is to fire unless I say so or they start shooting at us. And, Carlos, keep your wits about yourself this time. Don't do something rash."

As they rode down the dusty street of Lincoln, men left their chores or hiding places, all following on foot, some on either side of the trail and others beyond the adobes that lined the streets. The street was empty of women and children. A few chickens fluttered out of the way, and a short-tailed tomcat dashed by to hide. Wes studied the fortress that was Murphy's store ahead. At the far corner of the building stood the wagon Luther had driven from Arkansas. The Murphy FOR SALE sign on the sideboard still galled Wes, and he intended to reclaim the rig.

At the hitching post this side of his wagon, Wes counted seven horses. He understood other men might have stabled their mounts at the Wortley, so there could be fifteen or twenty men inside, all well-armed and with an unlimited supply of ammunition from Murphy's stock. Beyond the imposing building, he observed two Hispanic men picking up a load of firewood that had fallen from a donkey. Three more rested in the shade of a tree. Behind the store, Wes noted other Mexicans slipping out from the cover of juniper and piñon bushes dotting the mountain that scowled down on the structure. All the Mexicans carried weapons, a few with carbines, several with shotguns, and most with pistols. It was a ragtag army with little fighting familiarity, but the numbers—seventy or more Hispanics by Wes's estimate—might intimidate Murphy and his henchmen.

Beside him, Carlos counted the men and nodded, confident of victory.

Wes had been in too many battles during the War Between the States to be overconfident. Experience carried the field as many times as numbers, and Murphy's hard cases had practice in intimidation. The Mexicans might have right on their side, but sometimes even all the prayers of a frightened woman could not guarantee virtue's victory.

Reining up outside the store's front door, Wes stood in his stirrups and took a deep breath while Carlos halted the mules. Looking around him, Wes observed other Mexicans taking positions opposite the store. Wes settled back in his saddle, certain than no one had ever led a more decent group of men into a confrontation. He sighed, hoping none would get injured, then dismounted, giving his reins to Carlos. So far, his small army had gone undetected. It was time for that to change. He spoke softly to Carlos. "Do not fire *unless* I say so or they shoot first. Our chances are better if we scare them instead of fighting them. Too many of your people could die if shooting breaks out."

Carlos nodded. "I understand."

Walking to the mules, Wes untied the lines strapped to their harnesses. With the reins, he directed the animals toward his wagon, walking beside the mules to screen himself from the building in case shooting started.

"Murphy," Wes yelled, "I've got business with you. Come out and talk."

Wes saw flashes of faces at windows in the store but fortunately no gun barrels. He heard shouts from inside the building, Murphy's Irish voice mixed among them.

"Just a little unfinished business to settle with you, Murphy," Wes shouted. "Step outside and discuss it. Then I'll be on my way."

Moments later the door cracked slowly, and Murphy stepped out cautiously, his lip curling in anger. "What ye want, Bracken?"

"My wagon. I came to claim my rig back."

Murphy moved to the front of the plank walk, his gaze moving from Wes to Carlos and back. "It'll take more than ye and a

greaser to claim that wagon, six 'undred dollars to be exact."
He waved his hand, and a dozen men stepped outside, lining
the porch beside him with drawn revolvers.

"Easy, Carlos," Wes whispered, maneuvering the mules closer
to the wagon.

"Don't try to 'itch them up unless ye want to die," Murphy
called out with a laugh.

"You'll die first, Murphy."

The smirk died on Murphy's lips as he looked at the men
converging on the store.

Two Hispanics who had been picking up firewood spilled
from their donkey advanced with carbines leveled at Murphy
and his henchmen. From the shade of trees and the corners of
adjacent buildings appeared other men from town and from
miles around, their pistols, shotguns, and rifles aimed at Murphy and his hired guns.

"What were you saying, Murphy?" Wes taunted the Irishman.
"You can't fight all of Lincoln County. The only friends you've
got are those you've bought or the ones who've never done an
honest day's work in their lives." Wes backed the mules up to
the wagon. "If you want to die, have your men start something.
You're outnumbered five to one or more."

When Wes glanced at Carlos, he spotted a wide grin across
the youth's face, his carbine pointed squarely at Murphy's chest.
There was satisfaction in his eye and a longing for an excuse to
pull the trigger.

"I'll 'ave the law on ye and these greasers," Murphy challenged.

Wes laughed. "These men, not your law, drove the Horrells
out of Lincoln County. There's enough of them to run you out
if it comes to that. And if anything happens to a single one,
we'll come back and hang your worthless Irish hide from a
tree."

Murphy's cheeks bloated up like a frog's, then reddened with humiliation. "Ye take me wagon, we'll come for ye."

"Why wait, Murphy? Stop me now!" Wes challenged. "You know you stole this wagon from Luther, just like you've cheated these folks and made their lives miserable. Let's settle it today, if that's what you want."

Murphy scowled at Wes, crossing his arms over his chest.

As he backed the mules toward his wagon, Wes smiled. The bluff had worked. Murphy was too scared to challenge this ragtag army. Wes hooked the harnesses to the wagon-tongue, then tossed the reins into the seat.

"I'll not forget ye, Wes Bracken," Murphy challenged.

Wes climbed into the wagon box and tipped his hat. "Neither will these good men," he said, sweeping his arm toward the Mexicans surrounding the building. "You threaten any of us, you threaten all of us. And if it takes it, John Chisum's men will help, too." Taking the lines, Wes clucked his tongue and rattled the reins. The mules lurched ahead, the wagon rattling and creaking as it pulled away from Murphy and his store.

Carlos, holding the reins to Wes's mount, turned his chestnut and Charlie to follow Bracken.

Behind him, Wes heard the curses of L. G. Murphy, then the slamming of the door at Murphy's store. When he glanced back over his shoulder, Murphy and his gunmen had retreated inside, and the Hispanics were dispersing or following Wes down the road. Their faces wore broad grins. Wes sensed a confidence in their newfound power. Wes knew Murphy wasn't defeated, just taken down several notches. Murphy would strike back, but maybe this show of unity would delay his response for awhile. Perhaps with the Horrells gone and Murphy subdued, at least temporarily, the decent people of Lincoln County could get through a planting season and maybe even a harvest without having to worry about anything other than the rains and the insects.

As the wagon passed the Wortley Hotel and left Murphy's store behind, women and children emerged from their adobes with smiles as wide and white as those of their fathers, brothers, husbands, and sons, the men who had stood up to Murphy. These newcomers to the parade looked in awe at Wes, leaving him uncomfortable, even more so when a few of them waved shyly. They were good people.

Beside him, Carlos enjoyed himself, waving and making eyes at the señoritas among the women and their offspring. Wes decided Carlos had a right to gloat. For once, he had held his emotions in check, not starting a gun battle back at the store. Carlos had stared into the barrels of a dozen guns and not flinched. His bravery would enhance his reputation with the young ladies.

When the wagon was beyond rifle range from the Murphy store, Wes drove it under the shade of a tree and waited for the men to gather. They came in twos and threes, talking rapidly in Spanish and patting each other on the back, grinning at their wives and sweethearts gathering in a circle all around. As they congregated, Wes jumped from the conveyance, took Charlie's reins from Carlos, and tied his stallion to the back of the rig. Then he climbed back in the wagon box.

When more than eighty men, women, and children had congregated, an old man stepped forward and took his hat off. By his toothless smile, he seemed likely to be the oldest man in the crowd. Holding his hat over his chest, he spoke in halting English. "You . . . have shown us . . . our dignity. *Gracias.*" Everyone nodded in agreement. "How can we . . . repay you?"

Wes removed his hat and stood up from his seat. "You are good neighbors. That is enough."

Carlos translated his words for those who did not understand English.

"Please," the old man continued, "let us . . . show you . . . our thanks. What can we . . . offer you?"

The gesture touched Wes for its sincerity, and he took a moment to consider. When it dawned upon him what he should request, he was embarrassed at first. He gripped the brim of his hat tighter and stared straight at Carlos.

"Are any of you from San Patricio?" he asked as Carlos translated.

"*Sí, sí,*" answered several men, looking more attentively at him.

"Tomorrow afternoon," he said, still staring at Carlos, "I should like to use the chapel in San Patricio if a special lady of your people will say yes to my proposal."

Carlos grinned and nodded.

CHAPTER 32

The sun was sinking behind the mountains to the west when Wes turned with the road and viewed the Mirror B. The sight invigorated him, not just the place that was his, but a familiar horse tied to the hitching post. Jace Cousins had returned.

Wes slapped the reins against the rumps of the mules, and they danced ahead, following the road's gentle incline to trail ruts that led to the house. As the wagon started down the trace, the door of the adobe opened, and Cousins stood there waving his hat at Wes.

"Good to see you, Jace," Wes called out as he jerked on the lines, bringing the mules to a stop in front of Cousins. Wes set the brake, tied the reins, and jumped to the ground. In two strides, he was beside Jace, pumping his hand and slapping him on the back.

"Where'd you buy the wagon?" Jace asked, then scratched his chin. "Surely not from Murphy, did you?"

"I—we—took it from Murphy. Didn't pay a cent. It's the one Luther brought from Arkansas."

"Who's 'we'?"

Wes laughed. "The men that chased the Horrells out of the county. Them and Mexicans from all over the Hondo valley helped me bluff Murphy. He'll have his tail between his legs for awhile."

Cousins whistled. "Good for them and good for us."

"What about Jesse Evans?"

Cousins shook his head. "Jesse, damn his hide, got away. His two partners weren't so lucky. Fortunately, there were no witnesses. I don't know if Jesse'll come back or not, but if he does, I'll be waiting. That is, if the offer still stands for us to go together in the horse business, though I think we need to add cattle to our plans."

Wes nodded. "But I plan to take on another partner as well."

Cousins's face drooped for a moment.

"Sarafina Zamora, if she'll have me for a husband."

Cousins stared at Wes with an inscrutable face, then grinned, grabbing his hand and rattling it. "Well, congratulations, you old buzzard."

Wes flushed with embarrassment. "I'm taking her to San Patricio tomorrow afternoon, if she'll go along."

"She's a pretty woman, and she'll make you a fine wife. Fact, I'll ride up to Casey's Mill and let them know so they can attend. I stopped there on the way in, and Casey said you can have the run of his store for driving the Horrells out of the county. Not a bad gift to start a marriage on, now is it?"

Wes shrugged. "I was only trying to do right by me and my neighbors. And tell Casey when you see him, I won't be borrowing his wagon any more since I reclaimed mine from Murphy."

Cousins laughed. "Way things are going, Lincoln County'll be your kingdom in a few years."

"Murphy wants a kingdom," Wes replied. "All I want is a place where I can do honest work and raise a family."

As he aimed the wagon for the Zamora place, Wes swatted the road dust off his shirt. A knot in his throat, he wondered if Sarafina would agree to his proposal, though he knew Carlos had likely tipped her off it was coming.

Before Wes drew up outside the adobe, Carlos emerged, grinning widely. He stood with hands on his hips until the wagon halted. "You nervous?" He laughed.

Wes nodded.

Behind Carlos, the door opened, and Sarafina came out into the sunlight. She was dressed as she had been the night of the dance in Lincoln, only now in the light of day she seemed so much more beautiful.

Carlos slipped toward his new corral, where his chestnut strutted about. He worked at saddling his horse, taking his time as if he were ignoring Wes and his sister.

As Wes dropped to the ground from the wagon, Sarafina stepped over to meet him.

"My prayers were answered," she said, her voice breathless, as if she had bottled up inside her all the emotions of the day before and only now released them.

He took her in his arms and squeezed her tight against him. She turned her head and placed her soft cheek against his chest. It felt so natural, Sarafina in his grasp, and yet so difficult to pose the question he wanted to ask. He stood holding her, enjoying her softness and her aroma.

At last he spoke. "Sarafina, I have told the men of San Patricio that I might want to use the chapel this afternoon, if you would marry me."

Sarafina's arms tightened around him, and she looked up with moist eyes.

Wes continued. "I will respect you and care for Luis as if he were my own son. That I can promise you. I can't promise you wealth, or fancy clothes, but I can promise you as long as I live you will have a roof over your head and food on your table. And Luis and our children will be taught right from wrong."

Still Sarafina said nothing, her only response being the tears rolling down her cheeks.

Wes stood helpless at her silence. "I will—"

Before he could say more, Sarafina touched his lips with her finger. She nodded. "Yes, I will marry you, Wes Bracken."

Wes pressed his lips against hers.

At that, Luis cried out from the adobe. Sarafina broke away from his kiss, giggling. Wes laughed, too, as Sarafina retreated inside, returning in a moment with her fretting son. "This man," she whispered to her son, "shall be as your father."

Behind him, Wes heard Carlos riding out of the corral. When he turned, Carlos was laughing. "You look even more nervous. I'll see you in San Patricio after I tell folks to come to a wedding." He spurred the gelding and galloped toward the town.

Wes helped Sarafina get into the wagon with Luis. He walked around and pulled himself into the seat. Sarafina scooted over next to him and rested her head upon his shoulder.

The ride passed quickly with anticipation, and when San Patricio came into view, Sarafina caught her breath. By the chapel at the cemetery stood more people than lived in San Patricio. In addition to the villagers, Wes spotted Cousins, plus Bob Casey and his wife as well as others he did not know by name. They lined the path leading to the door of the church. "They have come to see you, to thank you," Sarafina said.

"No," Wes answered, "they are here to pay respect to you and our son."

Sarafina dabbed at the tears overflowing the corners of her eyes. She seemed dazed, even more when the wagon came to a stop. Men and women crowded around to help her from her seat. Wes held Luis in his arms, then gave the infant to Sarafina and climbed down. He slipped his arm in Sarafina's and nodded to those celebrating the marriage with them. The path to the door was lined with smiling people, but Wes broke through the crowd and guided Sarafina toward a wooden cross in the little cemetery. For a moment, Sarafina failed to realize where she stood. As Wes took off his hat, Sarafina knelt at the grave of

Bonifacio, bowed her head, and said a silent prayer. Wes knelt beside her.

As she lifted her head, she leaned forward and kissed the cross of her late husband and then their son. She looked at Wes with bright eyes and a gentle smile. Wes arose and helped her stand with Luis, escorting her back through the onlookers and into the small chapel, where they took their vows with the baby in Sarafina's arms. When they emerged from the tiny church, their neighbors cheered and clapped. At the wagon, Sarafina gave Luis to Carlos to hold as Wes helped her into the seat. After Carlos passed the baby back to his sister, Wes climbed into the wagon seat and took the reins as Cousins approached.

"Wes," Cousins said, "I'll spend the next few nights with Carlos until we can figure where I'll bunk, then we'll start our partnership."

"Obliged, Jace," Wes responded. "We'll work something out, just not on my wedding day."

Cousins laughed as he stepped back to make room for the Caseys. Both congratulated Wes and Sarafina, with Bob informing the Brackens that they could have the run of the store as a wedding gift.

"*Gracias,*" Sarafina said.

Wes looked at everyone celebrating the ceremony, then stood up from his wagon seat. "*Gracias, gracias,*" he said. "Sarafina and I thank you all for making this a memorable day."

Wes sat beside his new bride, lifted the reins, and started toward their home. They rode without speaking, the occasional frets of Luis the only noise.

Halfway home, Wes saw a rider approaching on a dappled gray horse. The horseman wore a broad-brimmed hat and a wide smile that accentuated his two front teeth. He cradled a Winchester in his arms, but as he neared the wagon, he slid it back in its scabbard and removed his hat. He angled his gray off the trail and reined up his gelding.

Wes stopped the rig and eyed the fellow, who was little more than a kid, maybe in his late teens at most.

"Greetings," the rider said. "I'm seeking work. You wouldn't have any jobs or know of anyone that does, would you?"

"This is my wedding day, son, so I can't help you today."

The horseman eyed the baby, then grinned at Wes. "Looks like you're nine months overdue for marriage."

Wes knew he should've been insulted, but something in the kid's lively eyes and innocent smile brought a laugh to his lips. "It's not what it seems."

"It never is when it comes to women, but you have a fine looking bride, mister . . ."

"Wes Bracken," he answered. "This is my wife, Sarafina, and our son, Luis. As to work, I can't help you today."

"Well, if you hear of anything, I'd be obliged to know."

"Sure thing, young fellow, but what's your name?"

"Bonney, Billy Bonney," he responded, then replaced his hat and tugged it down over his brow. "Thank you, Mr. Bracken, and congratulations to you, your bride, and your boy." Bonney nudged his gray with his knee, and his mount trotted toward San Patricio.

Wes twisted in his seat and watched Bonney ride away. The rider never looked back but did pull his carbine from his scabbard and cradle the Winchester in his arms again.

Sarafina slipped her arm in his and leaned against him, resting her head on his shoulder. Wes shook the reins, and the team started toward their modest home.

His bride sighed. "I have never known such peace," Sarafina said. "May Lincoln County be blessed with a tranquility such as this from now on."

Wes nodded but said nothing. He feared peace might not be possible for Lincoln County, but whether tranquility or trouble lay ahead, he could think of nothing better than sharing the rest of his tomorrows with Sarafina.

ABOUT THE AUTHOR

Preston Lewis is the recipient of two Spur Awards and a Will Rogers Gold Medallion Award for written western humor. He is a past president of Western Writers of America and the West Texas Historical Association, which has awarded him three Elmer Kelton Awards for best creative work on West Texas. He is best known for his comic westerns in *The Memoirs of H. H. Lomax* series. Lewis and his wife, Harriet, reside in San Angelo, Texas.

The employees of Five Star Publishing hope you have enjoyed this book.

Our Five Star novels explore little-known chapters from America's history, stories told from unique perspectives that will entertain a broad range of readers.

Other Five Star books are available at your local library, bookstore, all major book distributors, and directly from Five Star/Gale.

Connect with Five Star Publishing

Visit us on Facebook:
    https://www.facebook.com/FiveStarCengage

Email:
    FiveStar@cengage.com

For information about titles and placing orders:
    (800) 223-1244
    gale.orders@cengage.com

To share your comments, write to us:
    Five Star Publishing
    Attn: Publisher
    10 Water St., Suite 310
    Waterville, ME 04901